Exclusi

J. M. Hewitt

First published 2016 by Endeavour Press Ltd.

Table of Contents

Acknowledgements
'The Snowball Effect'

Although I've been a published author since 2010, a couple of years ago, something happened that I like to call The Snowball Effect.

In August 2012 I read a book called The Wicked Girls, and I was so struck by it that I emailed the author to say just how much I had enjoyed it. The author was Alex Marwood, and that was my real introduction to the world of crime fiction. Alex Marwood responded to my email and encouraged me over to Facebook to connect there. Later, Alex Marwood recommended a crime fiction author, Sarah Hilary, and her debut novel Someone Else's Skin. Imagine my delight when I learned that both Alex and Sarah were appearing at my local book festival in 2014.

I accosted them, both of them, listening enraptured at Alex's talk and earnestly attending Sarah's workshop. And Alex was appearing with an author from my hometown, Ruth Dugdall, whose friendship I immediately added to my growing collection of crime fiction authors.

The next year I was lucky enough to have my own event at the Felixstowe Book Festival alongside two other independently published authors, SJI Holliday and Jane Isaac, two lovely women who I also put in my collection. Ruth told me I should go to the meetings of the Felixstowe Scribblers, a writing group consisting of the loveliest bunch of supportive people. And through Susi Holliday, I found THE Book Club on Facebook, a group led by the unstoppable cyclone that is Tracy Fenton with around 4000 followers. And this snowballed and I met the wonderful Noelle, who is a self-confessed CrimeBookJunkie and a firm friend, and then a new friend was collected in the form of Carole Blake and her fantastic workshop, a day in Dragon Hall in Norwich which was simply superb. And I followed the meteoric rise of Marnie Riches and her award winning series *The Girl Who...* which was a story that I adored and which contained the type of writing I wanted to put out there. We connected and, just like all the others, the support given is heartfelt and without agenda. There are many others that I've gathered up over the years along what could have been a lonely road; Bluewood, the ones who took a chance on my work many years ago, Darren Walne, my own personal I.T, branding and marketing material consultant as well as a great giver of emotional support and encouragement. Most recently, Louise Beech, who's debut novel How To Be Brave really resonated with me – and the author turned out to be just as lovely as the book. Cornerstone's Literary Consultants, and the agents who although rejected, still took time to give a little nugget of priceless information or feedback. And then there were other events and other people, Daniel Pembrey who also came to be a firm friend via Ruth Dugdall and their Luxembourg connection, who always has words of support and kindness, and who I have met several times at numerous gatherings, BritCrime in the summer of 2015, where my tentative competition entry won, and I got to hand a manuscript in to Madeleine Milburn, and whose feedback and advice I took on board. That feedback led me in August 2015 to begin writing an entirely new novel from scratch, and that novel is the one that you are about to read.

And that, lovely readers, is what I like to call The Snowball Effect.

This book is dedicated to
Janet Hewitt (nee Wozny)
And Keith Hewitt.
They are not just my mum and dad, they have always been the best
teachers' I've ever had and also, my best friends.
If I had a flower for every time I thought of you...I could walk through
my garden forever.
Alfred Lord Tennyson, Poet.

Chernobyl 2015

With no law enforcement willing to go in the Exclusion Zone, a spate of murders are going *almost* unnoticed.

*

Pripyat, Chernobyl, April 26th 1986

"Wake up, the roof is on fire!"

I am so far in sleep that she actually appears in my dream and I carry on in blissful slumber, only stirring when she shakes my sleeping form.

"Sissy, wake up!"

I groan and poke my head out from the blankets that cover me. My sister's face looms close in the moonlight, eyes wide, her hand covering her mouth, fingers splayed and shaking.

Her words hit home; our roof is on fire? We live in a thatched cottage, the frame made of wood, the house surrounded by forest, are we in the process of being burned alive?

Throwing the covers off I look upwards, seeking evidence of the burning roof. When I neither see nor smell evidence of a fire, I turn to my sister with a quizzical expression.

"Afia, what are you talking about?" I ask her.

Afia sucks her lips and rolls her eyes, pulling me off the bed and over to the window. "The factory, stupid girl," she hisses, and points a trembling arm to the west.

Now I see the smoke. It billows through the night sky, casting a shadow across the moon.

"Father?" I clutch Afia's arm.

"He's gone to the factory to see if he can help," she replies, as she struggles to open the window.

I pull her back, worried that if the window is open all that black smoke will engulf our room, drag us down, and swallow us whole with the noxious gas. "Don't open it, Afia. Come away from there."

But Afia swats me away like an irritating fly and moves towards the door. She pauses, her hand on the door knob and, with her back to me, she speaks.

"Look out for mama; she's going to need you, Sissy."

*

These days, almost thirty years after that night, I go over those words time and time again. When I used to hear sirens, which was most days and nights when I lived in London, my heart would race and I would hurry to a window to seek evidence of a burning building or a national disaster. Even when the sirens faded away I'm there, stuck in 1986 in my town of Pripyat. I'm watching the nuclear plant burn and only half listening as my sister says her goodbyes. If I had have known that they were the last words she would ever speak to me, I would have listened a lot harder.

Chapter 1
Alex and Elian
London, June 2nd 2015

He watches her for a while before he plans his move. And from watching her he understands that, although she appears timid and reserved, there is an underlying core of steel.

He appreciates her physically. She is not conventionally pretty like the blond, catalogue model types he usually pursues, but rather striking; edgy and fascinating. Her mixed-race skin is smooth and well cared for, with the springy appearance that only comes from youth. But he is not interested in wooing her. It might be a by-product, it might actually be necessary, but only a means to the end.

He follows her for weeks. He knows that she uses the Italian launderette and he wonders why. Has she not got a washing machine in her flat or a communal laundry for the residents? She shops regularly at the Tesco Express in New Cavendish Street, late at night when the fruit and bread are reduced. Once a week, usually on a Saturday, she allows herself a meal out, either at Scandinavian Kitchen or Picture. Frequently she visits Rollo, Josh Lilley or the Woolff Gallery, but he suspects this is more out of boredom than a genuine love of art. Wherever she goes, she stays within a three mile radius of her flat.

The flat is a mystery. It is hers, mortgage free, which leads him to wonder how she can afford a million pound property in the suburb of Fitzrovia in the nation's capital. She can't afford it on her salary. He knows this because he knows what she earns. He knows what she earns because he is her employer.

He watches her at work as well as in his own time. She is not disliked, but she does not have friends here. She does not go to The Harp pub on a Friday night with everyone else. She does chat to the Romanian cleaners when they come in of an evening. She talks in their language, a fact that heightens his interest, since she is so careful during working hours to hide her Eastern European link. Sometimes she works until nine o'clock at night and leaves the office with the cleaners, Greta and Paulina, and they walk down Oxford Street together before parting ways at Great Portland Street. Greta and Paulina seem to be her only friends.

His own home life is not affected by his pursuit of her. His work is his life and everything else is secondary.

He pulls her personal file at work. She is only nineteen; he is sixteen years older than her. But, although she is extremely youthful in appearance, her demeanour is that of an older woman. Her work records tell him the bare minimum. He already knows more about her from following her than he discovers from her file. She keeps a low profile, at work and at home. She is a tough nut to crack. But he will break her.

He waits. Although he is impatient, he uses his immense self-control and when the time is right he picks up the phone and dials an internal extension. The voice that answers is quiet, meek and nervous. He smiles to himself in order to inject warmth into his tone as he speaks into the receiver.

"Elian, its Alex here, Alex Harvey. Can you come up to my office please?"

*

Elian Gould sits across from Alex and glances down at her hands folded neatly in her lap, before looking up and around his office. It is all chrome and wood, except for hints of spring green here and there, the chair, the telephone, the desk lamp. Downstairs everybody's desks are covered in paper, notes, back copies of the magazine and proofs. The carpet on her level – the hub of the place – is worn thin in places. Up here the floor has been stripped back to the natural wood and varnished to a shine. Alex Harvey's office is ultra-modern and expensive, just like he is. She has never been up to his office before, in fact, she is shocked that he knows her name. Nobody in this place, except the Eastern European cleaners who come in after hours, really converses with her. She worries that she has been caught doing something that she shouldn't. She thinks back to the last time she cleared her browser history.

"Elian, that's an unusual name. Is it Ukrainian?" Alex's voice is pleasant enough, but she bites her lip, unaware that anyone here knew of her Ukraine connection.

"No, it's . . . not." She is about to tell him the origin of her name, but something stops her. "Can you tell me why you wanted to see me?"

"It's housekeeping, official stuff."

Before she can reply he throws his hands up in the air and rolls his eyes. "I know, boring, boring, but we have to keep on top of it. I don't do it as much as I should, so I'm getting on it before the top brass come down on me."

Elian is silent, housekeeping to her is what her Eastern European friends do each evening. But something tells her that he is not talking about cleaning, but using the word in a different context, so she keeps quiet, looks at a spot on the wall behind him and waits.

"It's all to do with the pay slips, tax codes; like I said, boring." He smiles at her as he continues. "I'll need your identification, to take a copy. Passport works best, do you have a passport, Elian?"

She blinks, shifts her gaze back to him and remembers her bag lying at her feet. She pulls it up, roots around in her purse and pulls out her driving licence. In the bottom of her bag she sees a crumpled gas bill and she puts them both on his desk. She feels triumphant, but does not know why.

Alex looks at the two documents as she watches him carefully. His jaw works and there is a long silence before he pushes them back towards her.

"A passport would be better," he says. His voice now quiet, but with a firm undertone to it. "Photo ID, you see."

Elian grabs the bill and the licence, puts them back in her bag and stands up.

"Tomorrow will be fine. No hurry."

She nods, wanting to point out that the driving licence has her photo on it, but not daring to, and without another word she backs out of his office and returns down to her floor.

Elian sits at her desk, chewing on the end of her pen and sneaking glances at her work mates. As an editorial assistant, she has worked her way up from a junior designer and, before that, general dogsbody. When she first landed a job here she was still at school and she came in on Saturdays. Because of her professionalism and quiet, hardworking nature, it was made clear that when Elian was finished with her studies there would be a job waiting for her here at *Edge*. Her role is not important enough to sit upstairs with the likes of Alex, but she likes what she does. When she first got this job she was lucky if she did anything other than make tea for her colleagues and visitors. But someone, probably upstairs, saw a couple of pieces she had worked on and now everyone uses Elian for her research skills. Sometimes she edits copy and, more often than not, they use her piece. There is no recognition, aside from her name sometimes showing up in the by-line. But recognition is not what she wants. Elian prefers to stay under the radar.

But now she has been spotted, by Alex Harvey of all people, and she is pretty certain that he wants more from her than just her passport.

Chapter 2
Sissy

Chernobyl, April 26th 1986

By the time I put my clothes on, and get downstairs, our cottage is in disarray. A dozen women are crowded into our small home and I fight through the masses, calling out for my mother.

"Sissy!" Mama sees me and pulls me over to the open kitchen door. "What is your sister doing?"

I glance outside, see nobody and push the door closed against the biting April wind.

"Where is Afia?" I ask. "And what are all these people doing here?"

Mama shrugs, pulling her shawl tighter around her shoulders, and moves over to the hearth. "Something at the factory, some trouble." She flings more logs on the fire and looks scathingly at the women gathered in her lounge. "And so, there is trouble, and they all come here, to me. My home, my drinks, my heat."

With each bitterly spoken word she tosses another log on to the fire and I look behind me, worried that our neighbours may overhear her caustic words.

My mother and father are originally from East Africa, and when we moved to Chernobyl our black skin was a big problem for the town folk. Afia was fourteen when we arrived in 1980, and her answer to our ostracism was to pretend that she was some sort of African voodoo queen. She scared our new neighbours witless with her make believe of sorcery and witchcraft. When my father found out what his eldest daughter was doing he took his belt to her. It was the first and only time he ever struck out at any of his precious girls.

In the six years that we have been here the villagers have slowly accepted us. My mother worked tirelessly, baking traditional African food, sharing the wares of her livestock, and keeping a smile on her face until one by one we were welcomed into their community. Which is why it is so ironic now, in the face of a potential tragedy, everyone has congregated here and, in turn, it has made her quietly furious.

"People just want me when there is trouble afoot," she announces now, wielding a log at me before hurling it into the range. "Nobody appreciates me. Look at your sister, leaving me to face this angry mob!"

I look again at the villagers. They are not angry, they talk amongst themselves in hushed tones. They are quietly worried and I wonder why. Is the fire at the factory bad enough to warrant this fuss? And, where is my sister? At six feet tall, with glowing, ebony skin, I usually have no trouble spotting her in a crowd. More so today that any other day, wearing her ridiculous red pant suit that she mail ordered especially from England.

"Where did Afia go?" I ask mama, taking yet another log from her hands and laying it gently back in the basket.

She throws her hands up and clucks, before returning to the main room to mingle with her guests. I feel a flicker of a smile, she is hard done by and put upon, but she will see to it that these uninvited guests are comfortable.

I take the opportunity to slip outside unnoticed and stand for a moment on the porch, watching my breath puff out, visible in the cold night air. I see the smoke in the distance, smell something rancid that catches in my throat, like burning plastic, and I cover my face with my sleeve.

I am about to go back inside when I see movement out in the road and I wipe my eyes, straining to see better through the gloom.

"Afia, is that you?" I call and skip down the steps, making my way over the dewy grass to the roadside.

Without the light coming from the cottage windows it is even darker down here and I shiver as I step on to the road, looking left and right. There is nothing now, no sound, no further movement. I feel a rush of anger towards Afia. Although, at nineteen, she is four years older than me, for as long as I can remember it has always fallen to me to be the responsible one. I am always the one that helps our mother. It is always me that covers for Afia; and, on these occasions, she doesn't even repay me by letting me in on her secret.

There is trouble afoot. The wind tells me that, with the acrid scent of burning, just as much as Afia's absence.

My thoughts turn from my sister to my father. He is not working tonight, but he has gone to the factory to see if he can help.

The aroma that comes from the direction of his workplace is fearsome, ferocious and it worries me. I cast a glance to my right and, seeing nothing, I decide to walk towards the factory. After all, perhaps that is where Afia went as well.

This is a walk that I do every day, twice a day to my school and back. I walk past the factory, sometimes my father times it so he will be there to exchange a wave with me. Sometimes he has a gift for me, a piece of chocolate or something as simple as a flower that he might put in my hair. I feel a pang for him now, and concern quickens my steps.

"Hey, Sissy!" A shadow looms suddenly across my path and a deep, male voice booms out, making me shriek with fright.

A shuffling of the trees on the verge, hands batting at the bushes, and in front of me is Ivan, the son of one of our neighbours. Ivan is only fifteen, but he is huge. He is not fat, but simply a bear of a boy. The children in Pripyat do not play with Ivan, not since he caught one of Jamma's new-born lambs and tried to turn it into a pullover. Everyone always knew that Ivan was a little blank in his head; although he was harmless until the lamb incident. All the parents said after that was it could have been a baby or a small child. They wanted to send Ivan away, but his mother, Sofia, wouldn't allow it. The community relented, as long as Ivan did not have any more 'incidents'. We don't see Ivan much anymore; he is more legend and folklore than sinister, resident monster. But now he is here, blocking my path, larger than life; but, strangely, not all that scary.

"Ivan, you startled me," I clutch my chest, lean over to catch my breath.

"I'm sorry, Miss Sissy," he drawls, his words elongated and slow. I'm surprised, I never thought that he would know my name.

"What are you doing out here, Ivan?" I ask, feeling very grown up that I am having a normal, adult conversation with the poor spastic boy that nobody else dares even to look at.

"They need help at the factory, they need more men, strong men."

Ivan is proud, flexing his arm and smiling at me. I am confused, as Ivan is not usually allowed to help with anything. But, before I can question him further, I see that he is clutching something in his meaty paw. I step forward abruptly. Now it is me that is scaring him. No sudden movements around Ivan. That's one of the rules that is drummed into us kids. But the warnings are forgotten now, and I tap his hand until his fingers open to reveal my sister's peacock pin. It is both her most treasured possession, and a family joke. Our father mocks her for preening and strutting the way a peacock would do and, when he stumbled upon the pin, at a market on his only visit home to East Africa, he had to buy it for Afia.

"What are you doing with this?" I shout. Ivan winces at the noise and backs away.

He gestures beyond the forest to the lake behind him, stoops down and brushes his hands through the undergrowth. Power of speech has deserted him, no doubt because I raised my voice to him. I look around, fearful that Ivan snatched this from Afia, remembering the lamb that, like Lennie, he had only really wanted to love but had held too tight. Other than Ivan's careful backward steps, there is no other movement.

"Where did you find this, Ivan?" I try to make my tone friendly as I hold out the peacock pin.

"Water," he replies quietly, looking down at the ground, lower lip trembling a little.

It makes sense what Ivan is saying. His home is near to the bay and he would have had to track along the water's edge to get to the lane. I squeeze the peacock pin in my hand, spinning around, calling for my sister in a stage whisper. When I turn back to question Ivan further he has vanished. All of his life he has been accused of being abnormal, too strong, a freak. Now the community needs Ivan, and they happily sacrifice him. Poor Ivan is so thrilled to be received and rejoiced at last by his neighbours, that he happily sacrifices himself.

Chapter 3
Alex and Elian
London, June 3rd 2015

The day after her meeting with Alex, Elian Gould does something she has never done before. She calls in sick to work.

She sits on the window seat of her third floor flat and watches below as the people scurry along the street to their places of work. She knows that Alex has zoned in on her for a reason, but she does not know why. If all he wanted was proof of identification then why was her driving licence and gas bill not satisfactory? Why, specifically, does he want to see her passport?

It is here, now, on the table under the window. She glares at it and, reaching out, she slides it along the table with her foot until it topples over the edge. She feels silly, hops off and picks it up, turning it over in her hands. It is a UK passport, because she is a UK citizen. It holds no key to any other life, because technically Elian has had no other life. Her family may have, but nobody needs to know that, especially not Alex Harvey. There is nobody to testify to her family's past. There was once, of course, but not anymore. They are all dead. Or gone, which is much of the same thing; either way, they are not in her life.

Yet, every day, she worries that someone is going to discover what her family did. Elian knows it is impossible, and she chides herself, forces herself to go into the big city of London, albeit not very far. She goes into shops and greets her neighbours in the hallway of the building. She talks to her friends, Greta and Paulina, and, to everyone else, she is normal. Not a fugitive or a criminal. But, the fear remains, and so does the truth.

But what of Alex, what is it that he wants? Could it be possible that he really is 'housekeeping' and simply wants her passport for that reason? Hope springs up and she chews on the edge of the passport thoughtfully. Just because she is so naturally suspicious, it doesn't mean everyone else is up to something.

Elian makes a decision and, shoving her passport in her bag, she grabs her Oyster card and hurries from the flat. Usually she walks everywhere, but today she runs to Oxford Circus to catch the tube to Charing Cross.

The walk to and from the office in Cecil Court is only twenty minutes, but the tube is just twelve minutes and as she is already late she decides on speed. They won't be expecting her, since she already called in sick, but she doesn't want to lose any more of the morning than she has to.

She arrives at the tube station just as a train pulls in, and she hops on, happy that rush hour has passed and she gets a seat. The carriage is half empty, but a man who gets on behind Elian sits in the seat next to her. She stiffens, disliking anyone invading her space – especially unnecessarily – and sneaks a look sideways at him. He is wearing a leather jacket and a green woollen ski hat, definitely not needed at this time of the year. It is an odd combination of clothing as well. He does not look her way, but she notices that he clenches his fists and cracks his knuckles, one at a time. The sound reverberates through her and she winces, moves as far away from him as she can and averts her gaze. She is thinking of moving seats when, at Piccadilly, he rises abruptly and steps off the train. She breathes out. Putting her bag on the seat next to her, so nobody else can sit there, she stares unseeingly at the window until the train slows for Charing Cross Station.

Elian hurries from the tube, but stops when she reaches Cecil Court. She likes to take a moment here to pause and survey the land. She does this every morning and, for once, it is not because of her suspicious and fearful nature. It is an appreciation of where she has come from to end up here. Cecil Court is history that has persevered throughout all of the other changes that this city has seen. A seventeenth century street, it is home to antiquarian and independent bookshops with traditional signage that hasn't changed in a century. *Edge*, where Elian works, is situated on the third floor above Goldsboro Books. The magazine is only five years old but, since debuting in 2010, it has rivalled *Down & Out* and *Brick Magazine* for features and thought-provoking articles. She was here on the first day when they cut the ribbon, and never does she forget to appreciate where she is now.

Boosted by her earlier confidence, Elian heads straight up to Alex's office. She is about to knock on the door when Joanna, the deputy head of editorial, comes out of her office. She looks at Elian, a full once over, the kind of look that usually makes Elian feel she is being judged.

"He's not in there," says Joanna, as she walks past, and then she stops and turns back. "What do you want with Alex, anyway?"

"He asked to see me," says Elian, as she backs away from the door. "It can wait, I'm sure."

But Joanna's fleeting interest has dissipated and she has already moved on down the corridor.

Elian goes back down to her desk and switches on her computer. Her in-tray is full and she pulls out the pile of paper. While sorting through it she looks around the room. Her colleagues pay her no heed and she shakes her head. She has called in sick *and* is late, but nobody has even noticed her coming in. Unexpected tears fill her eyes as she logs in to her email. She shouldn't be hurt; after all, anonymity is what she strives for, but, still, it wouldn't kill one of them to stop by her desk and ask after her.

Her train of thought is brought to a sudden halt as she sees Alex's name in her in-box. He has emailed her. What does he want? Is he chasing her passport? Hurriedly she clicks on it.

Elian, I've had to leave the office today. Meet me at The Porterhouse when you get this. Alex.

She blinks and looks around the office, wonders if it is a joke being played on her. Fury flares inside her and she switches the computer off and stands up. Whatever game Alex is playing needs to be stopped now. She has managed to live a peaceful and drama-free life in the last few years and now, suddenly, Alex Harvey has got an eye on her.

She leaves quietly and starts to walk in the direction of The Porterhouse. She knows where it is, but has never been there. As she walks she feels a steely determination build. She will give Alex her passport, he can do whatever he needs to with it, and then she will tell him to leave her alone. She is more confident now, telling herself, as she picks up speed, that he can't know what her family did, nobody knows, and once he sees that she is not an easy target he will back off.

She stops abruptly when she reaches the pub. He is sitting outside, enjoying the sun at one of the lime-green tables. He is wearing aviators and baggy shorts, teamed with a white Levi's T-shirt. Elian, not one for romance or dating, draws a jagged breath at the sight of him. With his closely cropped blonde hair and designer stubble, he is drawing the attention of the majority of females that walk past him. He seems impervious to this, however. He is used to it, she thinks, somewhat bitterly.

At that moment, when her mouth is twisted with scorn and dislike, he looks up and sees her. He stands, raises his hand in a wave and calls her over.

With both confidence and fury suddenly gone, it is a meek and subservient Elian Gould that walks over to his table.

*

Alex's heart does a little jump when he looks up and sees her. She is standing on the corner, dressed in a fashionable crochet-knit cream dress which accentuates her dark skin nicely. Her long Afro hair is pulled back in a loose plait and the Converse trainers she wears should look wrong with such an outfit; but, somehow, the style suits her.

"Hello, Elian," he says, and sits back down when she walks over. "What would you like to drink?"

"Nothing, thank you," Even with the murderous look on her face, she is polite and Alex is amused.

"I'm glad you came."

"I'm not staying." She cuts him off, and pulling her passport out of her bag she slaps it down on the table in front of him. "I just brought you this, you wanted to see it. So you can look at it and then . . ." Elian tails off and Alex, safe behind his shades, studies her face.

He opens the passport and leafs through, taking a moment to check every page. There are no stamps on it. He knows they don't stamp the passport usually when travelling through Europe, and it doesn't look like she has been anywhere else recently. He looks at her passport photo. She is face on, her skin appearing paler by the camera flash, her eyes large, her expression one of fear. He snaps the passport closed and puts it back on the table.

"This expires next August," he drawls.

"But it's valid now." She picks it up and puts it back in her bag. "Am I done? Can I go now?"

"Won't you have a drink with me?" He isn't pleading. Alex doesn't beg anything from anyone; normally he doesn't have to. He removes his shades, looks at her intensely, his blue eyes welcoming and friendly.

She softens, he can see it happening, and he breathes out. He thought for a moment he had pushed it too far, pushed her too much; but, to his surprise and delight, she puts her bag on the floor and sits down opposite him.

She orders a gin and lemonade, a strange choice, but he gets it for her and for himself another Jack and coke. The gin and lemonade sends a thrill through him, after tracking her for so long he thought he knew everything. She drinks it quickly and he orders another. He questions her about work, he praises recent articles that she has both researched and written, detailing them so she knows he has really read them. He stays clear of certain subjects and deliberately avoids talking about her past. It will surface in good time. For now, he needs to have his game head on; but, as the spirits move on to cocktails and then back to shorts, he is struck by the realisation that he is actually enjoying himself. It is a revelation, one that was unexpected because this impromptu drinking session was always supposed to be about one thing: business.

They share a hot platter of chicken, sausages and meatballs, and in the early afternoon decide they should try some of the ales that the pub is famous for. Elian exclaims that the beer is 'terrible', and returns to drinking gin. Alex, who appeared to have matched her drink for drink, but in fact had virgins during cocktail hour, switches to non-alcoholic ale. He does not tell her.

"Why did you want my passport?" she asks, coyly.

He regards her seriously and shrugs his shoulders. "I wanted a chance to speak to you, but you always seem so unreachable. I didn't know how to approach you and by playing the boss card, well, it seemed a good idea."

He is boyish, childlike all of a sudden. Playing her like a theatrical actor, but suddenly it doesn't feel like improvisation. In a heartbeat, his words are truthful, not the lines that he has so carefully prepared. He chances a look at her and she is surprised and puzzled, but does not seem to doubt his lies.

But are they lies? They were; but, through the small amount of alcohol he has consumed, his thoughts are muddy. She is beautiful and intelligent. She is, he finds to his delight, funny and quick.

Alex slips his shades on and snaps the lid shut on this Pandora's Box. She is a means to the end, she always has been and she will remain so.

The mood has changed, but she mistakes it for sexual tension. Now is the time for act two, scene one.

Chapter 4
Sissy
Chernobyl, April 26th 1986

Clutching Afia's peacock pin in my hand, I carry on towards the factory. I know this route like the back of my hand, but even if I didn't I could just follow the smoke. After I've gone almost a mile, helicopters buzz overhead. I can't see them clearly, but their spotlights cast a shining beam from the sky. In the light I can see water being dumped out of the helicopters, although it seems more of a solid mass, too slow-moving to be water. I know I'm close when I start to hear the sirens, and soon the heavy thud of boots and moving vehicles reach my ears.

My plan is to reach my father. Before anything else I must make sure that he is okay. I also need to find Afia. With people like Ivan roaming freely in the area, I need to ensure that she is safe.

I am annoyed at Afia, always in our home it is she that causes trouble. She is older than me, but she never leads by example. Instead, I learn how *not* to behave by noting everything she does that worries my parents, and doing the exact opposite. In the last year she has talked constantly of leaving Pripyat. She wants to go to Europe or America, and she wants to live a life filled with fashion and fun. My parents will not let her leave and, as loving as they are, we know better than to disobey them. Technically they could not stop Afia if she wants to leave, but, like me, she would never dream of going against their orders. Sometimes I wish she would defy them, just a little. For then, in the future, I might be able to as well, although I would never want to leave my home here.

This is not the first time Afia has vanished without telling anyone where she is going. Over the last few months she has left our home at odd hours: before sunrise or very late at night. I watch her from my window. One balmy night in the spring I actually followed her. At the end of our lane she stood in the shelter of one of the pines, checking her watch, fingering her peacock pin and looking left and right down the road. I stayed hidden behind the verge. As the youngest child, I was good at hiding. Eventually, at almost midnight, a man came to meet her. I didn't recognise him, but she said his name, Niko, probably a worker from a neighbouring town. She let out a puff of air as he walked up to her, relief I should think after waiting so long. He did not greet her, not with words anyway. He held her arms to her sides as he backed her up against the trunk of the pine. Then he kissed her. He seemed angry to my naïve eyes and then, as he pulled her skirt up around her waist and spun her around to face the tree, it occurred to me that he *sounded* angry too with the noises that he made. The whites of Afia's eyes were vivid in the night gloom and I closed mine. I didn't want her to see me, hiding, watching. But, also, I didn't want to see her like that.

I stayed long enough to make sure he wasn't in the process of killing her. After they had finished being angry with each other, they spoke softly, too quietly for me to hear them. I crawled carefully away and made my way back home.

Now, as I walk towards the factory I look around me at the trees that line the road. I'm seeking my sister and, if I see her against a tree and conjoined with Niko or some other man, this time I won't stay hidden.

But, I see nobody else and when I reach the site of the factory I stand, hypnotised by the circling helicopters and the smoke that rises up in plumes. A man clutching a shirt to his face rushes past and I reach out and grab him.

"What has happened?" I ask.

He slows to a stop and sags against me. I push him upright and he teeters for a moment before dropping to his knees. The shirt falls to the ground and I stare at his bloodied face. I pick up his shirt and press it into his hands, silently willing him to cover up the macabre mask that used to be his face. He flaps the material at me and I lurch away from the drops of blood. He tries to get up, stumbles back to the ground and crawls away from me.

As I walk onwards I see more men like him. They line the road, dazed and bleeding. The closer I get to the building the worse off they seem. At the gate to the factory there is a man sitting in the road. He claws at his face, his mouth stretched in a silent scream. He does not see me as I approach as he is too busy trying to hold the skin onto his face. Muscle, skin and bloody tissue slips through his fingers.

I am aware that my balance has gone, I am light headed and I drop to my knees and pull myself backwards away from the gate. Now I too am dazed, just like the men who litter the road around me.

Last year, I thought what I witnessed between Afia and Niko was the worst thing I could ever see. Now I know I was wrong. That carnal act, although brutal and violating, was life. This, what I see before me now, this is death.

Chapter 5
Alex and Elian
London, June 3rd 2015

Never before has she bought a man back to the Fitzrovia flat. She has had men, not many, but a few. She never brings them here though, this is her sanctuary, her peaceful safe place. As they move quickly up the stairs, she wonders if she'll regret this. Not just sleeping with Alex, but bringing him here, tainting her home. It is a half-hearted worry, one that, in her drunken state, she dismisses as quickly as the thought arrived.

At the front door they pause while she fumbles for the keys. There are three locks and she sees him looking at them as she turns each key. In the hallway she closes the door behind them and slowly, laboriously, she inserts the key in the three locks all over again. She slips the chain on and then turns to face him. Sobriety has hit fast and Elian doesn't know if this is a good thing or not.

He's something else though, to look at, that is. He is older than her, but the way he wears his clothes and his hair and the whole attitude he exudes gives off a vibe of confidence. He knows what he looks like and suddenly the bitterness is back as she bites her lip and studies him. She reckons he doesn't spend his life looking around dark corners, cringing at the thought of a bad history jumping out at him, catching up with him. And if it did, he'd take out that fancy money clip of his, chuck a wad of cash at the problem and wave it goodbye.

And so it is, with a feeling of something akin to anger simmering below the surface, when she finally reaches for him. She pulls at his shirt, manages to undo two buttons before impatiently reaching for his belt buckle. He knows what he is doing, she realises; as, with a stroke of his strong hands, he all but massages her discontent away and the fury is gone and now she just wants *him*. He pulls her lovely dress up and over and off and she kicks one shoe off. Clothes and accessories trail down the hallway as she leads him to her bedroom and she laughs delightedly at the movie scene vision.

On the bed – for there is no time to get in it – they fuse together. There are no questions about condoms or contraceptives, she will think later that this is most unlike her. But, Alex Harvey has breathed life into that part of her that she thought was long dead. There is no first time awkwardness, they blend and they bond.

*

Later, Alex looks at the sleeping Elian for a long time. He clenches his fists, drags them through his hair and finally slips off the bed and quietly gathers his clothes together. When he is fully dressed he looks at her again and finally pulls a thin blanket over her naked, sleeping form.

He goes to the lounge, keeping quiet as it is only next door to the bedroom and at the front of the building. He looks out of the window, drums his fingers on the glass and closes his eyes.

"Come on, man, do what you came here for," he hisses at himself.

Pulling himself upright he forces himself to look around the room. He goes to her bookcase, sees her laptop on the top shelf and, pulling it down, he flips it open. It springs to life with a password request and he closes it and returns it to the shelf. He pulls a few books out at random, shakes them by the spines. Nothing falls out he runs his hands over shelves and opens the cupboard under the television. Increasingly desperate he turns in a circle, surveying the room. It is more than neat; not a cushion or coaster is out of place. It's quite impersonal too, anyone could live here. There's nothing that points to Elian at all.

He pads silently down the hall to the kitchen, looks in the bedroom on the way. She sleeps on.

In the kitchen the orange biscuit tin is the first thing he sees and he carefully picks it up and, sitting cross-legged on the floor, he opens it. It is full with papers and he lifts them all out and sifts through, one by one. Some are old bills for this flat and he tosses them aside. There is a wad of envelopes, bound with a yellow ribbon, and he unties it, his excitement growing with the possibility of what he has found.

There is a single one dated 1996, addressed to a bed and breakfast in Watford of all places. A few letters, sent between 1989 and 1991, were posted to somewhere in the Ukraine. The age of the Velvet Revolution, Alex muses, and before Elian's time. He opens the first one and grinds his back teeth, it's written in some other language, not the English, French or Spanish which he would be able to read. He flips through the remainder, pulling out random dates and putting them in his back pocket. As he is putting everything else back he hears a noise from the bedroom.

He takes a deep breath and stands up, the biscuit tin in his hands, and turns to face Elian as she comes into the kitchen.

She has put on a white vest and a tiny pair of shorts and she tilts her head to the side as she looks at him holding her tin of most valuable possessions.

He waits, holding his breath, and fixes his eyes on hers. He wishes he had looked away when he sees the flash of pain cross her pretty features.

She steps around him and fills up a glass of water from the tap. She takes a long drink. He notes her hands are shaking, and when she finishes and turns back to him she has changed. Gone is the weak woman. She has steel at her core, just like he knew she did.

"So, Alex," she says quietly, her nostrils flaring slightly as she speaks his name. "Why don't you tell me what it is you really wanted from me?"

Her anger, coupled with her vulnerability, is breathtakingly beautiful and he averts his eyes.

"I'm a PI," he says. "A private investigator, and I want your help."

She blinks at him and he knew that wasn't what she was expecting to hear.

"A PI?"

"A private investigator. My aunt is the owner of *Edge* and I use the office. I do work at the magazine, too, it's not just a front." He stops, wonders why he is explaining himself to her in more depth than he had planned. "I've got a case in the Ukraine and I know your connection to it. I want your help," he repeats, and then he waits.

"Get out!" She startles him. Suddenly she is in his face and the Elian he thought he had got to know has totally gone.

And she is still coming, right at him, her hair wild and her voice so very loud. He doesn't want to provoke her further, not now. Best to let her cool down. He backs up, slips out of the kitchen and she follows him, bouncing around him like a boxer.

"Elian, I'm going. But, please, when you've calmed down . . ."

"Calmed down!" She pushes roughly past him and violently begins to open all of the locks.

He swallows as he looks at the overwhelming security again. The door is open now, and she is standing to one side, arms folded. Her eyes are downcast now and suddenly he has to leave before he sees her cry.

Elian slams the door behind him with all her might. She sinks to the carpeted hall and buries her head in her hands. As she curls into a ball, she sobs. After three years of being totally alone, it had felt *so good* to let him in. For she has been lonely, not daring to open up and let anyone in lest they, too, leave her.

Fury chokes the tears away and she scrambles up and races through the lounge to the window. He is outside, head down, hands stuffed in his pockets as he walks away. She imagines the smirk on his face and she slams her hands on the window, and then backs up in case he heard it.

And what did he want? Her help? He admitted that much. But, help with what? She sinks onto the sofa and thinks back over the events of the last ten minutes. He said he was a private investigator, of what? She grows cold as it becomes clear; he is investigating *her*. Of course, and that's what he was going through her personal possessions for – evidence to use against her in court.

Crying freely now, she staggers into the kitchen and grabs the tin. It has been so long since she read these letters, but she knows the contents of them without even reading them. They are her history, how she came to be, and she clenches the envelopes together and stares out of the window. She has always known that some day somebody was going to find out about her past, that they would come after her and take away her home and her life. And, to Elian, it is so unfair, because none of this is down to her. But, those who are to blame, her mother and her aunt, they are not here anymore to accept fault. Like everybody, they left her too.

*

Not wanting to face anyone at the office, Alex decides to head home. Home for him is a three-storey five-bed house in Putney. It belongs to his aunt. After his parents moved to Portugal, three years ago, he came to stay while he looked for a flat, and simply never left. Over the years Alex took over the top floor as his own and, although he pays his way, it suits him that he doesn't have the responsibility of the upkeep. Selina, his aunt, never married and, although they were not close as he was growing up, these days she is the perfect housemate. He thinks now, as he wanders up to the Putney house, this is the perfect house. Over the years Selina has spared no expense; from the floors which are stripped back to the natural wood, the mod-con kitchen extension complete with atrium to the stained-glass double fronted door.

When he lets himself in, Selina is in the hallway, peering at him over her glasses, wild red hair escaping from her headscarf and reminding him in a way of Elian's Afro.

"Hello, darling!" she exclaims, as he closes the door behind him.

He smiles at her, raising his eyebrows as he takes in the watering can in one hand, gin in the other, a paperback under one arm and the cigarette jammed between her lips.

"Aunty," he rescues the watering can and she murmurs gratefully. "What are you doing?"

"Well I was watering the plants in the living room," she says, as she knocks back the gin. "And while I was watering I was remembering a book I've not read for years, and I had to find it. I just couldn't remember the title." She waves the paperback at him and he grabs it.

"*Brave New World*," he comments. "This is what you were looking for?"

"No." She takes the book back and rewards him with a smile. "But while I was looking I found this and want to read it again. Why are you not at work?"

"Research," he smiles weakly, and grimaces as he remembers Elian's anger.

"You look like you could do with one of these," she waves the gin at him.

He shakes his head. "I've got work to do. But, before I go, do you know anyone who can translate Ukrainian?"

"Adam Bartosz," she replies immediately. "He's actually Polish, but his home was Lviv, blurred borders, you know how it was."

He opens his mouth, but she holds up her hand. "I'll find his number for you."

"Thanks," he says, and makes his way up to the third floor.

In his own sanctuary he pulls the few letters that he stole from Elian out of his pocket and puts them to one side. Firing up his laptop, he logs in to his emails and re-reads the new work instruction. The email address was a combination of the signature at the bottom, BA, with the number 8696. It was a simple Hotmail account, but the IP address seems to be untraceable, Alex has already tried. The note is short and concise, informing him of multiple missing persons and at least one murder that has taken place in the town of Pripyat. Under normal circumstances Alex would have assumed it was a joke and ignored the email. If it hadn't been for the retainer, that is. Fifteen thousand euros paid up front, with another fifteen thousand promised upon completion. The payment gives no clues to the identity of the person who has hired his services. Again, it is signed BA and, again, it is untraceable.

There is a knock at his door and Selina pokes her head round.

"Adam's number," she says, holding out a piece of paper. "If you arrange to meet him, let me know, it would be nice to catch up with him."

"Will do, thanks." He takes the paper, puts it on top of Elian's letters and goes back to his email.

Not for the first time he wonders who BA is. There is one portion of the email that really got his interest. At the end, almost as an afterthought, BA suggests that Alex pays a visit to the home of one of his employees. That employee is named as a Ms Gold, misspelled; but Elian Gould was the only employee who he could pinpoint as being the one that the email meant. Elian's connection to Alex is obviously the reason that his services were sought, rather than one of the many other PI agencies. But BA, his mysterious client, what is their connection to Elian? It's just one of the many unanswered questions and, now, with the Ukrainian letters, the mystery has hooked him.

He stacks the papers in a neat pile and turns off his computer. His face feels flushed at the excitement of a new case and he puts his hands behind his head and closes his eyes. Elian's face, wounded and hurt, pops into his mind, and he snaps his eyes open. What has happened here? This is business, always it is only business, a means to an end, his own personal mantra that he lives by. But if that is the case, and it is the thrill of a new client and mystery to solve that has hooked him, how come it feels like Elian has hooked him too?

Chapter 6
Sissy
Chernobyl, April 26th 1986

I sit on the roadside watching death, until a man approaches me.

He puts his hands on his knees and crouches down. "You can't be here." His voice is gentle, such a contrast to our surroundings, that I look up.

He is wearing a suit and holds a face mask in his hand. I wonder why he is not wearing it. Has he not looked at the other men here and the state they are in?

"I have to find my father, his name is Jengo Bello," I say. "Will you help me?"

He doesn't know me or my family and I see him looking with intrigue at my black skin. Here in Pripyat everyone knows us now, but with the demographic of this place being 95 per cent Ukrainian and Russian, we can be a surprise at first.

"We are locating everybody, but please, you must move back."

He herds me backwards and I struggle weakly against him, but he's a strong man. I don't stand a chance against him.

"It's all right, this is not a major incident." He is casual, smiling and calm, but his eyes tell a different story.

And more people are coming out of the factory, we look at them. I'm still looking for my father. The man forgets me, goes to the new people and pulls them away from the building. Unobserved, I sneak past him and walk through the factory doors.

The building is quiet, the normal hustle and bustle gone. I can hear a groaning noise, like metal scraping on steel, and I realise it is coming from above. I shouldn't be here, I feel sick and I need water; my throat hurts.

"Sissy! What are you doing here?" The voice that calls my name is dearly familiar, and before I even turn around I am crying.

The further relief of seeing my father, apparently unharmed, is overwhelming and I charge at him, wrapping myself around him.

He is angry at me for being here, but I don't care. I recall the man outside whose face was slipping through his fingers and I cry harder, thinking that could have been my father. He is hustling me out now and I see the suited man looking at us, about to speak, but Father holds up his hand and the man lets it go.

"We can't find Afia," I whisper through my tears.

Father's attention has been captured by the men who sit vomiting and bleeding outside the factory. I remind myself that these are his workmates and his friends.

"Pappa," I say, my tone pleading. "Come home, help us find Afia."

But he is disentangling himself from me, telling me to go back to my mother. My heart sinks; my father is proud and loyal and he will stay with his friends and ensure that everyone is safe.

"Sissy!" He calls my name. "Find your sister and take her home. And stay in the house. And close the windows."

I start the walk back home, and this time the forest and roads are not so deserted. News of the fire has spread like, well, like wildfire, and information is traded. Despite the harrowing scenes back at the factory, there is still no huge sense of urgency.

I ask everyone who I pass if they have seen Afia, but all I get are blank looks and negative responses. I finger her peacock pin in my pocket and soon I am back on our road. Everyone has left our home now and my mother is alone in the kitchen. She looks up sharply as I enter, but hope fades when she sees it's just me.

Suddenly I feel weak again and I sit in the chair by the window and look outside. The grey fingers of dawn are breaking over the forest and with the sunrise comes a sense of foreboding.

I shiver.

Afia, where are you?

Chapter 7

Alex and Elian
London, June 5th 2015

Adam Bartosz returns Alex's call and suggests that Alex and Selina meet him at Scandinavian Kitchen. Knowing that it is one of Elian's haunts, Alex hesitates. But he reassures himself; it is Friday and Elian will be at work. When he arrives at midday Adam has got a seat outside, Selina is already with him. Adam introduces himself, shaking Alex's hand firmly.

"I'll be doing my shopping here later, but first order! Eat!" Adam passes menus around and Alex is instantly won over by the man's exuberance.

"I need your assistance, Adam," says Alex, and takes the copies he has made of Elian's letters out of his messenger bag.

Adam takes them and, starting from the earliest letter, he begins to read. Selina glances almost sternly at Alex before addressing Adam. "I'm sure you can take those away with you, this isn't a working lunch."

Alex is about to agree when, looking up, he sees Elian walking down Great Titchfield Street. He glances at Adam, now in conversation with Selina and waving the letters that he is holding around to emphasise a point. It has been two days since he saw her and he has purposefully left her alone before attempting to make contact. Now she is here, and she's spotted him; so, improvising and feeling like the smooth-talking pro he believes himself to be, he hurries away from the table to meet her, wondering why she is not at work.

"I saw you here," she says quietly. "I want to know what you want from me, and what you're going to do with the stuff you know about me."

Alex is surprised, this is unexpected. Elian is frightened and Alex realises that he is holding the cards again. He glances over at Adam and it strikes him that there is something very important, and possibly incriminating, in those letters that he holds. Interesting.

"Can I stop past later? I'll tell you all about it." Alex is careful to keep his tone level, he doesn't want to scare her so much that she does a runner altogether.

"No," she says, with a shake of her head, and he understands that she doesn't want him anywhere near her flat again. "I'll meet you, where?"

As Alex thinks of somewhere to meet, Selina catches his eye. She is sporting an amused look, watching the exchange between her nephew and Elian, and Alex has a brainwave.

"Come over to my house." At her startled expression he puts a hand on her arm. "It's private, and I promise I'll tell you everything, Elian."

She softens a little when he says her name and he wants to feel elated that he has won her over, but he is not.

"Give me your phone, I'll write my address in it," he instructs.

She roots around in her tote and hands him a Nokia. He stares at it, then at her.

"Are you kidding me?"

She looks up at him as he hands her phone back, all big wounded eyes. Alex grabs a passing waitress and asks to borrow her pen and pad. On it he scribbles his address and mobile number and, tearing off the sheet, he gives it to Elian.

"Come by later, I'll be in all evening."

She doesn't agree, he notices, but then she does not refuse either. He watches her tuck the piece of paper in her pocket and, with a brief glance at Selina, she carries on her way.

"And who was that?" Selina asks as soon as he sits back down at the table.

Alex doesn't answer and instead he directs his attention to Adam. "I'm going to need those letters translated as quickly as possible. Could you do it today?"

Adam shrugs his shoulders and Alex clenches his fists out of sight under the table. Old people are so slow; they have no sense of urgency, nothing that they need to hurry for. He takes a deep breath and tries not to sound impatient.

"Perhaps if I leave you now, you could drop them around to our house later. And, as a thank you, Aunty will cook you a nice dinner." Without waiting for a reply, Alex pulls some notes out of his wallet and leaves them on the table. "Thank you, Adam; I'll see you both later."

Leaving Selina and Adam somewhat surprised, Alex picks up his messenger bag and hurries off down the road in the same direction as Elian.

Walking fast, Elian cuts through to Oxford Street. She feels shaky after her encounter with Alex and wonders if she will go to his house tonight. As she plucks the paper with his address on out of her pocket, she realises that someone has also stopped behind her. She does not turn around; but, gripped by paranoia, she walks on in the direction of Hyde Park. It is a warm day and, desperate for some calm, she decides to walk through the park. After all, she had plenty of annual leave to use from work and her day is her own; until tonight that is.

The street is busy, as always, but Elian still has a sense that someone is tailing her. In fact, she has felt this way for some time now. She doesn't want to turn around in case she provokes whoever it is into a reaction. What do they want from her? Why does it seem that everyone is after something from her lately?

Up ahead she sees Marble Arch and the busy crossing. Perhaps she can lose him there. She walks as slow as she dares until she is upon the crowd of people waiting for the lights to change and she hangs back. As soon as the traffic lights turn red she pushes her way into the group of people, apologising as she breaks through the front and darts across the road. Head down, she grips her bag tightly and jogs into another throng of tourists, hoping that her assailant has lost her in the crowd. She walks in their midst for a few minutes and when she feels that it must be safe she moves away and through the park gates. Putting a hand on her pounding heart she looks discreetly around. Nothing seems out of the ordinary, so she walks on, slower this time.

She heads for the Serpentine, musing that it is further from the flat than she usually goes. But, then again, all those years of being terrified that someone was going to find out about her, well, that has happened now, hasn't it? Realising that makes her feel almost free. There is no need to look over her shoulder anymore, worrying that someone is after her, because Alex *is* after her, and he has admitted this. With that thought she knows that she will indeed go to his home tonight and find out just what it is that he wants from her. If she gives him what he wants, maybe he won't turn her in to the authorities.

Going over it in her mind makes her feel a lot calmer. As she retrieves his address from her pocket she glances up and her blood runs cold, as she spots a man leaning on a bin up ahead of her. He is looking for someone, for *her*, but he is looking away from her. Elian leaps to the side of the path and stands behind the trunk of a huge tree and covers her mouth with her hand. Holding on to the tree she dares to peek around the trunk and looks at him. His ensemble is bizarre. He is wearing a leather jacket and a hat and, oh . . .! The memory strikes her, this man is the same guy who sat next to her on the almost empty train carriage two days ago. She squints at him, sure now of her conviction. He is wearing the same jacket and hat, the very ones that struck her as so odd, seeing as it is the middle of summer. She conceals herself behind the tree again, deep in thought, as another possibility hits her. Has Alex sent this man? Has he been tailing her everywhere she goes? Shaking, but with anger now as well as fear, she pulls her old mobile out of her bag and dials the number that Alex wrote down along with his address. She hears it begin to ring and then, *he* is there too. Alex, himself, strolling through the park about fifty metres from her. As he stops to answer his phone Elian ends the call and, shoving his address and her phone back in her tote and forgetting momentarily about the *other* stalker, she takes off towards Alex.

When she reaches him, hot tears are slipping down her face, but she is filled with a rare fury.

"Elian?" he blinks, looking from his phone to her. "Were you just . . ."

She cuts his words off by grabbing her bag in both hands and slamming it in to his stomach. It is not satisfactory enough and she does it again, using all her force, all her might. He accepts it twice and, as she goes back for a third, he catches her by her wrists and holds her at arm's length.

"What the fuck?" Alex shakes her, and she struggles against him.

"You're sending your people after me, why? I'm going to help you aren't I? I don't have a choice, so tell them to back off," she cries, still pulling against him.

"Hey, what are you talking about?" He pulls her closer and she sags against him, the fight leaving her and fatigue setting in.

As if sensing this, he lets go of her and she stumbles back.

"That man, over by the bin. I keep seeing him, he keeps following me." She glares at him, simmering now. "You can tell him to stop now. I'll do what you want."

Alex is looking over her head and she clucks impatiently and spins around, arm outstretched, finger pointing.

"Oh," she breathes and covers her mouth with her hand.

The stranger has vanished.

*

Alex had lost sight of Elian in the hustle and bustle of the junction of Oxford Street and Hyde Park. He thought he had caught a glimpse of her entering the park through Cumberland Gate and he had pressed on, no particular plan in mind, but thinking that he may as well keep walking anyway. He had gone through the park, heading in the vague direction of the Serpentine when his phone had started to ring. He pulled it out, saw an unfamiliar number which cut off before he could answer, and then Elian was on him, battering him with her little bag, a wildcat that was scared and cornered.

And now she is gesturing to someone who isn't there, the path ahead is empty and he waits for an explanation.

"He was there, and earlier this week, he was on my tube," she murmurs, and to Alex it sounds like she is trying to convince herself.

"I've not sent anyone to follow you," he reassures her. "I work alone. I don't use anyone else in my business."

This is not strictly true, he thinks. After all he is using Adam Bartosz right now, but certainly not to stalk Elian.

Elian remains silent, still staring down the path, her hands loose at her sides, and he picks up her bag that has fallen to the ground.

"Elian, come back to my house, you shouldn't be out here if you think someone is watching you."

At his words she turns to face him and an unfamiliar feeling grabs his insides at the sight of the tear tracks on her cheeks. She is dazed, incapable of making a decision. Alex makes it for her and takes her arm, gently this time, and leads her back the way they came. She complies, puts one foot in front of the other, and in silence they walk out of the park together.

From Marble Arch to Notting Hill Gate she says nothing, looks at nobody. Alex stares out of the window, watching the black walls of the London Underground. After the change they are on the final leg towards Putney Bridge and she becomes more alert, looking around, over her shoulder.

"There's nobody here to worry about," he says, reassuringly he hopes, but she simply flares her nostrils and shoots him a look.

After they alight at Putney he steers her down Putney High Street and they are almost at the river when he turns left on to Lower Richmond Road. They walk along the waterfront and she stops as he goes up to the front door of his home.

"You live here?" She asks.

"Yes," he smiles at her. "Are you coming in?"

She treads up the steps behind him and, for effect, he opens both doors. She glances behind her, grips her bag tight and follows him in.

"You live here alone?"

"No, with Selina," he says, and seeing her expression he explains. "She's my aunt, this is her house. I just came to stay one day and never left. You might have seen her earlier, we were having lunch at Scandinavian Kitchen."

She nods and walks through the large hallway. "Do you have a view of the river?"

"We do," he says, stupidly delighted at her question and wonders what the hell happens to him when he is the presence of Elian. "Would you like to see it?"

He guides her through the kitchen, noticing her looking in awe at the atrium. Through to the conservatory and they are on the side of the Thames.

"It's almost like a house-boat," she remarks thoughtfully. "Does the river ever rise?"

"Yes, but not enough for any damage," he replies, walking around her and studying her.

She wraps her arms around herself as she surveys the horizon. He wonders what she's thinking and feeling now. Does she shiver because she feels exposed, standing out here in the open? Does she imagine that whoever has followed her is lurking in every shadow, every doorway? Is something else going on with her, is that why her apartment is like Fort Knox?

He reflects back over the times that he has followed her and searches in the dregs of his memory, but he can't recall anyone standing out. Even if there was someone familiar, it would be a little odd, but not really that unusual, for Alex himself was tracking Elian's movements to get an idea of her routine. It could be that the other man's own daily routine corresponded with hers. After all, how many times on the commute to

42

the office does Alex see the same faces? Many times, so much so that over the years they exchange nods and pleasantries, remarks about the weather. But Elian obviously thinks that there is something off about this particular guy. Then again, she is blatantly paranoid about most of the aspects of her life anyway.

Alex leaves Elian looking out over the Thames as he retreats into the kitchen and sits at the breakfast bar.

Whoever this mystery stalker is has done Alex a favour, no questions about that. So spooked is Elian, she has come running straight into Alex's arms. No longer is he the villain, but the hero, and that is a role that Alex is sure he can play very well.

Chapter 8
The Boy
Ukraine 1976 – 1985

The boy does not know that his life is any different to all the other ten-year-old boys out there. He has never wondered if the children that he passes on his way to the market also watch their parents fighting. Not each other, not too much anyway, and when it is just his parents it is usually verbal, but with the other people that his parents bring back to their caravan home. He imagines that other children clean up the blood that has been spilt before it soaks in and stains the walls and floors forever. He learnt early on to always have a sponge and a bottle of bleaching agent to hand and, as soon as that red liquid starting seeping out through split skin or jagged knife holes, to pounce with his sponge. He does not do this out of a sense of cleanliness, simply by learning that he would be made to clean up the mess and it was a far easier job to do straight away. Much less scrubbing and elbow grease needed that way.

As soon as his age hit double figures the boy was moved on to cleaning his parents' tools. He removed the sinewy muscle and tissue from the axe head, pulled bits of tooth enamel from the pliers and made sure every last blood-soaked hair was cleaned from the claw end of the hammers.

When the boy was fourteen he had a growth spurt. His parents found other jobs for this surprisingly strapping lad. He moved the bodies, transporting them with ease on his shoulder into the woods when the night was at its darkest. He dug the holes of the final resting places, eight foot deep as per his father's instructions.

He did not go to school, but he learned all about life from his parents' victims, before the messy stuff happened, when the guests were still just visitors and happy to be there. Then, later, he learned about death from them too. On occasion they stayed in campsites and the boy started to learn about cars and engines. An old hippy taught him to weld and the boy found he wass naturally skilled at it. When the old hippy died, the boy kept his welding torch for himself.

They move around a bit, as much as they can without drawing attention to themselves, keeping within the Eastern Bloc, setting up camp in dark, dank forest areas; staying to slaughter and then moving on.

They stay on the outskirts of Cherniviv and, when the boy is nineteen, the inevitable happens; his parents, with no visitors to spar with, fight each other.

They have quarrelled before, but this is different. The boy stands in the doorway of the caravan and watches as they go at each other. He does not know what set them off, but there are no words. They just swing at each other using their fists or anything within reach.

His mother is called Janelle. She is of slight build and very thin. Her hair, usually lank and greasy, is plastered to her face, made dark by a mixture of blood and sweat. His father, Sergi, is the polar opposite of Janelle. In his youth he was a wall of solid muscle. Then the ensuing years caught him, and now he is distinctly flabby with a gut that hangs low over the waistband of his trousers. His chest and stomach are swathed in dark, coarse hair.

Janelle seems to have the upper hand in the fight. She is nimble and quick, darting in with the small boning knife that she has snatched up.

The boy watches with a sick fascination as Sergi roars when the knife pierces his skin. Janelle laughs in triumph and as Sergi picks up a small generator and raises it up to bring it crashing down into Janelle's laughing face, the boy gets his cleaning equipment ready.

Chapter 9
Alex and Elian
London, June 5th 2015

Elian finally comes in from the conservatory when a summer shower begins to hammer down. Alex glances up at her from his seat at the dining room table and beckons her to a chair. She sees the stack of papers in front of him and is inexplicably nervous. Finally she will find out exactly what information he is holding against her.

"Do you know whose initials are BA?" he asks as she takes a seat.

She thinks, draws a blank and shakes her head.

She is uncomfortable and without pausing to think about what she is saying the words tumble from her mouth. "Was it bad? Sleeping with me, I mean? Should we not have. . . ?"

He stares at the table and now she can see that he is uneasy. After a pause he looks up.

"It wasn't bad, Elian," he smiles, tenderly almost, and she blushes. "It was really fucking good. But I shouldn't have . . ."

It suddenly hits Elian that he most likely has a girlfriend and, well, why wouldn't he? He probably has dozens. And he probably doesn't blackmail them, she really must be special, she thinks, and is surprised that she can feel wry amusement as her life hangs in the balance. And she is glad that she has said something, because what he did – having sex with her just to gain information – that was more hurtful than anything.

"Show me what you've got," she demands, and braces herself.

Alex takes a deep breath and picks up the papers he has prepared. He takes the very first email that he received, having doctored it by removing the mention of Elian and reprinting it. She takes it from him and reads it quickly.

"Is that it?"

He passes her the receipt for the payment made and she whistles at the amount.

"But where do I come into this?" Elian waves the paper at him; but, before he can answer he hears a key in the front door. Selina is back and he takes the papers from Elian.

"Stay and eat with us?" His offer is genuine, but he also needs to stall for time, after all Adam has to translate the letters that Alex stole from Elian.

Before Elian can give an answer Selina bustles into the kitchen. She has her hands full of carrier bags and Adam is trailing after her.

"Adam is staying for dinner," announces Selina, and stops at the sight of Elian at the table. "Hello!"

Alex stands up and takes the bags from Selina. "Elian will be staying to dinner too. Adam, may I have a quick word?"

In the hallway Alex draws Adam down to the front door, closing the kitchen door behind him. Before he can speak Adam takes a notebook from his inner jacket pocket with a flourish.

"I presume this is what you are so impatient for?"

"You've done them already?"

"Yes, while your aunt shopped for ingredients for our dinner." Adam cast a glance at the kitchen door and lowered his voice. "And the lady in there, she is a part of this, no?"

"Yeah, but blissfully unaware at the moment so . . ." Alex raises his eyebrows.

Adam strokes his full beard and looks pensive.

"Don't worry, as soon as I have read these through I'm going to talk it all over with her." Alex claps Adam on his shoulder and steers him back to the kitchen. "And, while I'm reading, your job is to keep those two lovely ladies entertained."

Alex knows he's pushing his luck, but before Adam can answer Alex retreats to his upstairs sanctuary to start reading the translations.

He begins with the earliest dated letter of April 1989. It starts 'to my darling' and Alex squints to read Adam's untidy scrawl.

I am heavy with fatigue, I am so alone. They say there will be money given to us but who knows when? They say this, they say that. It is lies. Don't come back here, you are safer there.

But I miss you, I am alone here. I've lost everyone.

Alex wonders who it is for, and, reading it now in English, it seems more like a diary entry than a letter. With no clue, he moves on. The next letter is typed up, official looking – to the untrained eye that is. Alex looks at the original that he took from Elian's flat. It's fake, he is pretty certain. There is no water mark like there usually is on government papers, and the coat of arms, a gold trident on an azure background, is usually raised. This one, although in colour, seems like a poor copy.

The letter is addressed to Mr Bello, dated 1996, and Adam has handwritten the translation and paper-clipped it to the copy.

In light of the dosimeter readings and correspondence from Hospital 126, Kiev, funding has been reserved for the family of Jengo M Bello. In order to take receipt of your allotted funding it is necessary to attend the branch of a bank situated in the city of London, in the United Kingdom . .

.

Alex snorts and wonders if Jengo Bello fell for this. He casts it aside, glances at the clock and picks up the most recent letter, sent to the Watford bed and breakfast in 1996.

Sissy,

Thank you for coming to England, I know how much you hate to leave Pripyat. Here is the deal, you must go to the address at the end of this letter. That apartment is yours Sissy. But there is one condition, you must keep safe what you find in the apartment.

If you don't do this for me, I can see to it that the money that has been sent to the family is taken back. I do have this power, I don't want to have to use it. When you go to the apartment and see what awaits you I know in my heart you won't hesitate to do the right thing by me, your family and by God.

The letter is not signed, but it is dated 3rd May 1996. There is no postmark, which suggests it was hand delivered. Alex puts the copies and originals in his messenger bag. Wanders over to the floor-to-ceiling window and stares out over the Thames.

Who is Sissy? Who sent her that letter in the summer of '96? And what was waiting at the Fitzrovia apartment? These are all questions that Alex is sure he will have answers to eventually; but, for now, he is satisfied. He has the leverage needed to ensure Elian helps him. He catches a glimpse of his smiling reflection in the glass and takes a deep breath. It's time to put the next stage of his plan into action.

Chapter 10
Sissy

Chernobyl, May 1st 1986

Almost a week has passed since the explosion at the factory and I know now that my life has changed forever.

My father is in the hospital in Kiev. My mother is also in Kiev, trying to get allowed in to see him. Afia has not come home. The day after the explosion over a thousand buses came from Kiev. We were given two hours to pack our belongings and get on a bus. Because my parents were not here, nor Afia, I didn't know what to do; so I stayed in my house and hid. Our neighbours must have spread the word that my family had already left, because nobody came looking for me.

I thought I was all alone, but in between the evacuation and now, I've seen a few people, soldiers, mostly. I'm pretty sure they've seen me too, but they've let me be so far. I ventured out to the lane yesterday and saw Knor, an elderly man who has always lived on his own for as long as I've known him. He stared blankly at me, then recognition crossed his features and he asked me why I was still here.

I didn't know what to tell him, but where else would I go? Besides, somebody needs to stay here for when Afia returns.

As Knor shuffled off towards his dilapidated old shack, a thought struck me and I hurried after him.

"Knor, have you seen my sister recently?"

"Black, like you?" He sniffed, looked down his nose at me. "Not since the factory *sookakoorva* happened. Not seen anyone since that *blyat*."

I tried to ignore his cursing. "Where did you see her? Was it before the accident?"

"By the river, down by those bunkers, with that *zhyrnyy hivno*."

I'd got no more out of him, and now I sit at my window, wondering who the 'greasy shit' is that Knor referred to. The way I see it, I have to make my own decisions now. I have to go to the river and maybe there I'll find my sister and bring her back home.

It's hot outside and I pick my way carefully through the forest, avoiding the main road as I don't want to be caught by the soldiers who are patrolling the area.

Usually the river bank is a haven for children in the summertime, but now it's deserted. I find it eerie and I wrap my arms around myself as I head towards the bunkers.

One thing is clear, Afia is not here now. I touch her peacock pin. I've taken to wearing it in the past week. I know if she sees it on me she will be furious, and I'm kind of counting on it. I want her home, or at least I want to know where she is. Right now I'd be happy to have her angry with me.

Since I have nothing else to do today I walk along the side of the river. The bunkers here are deserted, once used by the people who came here in 1970 to construct the power plant and our man-made city of Pripyat. Fishermen sometimes camp in them, and during the school holidays children play here all day long. At night, lovers bring blankets and wine and watch the river by moonlight. My sister does not belong to any of these groups, except possibly the last. Although from what I saw of her and Niko, he does not seem like a candlelit romancing type of man.

Niko . . . Could he be the greasy shit that Knor was referring to? Was she still seeing him? But I have no idea where he lives, in fact I don't know anything about him, except that he does not live in Pripyat. I know everyone who lives here, or *lived* here, perhaps I should say, and Niko is not one of them.

I move into the bunkers, one by one, just to say that I have checked them. The first two are empty, save for a large, dead rat. I shudder and move on to the third and final bunker. It is dim in here, in the shade of the trees that overhang the river, and I wait while my eyes adjust to the light. There is something in the corner, shining in the gloom. I edge nervously towards it, poking at it with my foot. It rustles and I realise it is a plastic carrier bag. I crouch down, pull it towards me and, picking it up, I take it outside in the sunlight. It's soft, and I upend the bag and tip the contents out.

I have a similar feeling now to the one I had last week at the factory, when I watched the men slowly dissolving at the roadside. This whole situation is suddenly very real as I sit down by the river, tears pricking at my eyes as I look at the contents of the carrier bag. It's Afia's ridiculous red pant suit. Bright red and not worn yet through years of washing like all of my clothes. I wonder if there could be anything worse than finding my missing sister's clothes. Then I lean closer and know that, yes, there is something worse. I see that it is torn and slashed, spattered here and there at random places. Parts of the pant suit material are darker with recent stains of blood.

Chapter 11
Alex and Elian
London, June 8th 2015

Sitting in the departure lounge at Stansted Airport, Elian looks out of the window at the plane. Shivers of nerves and of excitement run through her. This is her birthright, this journey to Sissy's place and all of the Bellos who Sissy taught her about as she raised her. And would she find Sissy, her runaway aunt, back there?

Elian hides a smile as she recalls Alex's shock when he discovered that the mysterious Sissy mentioned in the letters he stole from her is her beloved aunt. It was also the time that realisation dawned on Elian that this blackmailing son of a bitch didn't hold all the cards after all.

Elian had been slightly put out when Alex had left her alone with Adam and Selina, two people she had never met before. But her discomfort had turned into something else entirely as she put herself to good use and helped Selina prepare the meal that she had been invited to; and Adam had been an unexpected delight. Without imparting any of her history she had conversed with him in Polish, her rusty language skills coming back to her at his gentle prompting. Not for the first time, she sent a silent message of thanks to Sissy for bringing her up alongside all the languages that she, Sissy, had known.

Later, when Selina and Adam had left for an 'evening constitutional' along the Thames, as Selina called it, Alex had laid his cards on the table.

"I want to know if you'll come to Chernobyl with me," he had asked, taking a seat opposite her.

"And what do I do once I'm there?"

"Your role is to translate for me, you'll be on the books, a paid employee of my agency," he had replied, eyes twinkling.

He had thought he had her, already, that she was that scared of his unspoken threat. *I'm not that easy*, she had thought to herself, bristling at his confidence. Well, okay, so she had been easy once, in his company, but that one mistake didn't mean that he owned her or had control over her.

"I want half of what you are getting paid," she said, as she pulled the email towards her and scans through it. "Seven thousand, five hundred euros, and when this is done, I want it in writing that you won't bother me. I want all my letters back, including copies."

He'd stared unblinkingly at her, digesting her demands, no doubt. "Two thousand euros."

"Four."

"Three."

She hesitated and he had held up a piece of paper, the one with the government crest on it. The fake. "Please don't forget which one of us is in charge, Elian."

She bristled, almost told him where to stick his job. Then she had remembered her family, the one who raised her and the ones she never met. All of those sacrifices made, and although they had left her, she couldn't blow that.

"Okay," Elian relented.

He had smiled, like a cat who had got the cream, but his victory was soon forgotten as he had gone back to musing over the file.

"If only I knew who this Sissy was." Alex looked up at her. "Any ideas?"

She recalled thinking that he doesn't know everything. Interesting. She had smiled, tried but failed to keep a laugh from bubbling out of her, and he'd looked at her in surprise.

"I know exactly who Sissy is, she's my aunt, the woman who raised me. The closest thing I ever had to a mother."

*

Now, at the airport, Elian feels like she had some sort of victory back then. The feeling is short lived as now, sitting here, looking at the plane she is about to board, she is terrified. As if sensing this, Alex nudges her with his shoulder.

"All right?"

Is she all right? Not really, not since her nice, safe life was snatched away like a rug pulled out from under her. In fact, her life has not been nice and safe for about three years, since the woman who had raised her upped and left without so much as a note. But how can she say that to Alex?

"Are you nervous of flying?"

She smiles bravely and shakes her head. Alex thinks she's not done anything with her life, not been anywhere. He is very wrong. Before Sissy left, when Elian was much younger, they would go everywhere. Europe, Morocco even, and how Sissy had loved spending time on the continent that had been her own birthright.

But there had only been one place that Sissy really wanted to go, and that was back home to Chernobyl. The one place that she could never go back to was the only home that she truly yearned for.

As their flight is called, Alex puts a protective hand on Elian's back. She looks over her shoulder, glares at him and he removes it with a tight smile. He does not how to act with her now. He is no longer her lover, nor her real enemy. He is not a friend or even really her boss any more. Although he *is* paying her, the role of employer doesn't sit right with him, too many boundaries have been passed for that.

He offers her the window seat and she slides in without a word, stares through the window at the dreary day.

Alex wonders what the weather will be like in Chernobyl. He wonders what everything will be like. From his limited knowledge he imagines toadstools as big as a horse, sheep with two heads. In fact, he is sure that he has seen a picture on the internet of an animal with an extra leg growing out of its spine. He shudders, dreading to think what the people who have stayed since 1986 will look like. And what if they reproduced? Oh God, they're going to be like the characters in 'Deliverance'; Mongol-like inbreeds, but with nuclear deficiencies instead of genetics.

"Did you take the iodine pills I gave you?" He asks Elian now, rooting around in his hand luggage for his own bottle, and taking two, even though he has already taken the quota for today.

"Yes, but I'm sure we'll be fine," she remarks, a patronising tone to her voice and a smirk on her face.

He sits back, uncharacteristically nervous. His professional life does not usually involve going into the heart of a city that has been cut off from civilisation for almost thirty years. Normally his work involves cheating spouses, employment checks, child custody or missing persons where the police just don't have the resources. On occasion he is even employed by the Metropolitan Police. It's not often they sub-contract their work, generally they don't want to waste their budget, but sometimes, especially in high profile cases where public opinion matters more than money, his services are called upon.

This situation is a tangled mess, a web with players that he does not really know. Even Elian is keeping some things quiet, her mother's identity for one. She proclaims that Sissy never told her, never even said if she, Sissy, was her biological aunt. But Sissy was Black, Elian is definitely mixed race, so they are linked by blood. Why the secrecy? And why did Elian never demand to know her parentage? He had asked her this, a couple of days ago, as they sat at Selina's table. She had shrugged, her eyes faraway as she forgot herself for a minute and started to confide in him.

"I asked her once, when I was old enough. She said she didn't know, she showed me the letters, the same ones you have there." She had glared pointedly at him. "She thought maybe I was her sister's child, but she thought – still thinks, that her sister was dead. She went missing long before I came on the scene. Let's face it, I could be anybody's."

It had set Alex to thinking about his own life and how uncomplicated it always had been. He knew who his parents were, that he was their only child, that as soon as they could they sold their share in *Edge* Magazine to Selina, his mother's sister, and retired to Portugal. It wasn't a great wrench for Alex. He has been independent for as long as he could remember. They are not and never have been a family to smother one another, but they are always there, on the end of a Skype call or an email. And if he ever feels the need to kick back and relax, he knows he can turn up on the doorstep of their villa on the Iberian Peninsula.

He looks at Elian now, remembering his shock when she had told him that Sissy had vanished with no warning one week after Elian's sixteenth birthday. He had been eager to hear more, he wanted to know it all, but she had clammed up and gone back to business. He can't imagine how she coped, alone in London at sixteen. She was provided for, obviously Sissy saw to that, what with the flat and ensuring Elian had a job. But still, she'd left a kid, *alone*. He glances at Elian and looks quickly away. Alex is not maternal or overly emphatic, but to do that to a kid? To do that to Elian . . .

And she is not in the mood for talking now, that much is obvious. So he sits back, watches the ground fall away as they take off, bound for an unknown land, suddenly wishing more than anything he had declined the thirty thousand euros and was taking a trip to Portugal instead.

Chapter 12
Sissy

Chernobyl, May 1st 1986

After I get back from the river, my sister's blood stained clothes in the bag where I found them, I'm suddenly hopeful when I see movement through the window of our house. My mother is home. I'm not sure what I was hopeful for, perhaps just the fact that an adult was suddenly, *finally*, present, and I could forget all of this and go back to being a kid. But that was a foolish, childish dream.

"Mama!" I cry, as I rush inside our house and find her in the kitchen. "You're home!"

I run to her, throw my arms around her and bury my face in her skirt. Hot tears prick my eyes and the bag that I am clutching knocks against her. She bats me away, looks at me over her shoulder.

"I'm not staying, I need to get some things for your Pappa," she mutters. "Are you all right, Sissy? Are you staying out of trouble?"

"Yes, of course, Mama." I reply obediently, trying not to let her see that her brush off upset me. "Mama, how is Pappa? Will he be coming home soon?"

"God willing, but he is very sick. Everybody is very sick. Nobody seems to be in charge, sometimes we are allowed in, sometimes we are not." She heaves a sigh, stops packing for a moment and rubs her hands over her eyes. "What about your sister? Is she looking after you?"

It feels like my blood freezes in my body at her words. She doesn't know that Afia is still missing. That she hasn't been seen since the night of the accident at the factory! I look at Mama closely, seeing now that she is exhausted. Her skin, always shining and glowing, seems an unhealthy shade of grey. Realising that I am still holding the plastic bag with Afia's bloodstained clothes, I visibly blanch. I can't heap this on my mother, not now, not with Pappa still in the hospital.

"Everything is fine here, Mama. Really," I reassure her, as sincerely as I can manage.

"And you two are okay here? Perhaps you and your sister should come to Kiev with me," she muses, as she zips up the large shopping bag.

"No!" My tone is sharp enough for her to look round and frown at me. "I mean, who will look after the animals, the neighbours? I saw poor old Knor this morning, he's on his own; somebody needs to keep an eye on those who are staying here."

Thankfully she has turned her back and I throw the bag of Afia's clothes over in the corner.

"I have to go now, pray to God that those soldiers let me back out. But of course they will, it's a miracle they let me back in! Sissy, I'll call on Knor's phone if there is anything urgent to tell you. If everything is the same I will come back in a week, hopefully with your father."

And with a quick hug she is gone. I watch her hurry down the lane, glancing furtively left and right, and then I see two women join her, our neighbours, whose husbands must also be in the hospital with Pappa.

Then there is silence, once again I am alone.

After inspecting Afia's red pant suit I decide to head over to Knor's house and see if he knows anything more about the man he saw Afia with.

He is home, a single light glowing in his shabby hut. I knock on his door and call his name, so he knows it is me and not the soldiers here to turf him out. I hear him shuffle to the door and he unlocks it, peers out at me.

"I need to speak to you about my sister, she's still missing, and I have to find her."

He looks me up and down, his gaze lingering on my bare legs in my summer shorts and I feel very exposed as he licks his dry lips.

"Please, Knor, tell me what you saw." I beg, hating my pleading tone, but having no choice.

He turns and walks back inside, but leaves the door open and, with a glance over my shoulder, I follow him in.

His home smells musty and damp. A thick layer of dust covers every surface and there are no pictures or mementoes, nothing to personalise this place at all. I wonder, fleetingly, if he ever had a wife or a family. What happened? Where are they now?

"That black bitch," he snaps suddenly, "that dirty, filthy black bitch."

My heart begins to beat too fast and my vision blurs. He is talking about my sister. He is standing in the centre of the room, facing away from me, his hands curled into fists. Vitriol dripping from him like perspiration.

"What do you mean?" I manage to ask, my shaky voice betraying me. "Why are you talking about her that way?"

"You come here and you pollute us with your filth!" He turns around, spittle bubbling over his lips, his face red. "Opening her legs for every man, laying in the gutter, bringing disease!"

"No!" Never have I heard anyone speak such terrible words, but my memory drags up a vision of Afia and Niko, against the tree in the lane.

"Klim Karpik!" He whispers the name of a local boy that I know. "She beds down with him, and then the next night, that filthy gypsy. Whore!"

I have a name, I know where Klim lives with his father and that is all I came here for. I back away towards the door, but Knor follows and, with an agility that beguiles his age, he raises his arms, pinning them either side of me against the wall. I recoil from his rank breath and screwing my eyes shut I turn my head away from him.

"And you, do you open these, like that black bitch?"

I feel his calloused fingers on my thigh, and to me it is an electric shock. My legs jerk out, my arms flailing blindly. My fist catches him somewhere and I drop into a crouch, roll away and scramble for the door.

"Bitch! Black bitch! Whore!"

I can still hear him shouting obscenities as I sprint down the lane back to my house, and I can still feel his hand on my thigh.

I need to regroup and think, make a plan and calm down. I intend to lock my house up tight tonight and then, at first light, I will make my way to Klim's place.

Feeling slightly better now that I have a plan, and with my heartbeat almost back to normal, my world is then shattered once more as I see a soldier waiting for me on the porch of my house.

Chapter 13
Alex and Elian
Kiev, June 8th 2015

Elian stands outside the airport and looks around. This place, right here, could be anywhere in the world. But she can see beyond the rows of rental cars and taxis to the city beyond. On the skyline, rows of medieval buildings with spherical towers catch her eye. It seems exuberant, rich and colourful and she feels a thrill run through her. Alex comes up behind her, sets his small case down and looks around.

"It's lovely, isn't it?" she says, still drinking it in. "Are we going to Pripyat now?"

"No, we're booked on a tour tomorrow, we'll stay here tonight."

"Where are we staying?" she asks. "Are we in a hostel?"

Alex glances over at her as if she suggested staying on the moon. "A hostel? No! I've booked us in at the Hyatt. Come on, here's our car."

Elian blinks. The Hyatt? And who gets their rental car delivered to them kerb-side instead of going into the underground garage lot to get it?

Trailing behind Alex, Elian realises that this trip is going to be very different to the ones that she took with Sissy.

"Hey, if we're going on a tour, what are we doing with the rental car?" she asks as she climbs into the front seat of the Mercedes.

"Hertz will collect it from the hotel," he replies, as he pulls out into the stream of traffic on the highway.

"You hired a car just to get from the airport to the hotel? We could have got a taxi or a bus!"

He looks over at her, smiles somewhat patronisingly. "Darling, Alex doesn't *do* taxi or bus. Sit back, enjoy the ride."

Elian can't think of a response. How can she tell this man that he is missing out the true culture by taking a car? He wouldn't understand that to get on a bus alongside locals is to truly experience whatever country he is visiting. She bets he has never taken a bus in his life; he only takes the underground in London because it's the fastest route. He probably had a chauffeur growing up, she thinks and snickers.

"What?" he asks.

"Nothing," she answers, smiling to herself.

She watches the scenery as it rushes past the car. There has been trouble here recently, fighting and politics like there seems to be all over the world. But, right now, there is no evidence of it. The fields are green, the buildings are still stunning, and the people continue to go about their daily routine. Kiev looks nice; healthy and well maintained and rich with culture. She wonders what Chernobyl will look like, imagines it to be overgrown, wild and out of control.

In no time they pull up outside the Hyatt Regency and as Elian gets out of the car she looks up at the impressive façade. Bold, black glass fronting that stands out as a contemporary among the Gothic architecture.

"Wow," she says, leaning back to take in the whole structure.

"Nice, isn't it?" Alex picks up both of their cases, hands the keys to an employee of the hotel who appears as if by magic at their side. "Come on. If you like the exterior, you wait until you see the inside."

"Have you been here before, then?" Elian hurries alongside him.

"Not this Hyatt, no, but they're all pretty impressive."

As he checks in, Elian sits on her case in the middle of the lobby and looks around. Alex is right, the interior is even more impressive, cream leather sofas and wooden tables. It is classy and opulent, palatial and rich. Very Alex she thinks, with something akin to a sneer.

"Ready?" He is standing in front of her now, expectant, and she follows him to the elevator.

They are silent on their journey up and she trails after him and waits as he stops at a room, unlocks the door and gestures for her to go in.

She starts when he enters the room after her, closes the door and puts his case down.

Elian looks around, sees the twin beds and turns back to face him.

"One room? Seriously, you expect me to share a room with you?"

He looks surprised, hurt even. "We're only here one night, its two beds. What's the problem?"

"You! You waste money on a ridiculous car for a thirty minute drive, book us into the most expensive hotel in the city, all that waste and then you can't fork out for another room?" Elian marches over to the beds nestling together and yanks them apart until there is a ten inch gap between them. "Just so there's no misunderstanding."

"Forget it, I thought we could be adult about this, but don't worry Ellie, I'll get myself another room," Alex retorts, and picking up his case he slams his way out of the door.

"And don't call me Ellie!" she shouts into the empty room.

After spending an hour sitting by the window there is a faint knock at her door. She slips the chain off, opens it a crack and then wider when she sees Alex leaning on the door frame.

"I'm next door," he inclines his head towards the next room. "If you need anything."

She nods, manages a polite smile, bids him goodnight and closes the door gently and goes back to her window seat. Was she too harsh on him? Was it reasonable for him to expect them to share a room? It's not like it was one double bed.

Elian sighs, wishes she had more experience with men, wishes she knew what went on inside their heads. She procrastinates on whether she should have agreed to come out here at all, but what choice did she have really?

She leans her head on the glass, wondering if life ever gets easier, or just harder and harder the older you get. She brings her focus into vision and looks down on the street. It is quiet now, the time between daylight and dusk. Too late to be out sightseeing in the town, but not yet time be out for dinner. She sees a lone figure walk out of the awning from the hotel and across the street. He turns, leans against the wall of the building opposite her and, looking up, seems to stare straight in at her window.

A scream gets caught in Elian's throat as her brain registers the green woollen hat and the battered black leather jacket. Pushing herself off the chair she bounces off the bed, rights herself and runs to the door as though her assailant is in the room with her.

She calls Alex's name before she is out of her room, lurches over to his door and hammers on it with all her might. She hears a bell, it's the elevator signalling that someone has stopped the lift at their floor. Elian shrieks, batters on Alex's door again and he opens it, clutching a towel around his waist. She dives through the door, colliding with Alex, gripping his arms that are slippery with soap and water. As the lift door opens, Alex catches her as they tumble to the ground and Elian makes one last ditch effort and kicks the door closed with her foot.

Chapter 14
The Boy
Ukraine, 1985 – 1986

After Janelle and Sergi are gone, the boy enjoys having the caravan to himself. He cleans it from top to bottom and then ensures it stays clean. This keeps him happy for a few months, but soon after he finds he needs to do more. He repairs the caravan, welding it in places and patching it up. He cleans the exterior as well as the interior, but still something is missing. He takes Sergi's hunting rifle and waits at night time for the deer and rabbits. He catches them, skins them, happy now that there is blood inside the caravan again, satisfied with his new routine of killing, skinning and cleaning.

One morning he is struck by inspiration about trapping. He digs his pits deep and with a pile of steel sharpened into claws, he sets the traps in place. Then he waits.

Getting up each morning and finding something new in the trap is the most enlightening feeling he has ever possessed. Sometimes it's a hare or rabbit, on occasion something bigger like a goat who has wandered away from the pasture.

It is late summer of 1985 when he finds something altogether more exciting in one of his traps. As he wakes in the morning the chill of autumn is in the air and, as he walks out of the caravan, he stops and sniffs. The scent is the beginning of decay, a season almost done making way for the new. And over the aroma of dying leaves and cleaning products, he can smell something else: blood.

He feels a stirring in his trousers and he walks down the path that he has tracked so many times before.

He finds it in the second trap he comes to. Stands over the pit he has made and peers in. The woman lying at the bottom, her leg pinioned by the steel is waxy coloured. She is clutching a pile of material and the boy wonders why. Is she doing her washing? Where is the bag for the washing? Why is she traipsing through the middle of the forest?

The material moves and the boy snaps to attention, holding out his knife in front of him instinctively. A tiny arm emerges at the same time as a cry and he drops to his knees, reaches down into the pit. It's not washing, it's a *baby*. As the baby stirs the mother, who the boy had presumed dead, lets out a whimper.

The boy sees a double opportunity now and he smiles, revealing an unexpectedly decent set of white teeth.

It is hard work getting the woman out of the pit. She awakes fully and screams like a banshee, but he manages it. She is reluctant to let go of the baby, who is also screaming now, but he unwraps her fingers and separates the two beings. Once they are apart he sets the child to one side and studies the mother. She is young, not as young as him but not as old as Janelle was. She looks poor, her clothes are worn and threadbare, but she is clean and her child looks healthy. Her leg is obviously broken and she pleads with him from between clenched teeth to help her.

Oh he will help, but he will help himself. After the lack of blood in the caravan, settling for the rabbits and deer, the thought of human blood is utterly intoxicating. He cuts her clothes off, deftly, swiftly and, when she is naked beneath him, he takes his hunting knife and tracks the blade down her skin. She knows, as the first blood bubbles up through the seam he has made, she knows what is happening. She tries to get up and he lets her, watches with interest when her broken leg fails her and she falls back down. He pounces, although he had wanted to savour it, he can't. He jabs in a frenzy at her torso, whooping as the blood splashes up over him. It's over too soon, but he is harder than he's ever been. He mounts her, pushing himself into her, thrilled at the thought that he will be the last thing she sees as the light goes out of her eyes.

He tidies up quickly and efficiently. Returns to the caravan and comes back with his sturdy shovel. Digs a grave, eight feet deep as he was taught, hardly breaking into a sweat such is his strength. Once that part is over he turns to the baby, it gurgles happily, watching him as he buries its mother.

The boy smiles, the mother was for his own personal satisfaction. The baby is another matter entirely. The baby is money.

Chapter 15
Alex and Elian
Kiev, June 8th 2015

Alex catches Elian as they fall to the carpet. She manages to slam the door closed with her foot and collapses back on top of him.

"Elian, what the fuck's happening?"

She clamps her hand over his mouth and he is surprised at her strength. She is petite, but she has him well and truly pinned to the floor. Under other circumstances he would not be asking any questions.

From his view on the floor he sees a shadow pass the door and he feels her stiffen. There is the sound of a door opening and then silence.

"Elian?" he whispers.

She rolls off him, sits against the wall and drags her hands through her hair. He sees that she is shaking and, rearranging his towel to cover himself, he grabs her hand.

"What happened?"

"The man, the one I saw on the tube, and then again in Hyde Park, he's outside, outside the hotel, *right now*."

Her fingers grip his, but he disentangles himself and stands up.

"I think that was him in the lift, he walked past this room, he might be in my suite." Her voice is rising in panic and he looks out of the peephole through to the corridor.

"Wait here," he instructs her, and oblivious to her cry he opens the door and slips through.

She is on his heels, clutching at his bare arm and he holds a finger to his lips.

Her door is ajar and he leans back and whispers in her ear. "Did you leave the door open?"

"I don't know," she replies, quietly. "I can't remember. I just ran."

Together they sidle into the room. Alex flicks the light on. Empty. Leaving Elian standing in the doorway he checks the bathroom, cupboards and even under the bed.

"It's clear, nobody here," he says and walks over to the window. "Where was he standing?"

She joins him at the window, points across the road to where the leather-jacketed man had been, but which is empty now.

"And you're sure it was the same guy?"

"I think so. I mean, the hat and the coat, even here it's still summer, it's a hot day like it was back in London. He stands out wearing a hat and leather jacket."

Alex sees her shiver, the feeling transfers to him and he suddenly feels exposed standing in just his towel.

"All right, you're staying in my room tonight. If this is the same guy who has been following you he might have seen you in this room. Come on, get your stuff together."

He had expected an argument, but instead she moves around, picking up the few items that she bought with her and putting them in her case. Still holding his towel, he picks up her bag and uses it to nudge her out of the room.

She is wide eyed, still looking at that damn window, properly spooked like she was in the park last week. He doesn't want her like this. He needs the steely side of her, because he is feeling freaked out enough thinking about where they are going.

"Look, Elian," he says, mock serious as he guides her into his suite. "I know you just want to see what's going on under this towel, but we agreed right? It's not going to happen."

She turns to him, startled, sees he is joking and her face dissolves into a smile.

"That's better," he says as she sits down on the end of his bed.

"I don't understand why this is happening to me," she whispers. "I mean, who is this man? What does he want from me? How can he be in London, and then here, too?"

Her voice is rising, her smile of only moments ago faded. Alex is caught, should he comfort her? Put an arm around her shoulders like any normal person would? But she might interpret that as something else, so he sits beside her on the bed.

"I think we should go out, get some dinner."

She looks at him like he is crazy. "What if he's there, out there? Watching us."

"Good!" Alex exclaims. "You forget I've not yet seen this dude, I'd like to find him out there, ask him what the hell is going on."

Elian feels calmer as she sits in *Shoti*, an upscale restaurant on Mechnikova Street offering traditional Georgian food.

"This is good," she says, as she stuffs another piece of *pampushki* into her mouth and chews enthusiastically. "I feel much better. Thank you for making me leave the hotel."

Alex smiles as he eats his *varenik*, offers her a bit of the stuffing-filled pie. She accepts it gratefully.

She imagines that they could be any young couple out for a romantic long weekend away and, for a moment, she lets go of the problems that brought her here and lets herself daydream. But, it's not a mini-break and Alex is not her boyfriend. And, outside, somewhere, a man is watching her. She shudders, her mood altering and Alex leans over the table, pours her another glass of *kvas*.

"Perhaps we should have got something stronger," he mutters, as he looks at the non-alcoholic drink.

"No, we need to keep a clear head," she replies sharply, remembering what happened last time Alex got her drunk.

"All right." Alex pulls his chair in closer and touches her hand with his finger.

Elian shivers, but doesn't move.

"We need to get real here, what we're going in to is dangerous, it's about *murder*, Elian, and there's someone out there that you think is watching you . . ."

"He *is* watching me!" She slams her glass down. "You think I'm making it up?"

"No, Christ, no. Just, I don't know, maybe you should tell me about . . . you and about Sissy, everything that you know. I just want to . . . be prepared."

"But my aunt is nothing to do with this," Elian looks up at him. "Is she?"

"I don't know, you're the one holding back on me. Every time I ask you about it you clam up on me."

She doesn't feel that she's holding out on him, he knows everything that he needs to. How can she tell him that anything else she confides will be deeper, emotional? But, on the other hand, how good would it feel to finally offload? She's never actually told anyone what happened, not even her two friends from the office.

"I came home, just after I finished my exams, Aunt Sissy was gone." She blurts it out before she has fully decided that she's going to tell him.

"So she raised you, for sixteen years in the Great Titchfield Street flat, then she just left. Did she leave a note?" Alex's tone is disbelieving.

"No. Nothing," she replies, already regretting telling him.

"So how do you know she left willingly? Did you go to the police?"

Elian laughs, but there is no humour in the sound. "I did not go to the police. People like me can't go to the police."

"Why? What do you mean, people like you?"

"You saw how she set up home here, fraudulently collecting money from a fake government compo letter. Cops would look into that shit. I got a life back in London, I can't be jeopardising that."

Alex looks well and truly stumped. He opens his mouth and then closes it again.

"But you're there legally, you've got a passport." He smiles. "I saw it."

"And Sissy was legal, too, but someone put her there *illegally*." She stresses the point, leaning forwards, close to him, speaking quietly. "And that someone was from my family, my mother, Sissy's mother, who the fuck knows? I still have to protect them, they're still family."

"You don't know? And you really don't know who your mother is?"

She is weary all of a sudden, so tired.

"Holy fuck!" Alex grabs her hand, making her jump. "Don't move, don't look up. Look at me."

He pulls her close, as though they really are a couple on a romantic mini-break. He had scooted his chair around the table when she first started talking about Sissy, now he pulls her close, burying her face in his shoulder.

She feels a chill run through her. "He's here isn't he? Is it the man with the hat and the leather jacket?"

"Yeah, he's here," Alex replies. "He doesn't know I've seen him, so keep cool okay?"

She nods, feeling herself begin to quake. "What do we do? What's he doing?"

She feels Alex tighten his hold on her. "When I give the word, we're going to confront him."

She tries to pull away, but he holds her in his grip. "What if he . . . ?"

"He's not going to do anything. You can stay here."

This time she does manage to free herself, but she stays close, takes Alex's face between her hands, still looking like lovers to anyone looking in. "No, let's end this now."

He takes her hands, looks into her eyes. "Ready?"

And, she is. More than ready to put this part of the mystery to bed so they can move on and do the job they are getting paid for. She is tired of running and hiding.

"Yeah," she says, eyes shining, a mixture of fear and excitement. "I'm ready."

Chapter 16
Sissy

Chernobyl, May 1st 1986

I'm still shaking from the encounter with Knor, I couldn't be less prepared for a soldier at my door if I tried. I think about turning and running, but that would be back in Knor's direction, and I'm sure this soldier is the lesser of two evils. Anyway, it's too late, the soldier has spotted me.

"Hey, wait there!" He marches down the porch steps and over to me.

He is young, this soldier, maybe in his early twenties. I wait as he makes his way up to me.

"You know you're not supposed to be here, don't you? Where are your family?"

"My mother is in Kiev, my father is in the hospital there. I'm leaving to join them later today." The lie comes frighteningly easy to me.

Before he can talk further I have a terrible feeling of foreboding.

"You've . . . you found my sister, didn't you?"

He stumbles over his words, confirming my suspicions without even forming a sentence.

"You found a body! Is she dead?"

"Is somebody unaccounted for in your family, miss?" He asks.

It is like the breath leaves me, and life along with it. It's all over. "Take me to her, I'll identify her for you."

He is unsure. I know what he is thinking, that I'm too young to handle this. But there is nobody else.

"Take me," I insist, and he relents.

*

The mortuary is makeshift, about a mile past the factory, not in the clinic that we would usually attend. This brings home to me just how many deaths must have occurred since the accident. I've been so preoccupied with Afia that I've almost forgotten about the nuclear disaster.

I wonder how she died. Was it like the factory workers that I saw, skin sliding off their faces and their lungs exploding in their chest? Or was this nothing to do with the factory? Did one of her misdemeanours with one of her many men go wrong? Why were her clothes at the river in the bunker? Was Afia murdered?

The young soldier drives me there in his station wagon and accompanies me inside the building that looks suspiciously like a haulage container. We pause at the hastily-erected reception desk while he checks a clipboard.

"This way," he mutters, and I follow him down the corridor to a big steel door.

When we go into the room I look immediately down at the floor. Even from here I can see that there are many beds, and I know that they all hold bodies. I raise my eyes and gasp. Twenty or thirty pairs of feet poke out from ill-fitting sheets. I look at the soldier by my side. He, too, has averted his eyes.

"All this is from the explosion?" I ask, dumbfounded.

He gives me a strange look. "This is just one of the rooms."

"But they said . . . there was no danger." I cry, simultaneously wondering how many more rooms there are.

We were told that only two men died, and that was because they happened to be practically on top of Reactor Four when it went up. Were we lied to? We must have been; after all I saw more than two men out on that dusty roadside that night and they were dying too.

The young soldier is consulting his clipboard again and he walks over to a bed, peels back the sheet at the top of the body and hurriedly covers it up again.

"That's her? Is that Afia?" I whisper the question and shuffle over to him. My feet are dragging as though they know I'm unsure if I can make myself look under that sheet.

With a sigh he lays his hand on the sheet.

"Wait!" I clamp my hand on top of his. "What . . . does she look like? I mean, is she badly injured?"

He shrugs. I've made him uncomfortable again. I feel bad, after all he does not have to do this, and he probably shouldn't even have let me in here. I nod for him to continue and I remove my hand as he folds the sheet down over her face.

I stare for a very long time at the dead girl on the gurney.

Chapter 17
Alex and Elian
Kiev, June 8th 2015

Elian pounds the pavement with her feet, surprising herself with her speed and stamina as she flies past Alex in pursuit of the leather-jacketed man.

He is fast though, and Elian is not sure how he got away so quickly. When they made the decision to confront him they were off the starting blocks and outside. But, as he was watching them, he knew his game was up and he was off before they even got out of the restaurant.

The idea of him fleeing from them was a red rag to Elian, and now she has started running she finds she can't stop. She can still see him in his green hat, up ahead, weaving in and out of the late dinner crowd. It's as if all the years of hiding and keeping her head down have fuelled her, and now she wants to confront this man, find out who he is, why he is stalking her.

"Ellie," Alex has caught her up and is wheezing alongside her. "Stop, we're not going to catch him."

She doesn't answer him. She is focused, determined. She *will* catch him. She *has* to.

Alex falls back again and Elian puts her head down, moves up a gear; a frisson of excitement as she realises she is gaining on him, just at the same time as she sees the street sign for the Metro. She can't let him get in there. He'll get on a train, speed away . . .

A group of American tourists exit a bar to her left and spread out on the pavement in front of her. She pushes through the throng, but they are all heavy set and slow moving. She swears, knocks them aside and suddenly he is there, her assailant, bent over, breathing heavily with his hands on his knees. She pulls up sharp, glances over her shoulder in search of Alex. The mystery man spots her, makes to run and as he darts across the road Elian shouts and grasps at his body.

Horns blast out into the night, momentarily stopping for the maniac who slams his hands on bumpers and staggers across the junction to the other side. The cars move again, no chance for Elian to get through. She watches the man as he disappears down into the Metro, his hands stroking his hair that flaps around his head, investigating the absence of the woollen hat that Elian snatched off his head and now gazes down at, holding it gingerly in her fingers.

*

When Alex reaches her, minutes later, he leans against her, catching his breath. He is aghast at how he couldn't keep up with her, and vows to exercise regularly on his return to London. Disgust at his inability to match Elian's strides gnaws at him. He's athletically built and healthy, but his day-to-day PI role does not usually involve chasing people, regardless of how the movies make it look.

"I might look fit," he wheezes, "but . . . I'm not!"

"Who said you look fit?" she asks, as she looks disdainfully at him.

She's getting an attitude now, he realises. Or maybe it's always been there, but now she's coming out of her shell it's more prominent. He likes this side of Elian he decides.

"What's that?" Now he can breathe he registers the material she is clutching.

Elian looks down at it, dazed. "I grabbed it off his head. I was that close to catching him."

He takes the hat from her and looks over at the Metro where the man has long disappeared. "What the hell would you have done if you'd caught him?"

"I don't know, I didn't think that far. It was strange though, it was almost like I knew him, like I'd seen him before."

"You have seen him before," Alex replies patiently. "You saw him twice last week, on the tube and in the park."

She waves away his words. "No, it's more than that. I can't explain, but what do we do now?"

"We sleep, and then we go to Chernobyl in the morning."

Turning around, they walk back to the Hyatt, Alex continuously stealing glances at Elian. She is quiet, reflective, but somehow she seems stronger.

He feels that he shouldn't have let her chase after their mystery man like that, it was irresponsible, and he tells her as much.

"You're not responsible for me. Don't treat me like a child. You can't blackmail me to come out here and then act like a knight in shining armour." She cuts him down to size, just like that. Her words are like punches to the gut, sharp and painful. But he is getting used to her now, he sees that she has spent so long taking care of herself, at the same time as living in fear, that she is desperate to let someone in. But, as soon as she does, she remembers that she shouldn't and up go the walls.

They go straight to Alex's room. Again, it has twin beds, the source of their earlier fight, but Elian seems to have forgotten as she slings her bag on the floor and crawls fully clothed into one of the beds. He perches uneasily on the other one.

"Alex, I'm sorry for being a bitch earlier," she says quietly.

He looks over at her and feels a little bit of his heart come undone. The feeling, entirely new to him, is worrisome.

"It wasn't you, it's my fault. I'm sorry for the rooms, and I'm sorry for everything bad that I've done to you."

As he speaks he realises that they are not empty words, they are true. This young lady is not somebody to be messed with. She is a fighter, despite her mild front. She is brilliant and, he's not sure that he dares to think it but he does anyway, she is important and special. On the other hand, she is young, a lot younger than him. Does that matter? What age gap is too much? Would she even want him? Would it work? With so many questions that he never expected to be asking, Alex suddenly feels quite shattered. He looks over at Elian. She is nodding off, smiling, and he eases himself on to the bed next to her and when he is sure that she is asleep he picks up her hand and holds it.

*

When Elian wakes it is dark in the room. She looks over to the window and sees that a strip of light is coming in from the street lamp outside. She becomes aware that she can't move her right hand, it's pinned down by something solid and clammy. Alex's hand, she realises, and looks over at him. He is asleep on his back, his right arm thrown back over his head, his left hand holding hers.

She smiles. She would never have had him down as a hand holder. She finds she doesn't mind it, actually quite likes it, despite not liking him very much recently. And, as his grip tightens on her hand in his sleep, she finds that she does actually quite like him as well. She can't forget what he has done to her, not yet. But he's not as tough as he makes out. She saw that when he was with his aunt. He is quite fearless though; after all it had been his idea to chase after the man who was watching them.

As her thoughts turn to him she frowns in the darkness. Who is he? What does he want from her? It must be something very important for him to follow her overseas from London to Kiev. Will he turn up in Chernobyl?

He's obviously not armed or, for that matter, dangerous. He could have taken her out easily, especially when Alex fell behind. And, at the moment when their eyes locked, what was with that feeling of familiarity?

Elian shivers, despite being under the cover. Closing her eyes, she tries to forget about the man and, pressing her fingers tighter into Alex's hand, she goes back to sleep.

*

When Alex drags himself out of sleep, daylight is streaming through the window. He lifts his arm to look at his watch and finds Elian's hand still attached to his. The movement wakes her and she looks up at him. Uncomfortably he lets go of her hand and clears his throat.

"What time is it?" she asks, burrowing down into the bed.

"Nine," he replies, and then, "oh, shit!"

"What? What time are they collecting us?"

"Nine," he says grimly as he jumps out of bed. "Hurry!"

She runs into the bathroom and he hears water running as he opens the window and looks out. Maybe the tour bus will be late. But, no, a minivan is parked on the kerb, engine running, a young, dreadlocked man standing beside the vehicle, rolling a cigarette.

"Mate, five minutes!" Alex yells out the window, holding up his hand with his fingers splayed. "Ellie!"

She pauses as she washes her hands in the bathroom, a smile creeping over her pretty features as he calls her. When did he start calling her Ellie? It sounds familiar and possessive and she shakes her head and splashes her face with cold water to get rid of the idiotic grin.

"Pull yourself together, woman," she whispers to herself, and then, louder to Alex, "I'm coming!"

"Put this on," says Alex, as he hurls a long red scarf at her. "Cover as much of your face as you can and put your shades on."

The scarf is silk and tasselled, not a thick winter one which would look odd in this heat. Elian does as she is told and watches Alex as he zips up his lightweight jacket to his chin, puts a matching cap on and finally his shades.

"And what is this disguise for?" she asks, as he herds her out of the door.

"Because the tour guides will be expecting to drive out of Chernobyl with the same amount of people they took in. We won't be on that bus, but two people dressed like us will be."

Elian shivers at this thought. With two people effectively taking their place, nobody will ever know if anything should happen to them in Chernobyl.

Together they run down the stairs, clutching half-packed bags and coats. Their driver and tour guide has discarded his cigarette and is climbing back into the van. Elian and Alex knock on the window, full of apologies, expecting the driver to berate them. Instead, he rolls down the window, a lazy smile on his face and the strong aroma of weed drifting out to them.

Elian turns to Alex, a smile spreading over her face.

He looks down at her, shrugs and smiles as their driver opens the door for them.

"After you, madam," he says, and helps her into the van.

They watch Kiev as they leave. Despite their follower, it has been safe here. Kiev is welcoming and friendly. Chernobyl is a different kettle of fish and neither of them really know what to expect once they get there.

Elian feels a shiver down her spine and she pulls her coat tightly around her. They are heading for the Exclusion Zone now, and there's no turning back.

Chapter 18
The Boy
Ukraine, 1986

The boy continues with his traps well into the spring of 1986. The more success he has, the more risks he takes. He moves the traps out further, closer to civilisation. After the sale of the baby, to a Russian acquaintance, he realises how much money he can make, at the same time as satisfying his need for blood.

The Russian is called Lev and he sells children, mostly babies, on the black market. Lev is not interested in the parents and the boy is not interested in the baby. Their partnership works very well.

Between autumn 1985 and early 1986 the boy has trapped and killed four adults and has sold on two babies, including the original one. He knows that the winter months will be leaner as there are fewer people out walking in the forest. But as long as he is prepared for that he can handle it. When there are no people in his traps he sits and thinks about the ingenuity of it. It is impossible for him to be caught and imprisoned. If anyone finds any of his victims in the traps before he does, then they have simply stumbled in there by mistake. After all, it's not illegal to set traps. If anyone should find him in the process of getting them out of the traps, then he is simply saving them. Hell, should that happen, he'd be a hero! But it's not likely to happen, for the boy is so in tune with the forest that he fancies he can hear a rabbit standing on a twig from a mile away.

It is very early in the year and the boy is out and about, walking the miles between his traps. In the smaller ones he finds a couple of rabbits and he ties their legs together and slings them over his shoulder. Heading back to his caravan he hears the sound of tread on the frosty ground and he stops, listens. And then, out from between the trees walks a woman. The boy feels his eyes bulge, she is like nothing he has ever seen before. She carries herself with a certain regal quality. She is tall, striking. And *black*. He has never seen an African before. He has heard of them but, this, this . . . specimen is a sight to behold. A moan escapes his lips and she stops in her tracks.

The boy fingers the knife in its sheath by his side, imagines cutting into that shiny ebony flesh. This woman would be worth a dozen of the white girls he has slaughtered. He steps forward into her path.

He expects her to scream and to run, but she only ignites his interest further when she smiles, tentatively at first, but then wide, showing two rows of gleaming white teeth.

"You startled me," she says, still smiling, and her eyes travel up and down his body.

He catches her look, he *knows* that expression; she is looking at him the way he looks at his victims before he kills them. Lust. Wanting.

And then she knows it too, and the scene is the most surreal he has ever known. She walks right up to him, eyes still locked on his. He slips his knife out of the sheath and the clean blade shines between them. She looks at it, back at him, licks her lips.

The boy takes in her clothing and again, her garments are like nothing he's ever seen. The material is silky, shiny blue. He holds the blade to it and it slices like a knife through butter. She gasps, still smiling as, very gently, he cuts the rest of the material. It flutters to the ground, until she is quite naked before him. Holding the knife carefully he brushes it, blunt side, over her belly. She takes his hand, their first physical contact and his fingers shake. She guides the knife, turns it over and trails it over her hip. He hears her sharp intake of breath as a thin trickle of blood escapes, dark red on black. He lowers himself to his knees, licks the blood. She catches his head in her hands and turns his face to look at her. He smiles at her; there is blood on his teeth.

And that's how the boy first met Afia Bello.

Chapter 19
Alex and Elian
Chernobyl, June 9th 2015

Their tour guide is called Yuri, and travelling with them are six other tourists. Yuri gives them a history of Chernobyl, safety tips and stern instructions not to wander off alone. They are not allowed to go into or near Reactor Four, but pretty much anything else is within limits. He drags deeply on his joint, as if to demonstrate his easy going nature.

"He's off his face, it's not going to be too hard to fool him," comments Elian.

Alex nods his head in agreement, but he still intends to be careful. He looks at their six companions and asks Elian if they are Russian. She listens to their conversation for a moment and confirms his suspicions.

"Does anybody still live in Chernobyl?" Elian pipes up.

Yuri's face darkens as he glances at them in the rear view mirror. "Yes," he answers in careful English. "They shouldn't, but some people just did not leave."

"Isn't that dangerous?" Alex joins in.

"Maybe, maybe not. Children born with defects, but anywhere this can happen," replies Yuri.

Alex turns to Elian and speaks softly. "We're going to be dropped just past the police checkpoint. If the authorities are there, try to keep your face as covered as possible. Hopefully they'll just recall the colour of your coat, your scarf and shades. We'll meet our doppelgängers a few hundred yards in; when I give the signal follow me. They'll go on in our place."

"Why would anyone do something like this for us?" Elian asks.

Alex doesn't answer, just rubs his fingers together in the universal sign for money.

With many more miles to drive, Elian settles back in her seat and closes her eyes. Alex watches her, amazed and a little envious of her ability to slip into sleep. He looks at her hand, wonders if he can hold it again, then looks out of the window to distract himself from such stupid thoughts.

Elian wakes with a start, surprised to see that the minibus has filled up since she fell asleep. She wonders what woke her, and then realises that the vehicle has slowed to a stop. They are at the police checkpoint. She sits up and looks at Alex. He has put his shades on and is looking down at the floor. A rush of fear pricks at her and this time she reaches for his hand. He looks up, startled, and folds his fingers around hers.

"I don't know why I'm nervous," she whispers. "We haven't even done anything wrong yet."

"We're not doing anything wrong, we're here to help," he mutters, as the police walk down the side of the minibus peering in the windows.

Elian is sure she looks guilty, so she tries to smile, but senses it seems very fake, so she shrugs her shoulders helplessly. Eventually, after what seems like an age, the police disperse and the van rolls on down the track.

"If the police are here after all this time, why doesn't your mystery man just contact them about the murders?"

"I don't know. Maybe the police don't go any further than this checkpoint." He looks back through the window at them. "I don't think they're even police, I think they are military."

Soon the van has stopped altogether and the group stands, stretches and climbs off the bus.

Elian looks around. They are in the town centre and here it doesn't seem too out of the ordinary. The buildings are run down, scrawled with graffiti and abandoned, the surrounding greenery is a little more overgrown than it would be anywhere else; but, apart from that, it looks . . . normal.

Yuri is speaking, gesturing for his group to gather round. Elian leans in to listen, before realising it doesn't matter what he says, they won't be with him for long.

Alex is looking around discreetly and when he tugs on her sleeve she looks up at him, and then over where he subtly gestures.

There is a shadow at the corner of one of the buildings and, when she sees a flash of red, Elian knows this is her doppelgänger.

Yuri leads them down the main road and Elian thinks of her ancestors and how they must have walked this route hundreds of times. She thinks of Sissy and wonders if she is here somewhere. Slowly, Elian and Alex fall back, until Elian becomes aware that they are being shadowed. When

Alex takes her hand she tenses herself in readiness and then he yanks her hand so hard she thinks her arm might come out of the socket. She swears her feet leave the ground as he pulls her off the road into the trees.

Their replacements walk past them, the male bumping fists with Alex as he passes and the younger girl giving Elian a curious look.

After a moment she hears Yuri yelling at them to keep up, and then the group is gone. Elian and Alex are alone.

Elian holds his bag as Alex roots around for the map they printed out before they left London.

"Do you even know where we're going? Are we meeting someone?"

"I know roughly where we're headed," Alex answers her question. "But I don't know who's going to be there."

Elian can tell that he is trying for a casual tone, making out there's no need for Elian to know he's even the slightest bit concerned.

Alex is peering at the map, cursing about not using the zoom button when he printed it, when they hear a noise. It is the sound of an approach, undergrowth rustling and twigs snapping. Alex puts down the map and, taking Elian's arm, pushes her behind him.

"You are Alex?" The man is calling out, even before he has entered the clearing.

"Yeah, was it you who contacted me?" Alex says, squinting into the shadows as they wait for the guy to show himself.

There is silence, and Alex clears his throat. "You want to at least tell us your name, man?"

There is a pause, a shuffling noise, and then he walks out of the trees, stopping a few feet away from them.

"My name is Klim Karpik," says the stranger, at the same time that Elian looks around Alex.

She blinks, stares hard and digs her hands into Alex's shoulders. She feels herself tremble as she looks Klim up and down in disbelief. "You?"

Alex has only seen him once, she remembers, but she has described him often enough. He is minus the woollen hat now, since Elian ripped it off his head yesterday. She senses Alex raking his eyes over the man called Klim, taking in his leather jacket and the pieces of the puzzle fitting together.

It's a trap, he wanted me all along, thinks Elian, too petrified to actually speak the words.

She feels the change in Alex as he shrugs her off. She reaches to pull him back, but he slips through her fingers. She feels a scream building inside her as Alex covers the ground between himself and Klim effortlessly and punches him hard in the face.

Klim rears up, and Elian's scream is finally released as she sees the glint of the gun tucked into the waistband of Klim's trousers.

Chapter 20
Sissy
Chernobyl, May 1st 1986

"It's not her."

The young soldier looks down at the body and then up at me. I can't believe it, but this is not my sister. I am ecstatic, just for a moment, then anger strikes.

"This woman is not even African!" I glare at him and, to his credit, he looks suitably abashed. "Did you not look at me, at my skin?"

He opens his mouth to speak. But, now I know this is not Afia, I no longer have time for this. The soldier's mouth is flapping uselessly, like a fish out of water. I suck my teeth, mimicking Afia without realising it, and before I leave I cover the young woman's face with the sheet.

Out in the open air I can breathe again. I look back at the building and suppress a shudder at all of the bodies in there. The young soldier comes out and hurries over.

"I'm very sorry miss, I should have realised," he barks a short, nervous laugh and rubs at his face. "I can't believe I was so stupid. Miss, can I drive you back?"

I surprise myself by accepting and when we are back in his car he introduces himself as Simon. He is English, one of only a few soldiers that have been sent here from the British Army. He is young, nineteen, the same age as Afia.

Simon seems genuinely sorry and I decide to use this to my advantage. I ask him to take me to the home of Klim Karpik.

Simon asks me about my sister. I tell him the truth, that she went missing in the night of the factory explosion and has not been seen since. He asks me who Klim is, and why would he know anything about Afia?

"I think he was a boyfriend of hers, one of our neighbours saw her with him. He might know where she has gone. She might even be hiding out at Klim's house."

When we drive up to the Karpik home it looks deserted. The whole family has probably left, but I need to check. I ask Simon to wait in the car and he agrees, reluctantly though it seems.

"Klim!" I call, when I reach his house and peer through the window. "If you're here, open up, it's Sissy, Afia's sister."

He comes around the side of the building, casting a suspicious glance at Simon, but heading straight over to me.

"Have you seen her? Is Afia all right?" He asks, taking my arm and looking anxiously into my eyes.

My heart sinks upon hearing his words.

"I was hoping that you had seen her, Klim. She's been missing since the accident at the nuclear plant," I reply, noting how his hopeful expression fades away. "Old Knor told me she was with you."

"She was," he says, glumly. "The night before the explosion she broke up with me."

I wonder if he had done something to Afia in a fit of jealousy, but then I remember that Knor told me he had seen her the actual night of the explosion with some sort of gypsy.

"Knor said she went to bed with you. Why would she do that if she was breaking up with you?" I ask, and the suspicion is evident in my tone.

Klim is embarrassed, and I know he's aghast at the thought of the old man spying on him in his most private moments. He looks down and kicks at the dusty ground with his shoe.

"I thought I could change her mind, I thought if I showed her how much I love her." He tails off, mournful now.

"Do you know anything of this gypsy she was seeing?"

His face darkens and he scowls. "He's a freak," he spits. "I'd do anything for Afia, I'd work my hands to the bone every day to give her everything she wants, but she picked him."

"What's his name? Where does he live?"

He shrugs, moody now, kicking at the ground again. "Somewhere over the water, but that's all I know of him. For all I know, she didn't want to go to him, he's got some sort of hold on her."

Suddenly I'm feeling very sorry for Klim. He's a good man, with a good family and a nice home. His words make my blood run cold, has this mysterious man taken my sister hostage?

"Are you leaving Pripyat?" I ask.

He shakes his head. "My family have gone to stay with my grandmother, but I want to stay here." He looks over my ahead, across to where the water lies. "I'll stay here until she comes back to me."

I squeeze his arm, thankful that it's not just myself and Knor staying in town. I walk back to where Simon stands like a sentry beside the car.

I give him my most winning smile, fluttering my eyes at him the way I've watched my sister do so many times. I have another favour to ask Simon, I want him to take me across the water, to see if I can track down the man who I'm pretty sure has kidnapped my sister.

Chapter 21
Alex and Elian
Chernobyl, June 9th 2015

Elian can't stop screaming. It's as though the gun in Klim's waistband is a trigger for everything that has happened to her in the last three weeks. Alex looks frantically from her back to Klim, as though he can't decide which situation to deal with first. Klim stands at the edge of the clearing, his left hand hovering near the gun.

Klim makes the first move. Taking the gun out he holds it up, then throws it carefully to one side. He turns to Alex.

"Make her be quiet. She's making too much noise!"

Alex runs over to her, folds her into his arms. She sees him and feels him, and eventually her screams drop down to a whimper.

"Who are you?" Alex's voice is angry and Elian takes comfort from it.

"I'm sorry, so sorry, I don't mean to scare you," Klim moves towards them with his hands out.

"You stay right there," calls Alex. "What the fuck are you doing with a gun?"

"The wolves, other creatures, you have to be very careful here, they are very dangerous and there are very many of them." Klim is tripping over his words to try and explain.

Elian wipes her face and moves out of Alex's grip, but keeps hold of his arm. "Did you contact Alex about the murders?"

Klim hesitates, looking at each of them. "You have to help us, people are dying, being *slaughtered*, and nobody will help us."

Elian glances at Alex, wondering if he picked up on Klim's words, how he didn't admit that it was him who contacted them, but Alex's face gives nothing away. She wants to speak to Alex, and she gestures to him. "Stay there," she instructs Klim.

"Well?" She asks Alex.

"I think we have to go with him, but we don't have to trust him," Alex replies.

The horror of seeing him suddenly appear in the clearing, after all of those half glances on the tube, in Hyde Park . . . she shudders, moving closer to Alex. Now they are supposed to go with this man, this stranger with a gun. But where else can they go? After all, they've come this far, their replacements are on the Chernobyl tour, there really is no way back.

Reluctantly she nods her agreement and, as one, they move back to Klim. "We'll go with you, but we'll look after that for you." She gestures towards the gun, tries to make her voice strong and superior, wishing hopelessly that she hadn't screamed and shown her weakness. Klim hesitates, but he probably figures it's his only way to get them to go with him, and eventually he nods his ascent.

Alex picks up the gun and, checking the safety catch is on, he puts it in his bag. Klim leads them out of the clearing and they begin to make their way through the forest.

It is overgrown, just as Elian expected it to be, and she picks her way carefully through the trail left by Klim and Alex who are in front of her. She studies Klim as he walks, he looks to be in his forties perhaps, though with his nondescript clothes and shoulder length hair it is hard to tell. At some point he would have been handsome, she can tell that much. But, although he is not old, he looks tired. He is gaunt and pale and she wonders if he is suffering from radiation sickness, a sure possibility if he stayed after the nuclear accident.

"Why were you following me back in London?" Elian asks as they walk.

"I had to make sure you would come here, after you were contacted. You could have just taken the money," replies Klim, as he bats the overhanging branches away. "It took us a long time to get the money; we couldn't afford to lose it."

She wonders who the 'we' is he refers to. Does he have a partner? Or is there a group of them, hiding from the local murderer, scraping together their funds to buy some help.

Elian pokes Alex in the back. "Why was he following me, if it was you he paid?" She hisses at him. "Nobody even knows that I know you. I was nothing to do with this until you made me come here."

Alex shushes her and she shoots him a look. She is cold now, and it is not just because she is out of the sunshine. One of them is lying. But is it Alex or Klim, or both of them?

"Do you know my family?" She calls to Klim. "Sissy Bello?"

He pretends not to hear or understand her, but she sees his spine stiffen in front of her. She catches up to Alex and tries to catch his eye, but he looks straight ahead.

Jesus, these two are in it together, she thinks. *They are both after me, for something, for some reason. Maybe Klim is the murderer, maybe he wants fresh meat. And Alex has been paid a handsome sum to deliver me.*

After all, what does she really know of Alex Harvey? Nothing really, and he has already lied to her. Maybe this is how he gets all his money, maybe this is why he is loaded, through trafficking young women around Europe and selling them on. Perhaps that's why he slept with her, to try out the goods for his customers further along the chain.

She hangs further back from the two men, deliberately slowing her steps until every time they turn a bend she loses sight of them for a moment. She wishes she had taken charge of the gun. As it is she has nothing to defend herself if – or when – they turn on her. But there is no sense in ifs or buts. Alex has the gun, Klim could have another firearm or knife. She has nothing. Nothing, except her will to survive.

Alex swears softly as he gets caught in the face for the third time by a tree branch springing back at him. He had envisaged this, this total and utter wilderness, but it surpasses his imagination. Klim seems to him half feral; unkempt and unsure on how to behave with other people. It is understandable, after all, there can't be many people still living here in Chernobyl. Alex is not sure what to make of Klim. The gun, the realisation that it is him who has been trailing Elian back in England and his sudden appearance in Kiev, it's a lot to take in. His explanation makes sense. Thirty thousand euros is a lot of money to give away with no action forthcoming. Of course someone would be watching the other end to ensure the transaction is completed. But Klim was stalking *Elian*, someone who had nothing to do with the transaction. Uncomfortably, Alex recalls the original email, pointing him in the direction of Elian. And, inwardly, he groans. What if this was all a ploy to get her here? But why use Alex? Why not just jump her, drug her and bring her here? Has he, Alex, unwittingly thrown Elian straight into the lion's den, all on account of his greed and love for money?

He needs to tell her, has to warn her to be on her guard. Klim is still walking ahead, thrashing at the trees to clear their path. Alex turns around, opens his mouth to speak to Elian, closes it, stops walking. There is nobody behind him. She has vanished.

*

Elian is running, reminded of yesterday when she was chasing Klim through the streets of Kiev. Now he will be chasing her, and when did this turn into a game of cat and mouse? This is not as easy as the Kiev chase though. Last night there were clear pavements and concrete. This sprint is fraught with wet, soft, uneven ground and nettles and branches that reach out to tug at her clothes and skin. She doesn't really know which way she is going, there is no footpath as the crow flies, just winding, twisting pathways. She stops for a moment, wrapping her hands round a tree trunk and leaning gratefully against it. She senses that she is some way off from the two men and she cannot hear them any longer. In fact, she can hear nothing now, not even birdsong.

Was she mistaken about Alex? Surely she was. No way would anyone go through all of this trouble to deliver her here, not even for thirty thousand euros. She smiles bitterly as it hits home, she has panicked. She is almost certain. After all, she's not worth that much, not to anybody.

She pushes herself off the tree, walks on. As she walks she silently chastises herself for thinking this was all about her. She can't explain why Klim was tailing her, that part of it is still a mystery; but nobody has sold her and delivered her into this land. And it hits home now, why she had begun to think so much of herself. It's Alex's fault, over the last few days he has taken care of her, treated her with kid gloves, made her think she was something special when she knows she's not. She's known that, since Sissy left her, she's nothing special. And, she had enjoyed it, the attention that Alex had bestowed upon her, spending time at his home, eating with him, travelling with him, sleeping next to him. She hadn't really thought about just how reclusive she had become in the last three years. She curses him softly, tells herself that, when she is reunited with him, she must not let his words and actions convince her that she means anything to him. She is being paid to be here after all, she is a translator, an employee.

She pauses to dig around in her shoe. A twig or a stone has worked its way in and she pokes at it, finally taking off her Converse and shaking it as she stands on one foot. Elian hears a noise of someone traipsing through the undergrowth behind her and she sags with relief. Alex and Klim have found her.

She turns her head, ready with her apologies, her stance business-like and professional, but it is not Alex who she comes face to face with. It's a wolf, and he looks more dangerous and deadly than Klim's gun had ever seemed.

Chapter 22
The Boy
Ukraine, 1986

At first, with Afia hanging around, the boy finds he does not feel the need to check and set his traps so often. Often he has sex with his victims, but it is so entirely different with Afia. She is willing for one thing, and she will do anything that he wants.

Seeing her fancy clothes and jewels, he knows that his caravan, although clean, must be a big disappointment to her. But, she denies this, with such fervour that he almost believes her. He enjoys lying next to her, marvelling at her ebony skin. He fantasises about cutting it again, and just imagining it turns him on. He insists that she is naked all the time she is in his home, even going so far as to turn the old gas stove up high so she won't get too cold.

On that first day they met, after they had retreated to his caravan and spent the afternoon there, when she said she had to go home he let her go. He couldn't believe he had done that, later on when he sat and masturbated and thought about her. He had actually let her walk away unharmed. Alive.

And then, the next day, she had returned. It was early in the morning and he had heard a gentle knock on the door, three times, like a little bird. It was her, looking a little shy, eyes downcast, smiling hopefully. She had brought some bread that her mother had made, and some *feijoada*, a stew with beef and beans, in an earthenware dish covered with a towel. He had accepted it from her, tasted it solemnly, not offering her any, but picking up the bread and wiping the dish clean with it. She had watched him with obvious delight.

With a full stomach he had carefully cleaned the dish, wiped his hands and then taken her there, standing up in the small kitchen area.

He had let her go again, and found himself wondering if she would come back; and, she did, each time bringing something from home, usually food. And she is here now, standing in the kitchen, chatting about her home, her family, her life. He doesn't want to know about her other world, he wants it to be that he is her life. He asks her to stay for the whole night. She shrugs, tilts her head to one side as she thinks about it.

She says she will have to go home, but she can sneak out again and spend the whole night with him. She does.

He makes her think that he needs her. But, for him, Afia is an excellent cover should anyone ever investigate any missing persons or by chance dig up one of his graves. If he has a steady girlfriend, someone affluent with a good standing in society, no fingers will be pointed at him. Besides that he has the use of her body whenever he wants and in any way he wishes to abuse it. She does not seem very intelligent to him, more interested in pretty things, a bit like a magpie. She would not discover his hobby. Hopefully she has inherited her mother's cooking skills; he must provide her with some ingredients and test her. She could be an asset.

In late February he finds a man in the trap furthest away from his caravan. And, upon close inspection, he sees that it is not only a man, but a small child, maybe two, three years old. A father out on a first hunting trip with his son by the look of the man's weapons. He stares down at them. Both are quiet at first, but the small boy's chest heaves with silent sobs. Through the pain of his broken bones, the man realises a shadow has fallen over him, and he looks up, shielding his eyes from the weak early morning sun. The man is relieved, thanking God that rescue has arrived. He is not relieved for long.

The boy pulls the child out first, sets him to one side as he turns back to the man. This man is young, his face is pale with a thin film of sweat. His eyes are red. Paying no heed to the man's cries, the boy uses his immense strength to pull him out. The man collapses on the ground, arm outstretched toward his son. The boy places his hand on the man's brow, notes that he has a fever. It seems quite excessive and, when the boy rifles through his pockets and pulls out a clear package filled with brown powder, it becomes clear, the man is a drug addict. With no way to prepare his fix, he is withdrawing.

"I have more," the man's voice is high and reed thin. "It's yours, if you help us."

Interesting. The boy has not even threatened yet, but this man is already begging. The boy does not want more, he does not need drugs. Blood is his drug and he shows this now as he takes out his blade and runs it down the man's chest. The cut is not deep. Too shallow to kill, deep enough to show the man what is going to happen. As the blood trickles out, the boy smiles, blissfully happy. The man screams. The young son watches, pale faced and serious, sucking on his fingers as he watches his father's agony.

Later he makes the transaction with Russian Lev. Lev looks over the boy.

"This is older than I usually like," he says. "It will be a reduced rate."

The boy thinks about arguing, but this baby money is a bonus anyway, regardless of the amount. The boy still gets what he needs, these children are simply a side line.

"What is that?" Lev's keen eyes look at the packet of brown powder that the boy has put on the table. "Are you selling it too? I pay a good price."

The boy thinks about it, but does not want to sell the drug. He will not use it himself, but something tells him it could come in useful. A plan is set into motion in his mind and he nods to himself. He knows exactly who will benefit from this little bag of heroin.

Chapter 23
Alex and Elian
Chernobyl, June 9th 2015

Elian is mesmerised by the wolf's eyes. They are azure blue, reminding her slightly of Alex's eyes. The wolf has come to a halt a few feet away, and it stares at her intently. She had always thought of a wolf as looking similar to a dog, but this is no canine. It is huge, on scale with a lion or a small bear. It is unnatural; born from the strange side effects of its particular society; it is hungry, and it sees her as food.

She can't believe that her time is up, not here, not like this. To lose her life to a wild animal rather than the dangerous mission that she has embarked on seems almost laughable. Yet still the wolf stands poised and motionless and Elian feels her body begin to tremble.

"Just do it, if you're going to, fucking do it," she whispers.

"Stay still."

For an absurd moment she thinks the wolf has spoken, but then she looks off to one side and Alex is there, with Klim cowering behind him. The wolf flicks its head in their direction, but does not take its eyes off Elian. Elian takes a deep breath in, her body shaking as it shudders out of her. She sees Alex's hand go in his bag, emerging with the gun. Quietly he slips the safety catch off and, with a steady hand, he raises the gun.

Elian closes her eyes. The shot rings out and she looks down at herself, feels no pain; sees no blood. The wolf is down and dead, a clean shot through the chest. Alex stands tall and firm and Elian breathes a sigh of relief. He saved her and, looking at him now, she wonders why she doubted him. She needs to feel his touch, feel his strong arms wrapped around her and for the first time and probably only momentarily, for the old walls may come back up, she trusts him utterly. She moves over to him, hurrying on shaking legs and he opens his arms, still holding the gun. When he holds her she feels the cold metal pressing into her back.

"Why did you run off?" Alex says, his voice muffled as he puts his face in her shoulder.

Elian doesn't answer. How can she tell him that, for a terrible moment, she suspected him of orchestrating this whole thing to harm her? And now she can feel him trembling a little bit too. There's something here, between them, right now in the aftermath of an almost disaster, she can feel it, just as sure as she can feel his heart thumping in his chest as he holds her tight.

"You're all right," Alex says, and keeping hold of her, as he passes the gun back to Klim, another moment of trust is formed, and they begin to walk back through the forest.

*

Later, at Klim's home, Alex sits as close to Elian as he can and casts frequent glances at her. He is shaken too, more so than he will ever let on to her. Coming upon Elian in the forest, and seeing the wild animal that would have killed her, has affected him in ways he didn't know were possible. He had known that he liked her, *more* than that, he had admitted it to himself just last night. But he hadn't realised just how much until it looked like he was going to lose her. He had not hesitated on pulling out the gun, and he knows he would have used that weapon on anything that had threatened her. Even another human.

Now they are at Klim's home, where he lives with another man called Sol. After pleasantries are exchanged, Alex realises that Sol is British, a fact upon which Alex comments, but receives no further explanation. Idly Alex wonders what their relationship is, if they are partners or simply housemates. They do not seem to be overly affectionate, and Alex doesn't know Klim well enough to ask. Sol is a large, solid man, with a clean shaven head and the apron that he wears as he bustles around preparing their meal is quite out of keeping with his demeanour. His dark brows are furrowed as he works. But, as soon as Klim or Alex mentions the 1986 nuclear accident, his expression changes to one of sadness.

"Were you here in eighty six, Sol?" asks Alex.

Klim answers for him. "Sol was in the army, but he came here very late, in 1999." He smiles almost tenderly at his friend. "Isn't that right, Sol?"

"Yes, I came here, I did my job. But, people stayed. At first I thought they were mad. But, as time went on, I too discovered the magic of Chernobyl. It was beautiful then and it is now." Sol's face darkens. "And now someone is trying to tear it apart, taking people one by one." He slams his fist down on the table. "Killing innocent people!"

Alex exchanges a look with Elian as she shifts a little closer to him.

"Tell us what you know," she instructs Klim, and as Sol turns the heat down on the wood burning stove, he comes to join them.

"There are not many people here, not compared to populations of normal towns. So we knew pretty much everybody. And, we lived like a normal town. People got married, started a family. And then, they started to disappear," Klim explains.

"Maybe they moved," suggests Elian. "If they had children, it's likely they wanted them to grow up somewhere that's not uninhabitable because of radiation."

Alex flinches at her uncharacteristically sarcastic tone, but Klim nods enthusiastically.

"That's what we thought at first. And some people did. But they still had family here, grandparents or cousins," Klim says softly, and leans closer. "But the ones they left behind never heard from them."

Alex feels his body sag with fatigue. This can't be why he was summoned here, for missing persons but no concrete evidence.

"There's more,' Sol speaks up. "Last year, some of the guys decided to try and get the gas pipes working. In eighty six, so much of our town was buried under concrete, we got hold of some diggers, the original ones that had laid the concrete. They didn't work. But we repaired them, got them working and started to pull up what they laid. On the edge of the forest, just before the concrete began, we dug up a grave."

Alex feels Elian tense beside him and he sits up straighter. This is what he has been waiting for. He leans forward, the others follow suit, until their foreheads are almost touching.

"The shovel was hitting something that wasn't rock or concrete or stone. So we killed the ignition and took a look. It was a woman." Sol passes his hand across his face, clearly remembering the horror. "She must not have been buried long."

"How do you know that?" asks Elian sharply.

"She had not decomposed much. Hair, clothes, skin, these were all intact." Klim drums his fingers on the table. "And, she had been stabbed."

Alex sits back and breathes out heavily. Sol gets up and comes back to the table, starts to dish out their meal.

By some unspoken agreement the conversation is halted as they eat quietly, all lost in their own thoughts.

"You wonder why we didn't go to the police," comments Klim. "Well, we did. After we had been once, it became very apparent that we couldn't ever go back to them."

"Why?" Alex asks.

Klim pauses, fork halfway to his mouth and meets Alex's eyes. "Because the first time we went, and what happened after, made it suddenly very clear that the police were involved in the murder."

*

Elian listens as the three men talk in low tones. Alex is going over old ground now, jotting down dates and names and times in his leather-bound notebook, the quintessential star investigative reporter.

She thinks over what they know, or at least what Klim and Sol have told them. She is still not sure that either of them are trustworthy. What these two men have imparted is that, as long as they can remember, especially directly after the nuclear accident, random people have been going missing. Not so unusual in itself, except they left with no warning, no goodbyes, not even to partners or parents or siblings. In a lot of the disappearances, young children have also vanished, almost always along with a parent or caregiver. Last year a body was found in a clandestine grave on the edge of the forest. The body had not decomposed much; it was a woman and she had clearly been stabbed to death.

"Who did you see at the police station?"

Sol looks up at Elian. "The Chief Inspector, a fat bastard called Arnja. He came down to the site, declared it suicide." Klim scoffs at this point. "We pointed out the stab wounds, the grave itself. How could anyone commit suicide and bury themselves?"

"So this Arnja is corrupt, did you try again?" Elian demands.

"Yes, we asked to see someone else, we said it was about a burglary. We waited in the room we were put in and, instead of some young wet-behind-the-ears cop, Fat Arnja comes along," replies Klim.

"We insisted that we would take it higher, to Kiev," chimes in Sol. "And that night our home, this house, was broken into. Klim was beaten to within an inch of his life."

Klim nods sagely and takes up the story. "It wasn't Fat Arnja, which just goes to show there are more people involved. After that night," Klim visibly shivers, "we had to leave it alone."

97

"Why? Why didn't you just go to Kiev? Or the newspapers? Blow this whole thing wide open?" asks Alex.

Klim's mouth had been set in a straight line, but now it works. He grinds his teeth and then pushes his chair back suddenly, stands and, without a word, slams out of the house. Sol looks mournfully at the empty chair.

"What happened, Sol?" Elian asks softly. "They didn't just beat him up did they?"

The minutes tick past and Sol does not answer. Elian exchanges a glance with Alex and he shakes his head softly. She catches the message; don't push him. Instead she sets about collecting the remaining dinner plates and stacks them neatly in the sink. As she makes her way back to the table, Sol begins to talk.

"I wasn't here that night. I'd gone to check on a couple of people, older residents, who live on a farm near the Red Forest. They waited for me to go out, and then they came in. They beat Klim so bad he was unconscious, and then they took him to the grave we found and," Sol pauses and swallows audibly, "they put him in it."

"Jesus!" Elian shudders.

"Klim was in such a bad way, barely conscious. He can't recall if the woman was still in there with him." Sol says as he casts a glance at the door. "We need to go back there, but Klim won't help me. He won't even talk about that night, and I can't really blame him."

"Do you think there are more bodies?" asks Elian.

"That poor woman was just the beginning," Klim says, startling them as he slips quietly back into the room and fixing his stare on Alex. "Now do you see? We need your help before anyone else is killed."

Chapter 24
Sissy

Chernobyl, May 3rd 1986

I had to wait two days until Simon is free from his work duties to take me across the river. During those two days I stayed in my home alone, rifling through Afia's things to try and find a clue to the other life that I've since found out she was living. Or *lives*, really, for none of us knew about Klim and her relationship with him; and, apart from the one night I spied on her, we didn't know about Niko either. I wonder if Niko is the gypsy that Knor referred to, and the man that Afia left Klim for. I can't understand why she would choose Niko over Klim. Klim is a good man, kind and obviously very much in love with my sister.

I've heard nothing from my mother since I saw her a few days ago. The town seems unearthly in its silence. Simon tells me that they are in discussion about the radiation that has leaked into the atmosphere and they may need to bury Chernobyl under concrete. He tells me that the people who have died have to be buried in lead lined coffins. I visualise this, standing at my window and looking out at the forest and the wildlife. It is inconceivable that all this is to be buried under tonnes of concrete.

While I wait for Simon I inspect Afia's red pantsuit. The blood has dried a rusty red and I stare at it, wondering what it means. Who did this? Was Afia waiting for the gypsy on the riverbank? But instead of him, did someone else come along and hurt my sister and, if so, why? Why remove her clothes? Where is she? Is she already buried beneath the surface of our poisoned land, soon to be buried again by the government and their soldiers? The questions circle my mind, endlessly, and I drum my fingers on the window, waiting for my British soldier. Finally, when he arrives, he is not alone.

Klim tags along behind him.

"He's been hanging around the factory. I thought it wouldn't be a bad idea to bring him. Strength in numbers and all that," says Simon hurriedly, as he comes up to the house.

I agree, there's no denying that we are going into the unknown. We rarely cross the water, we have no need to.

Simon has a boat for us and as we go down to the water I eye it uneasily. It's a simple rowing boat, but I reassure myself that we don't have far to cross in the rickety old thing. Klim takes the bow, Simon is at the stern and I sit in the middle of the two men. I can't help but imagine that I am Afia. This is exactly the sort of situation that she would aspire to be in; the African queen and her two suitors. I have had glimpses of her life, and it is only now that I feel like I'm really getting to know her.

Both men take one of my hands as they help me out of the boat on the other side. Silently we pick up a footpath and make our way into the forest.

I become despondent an hour into our trek. The forest is huge, many, many kilometres, and the pine trees that grow here don't help our search. The scenery is the same everywhere I turn. This is fruitless; but, as I pause to rest against a tree, Klim has an idea.

"I'll go west. At least if we separate we will cover more ground. We can meet back at the boat in three hours."

Simon and I nod our agreement and after synchronising our watches Klim hurries away from us.

Simon and I don't talk much as we walk along. He scans the trees for any sign of habitat, I look at the ground, scouring the undergrowth for evidence that my sister has been here. I worry about bears and wolves and seek reassurance from Simon's pistol that he carries on his belt. I wonder what Afia would have made of Simon. She would have flirted with him, fluttered her eyelashes at him and, if she were me right now, she would fake a fall or stumble. Then, when she was in his grip, she would divest herself of her clothes and lay down with him, right here on the forest floor.

"Are you all right?" Simon's voice pulls me out of my erotic daydream and I realised I have stopped moving.

How can my sister have such control over men? I am not much younger than her, but I don't think any man has ever looked at me the way they look at her. I catch up to Simon, flash a smile at him, but he looks forward, frowning slightly.

We carry on, walking in circles, widening them with each loop we make. Eventually we end up back on the river edge, standing by the small boat, waiting for Klim to appear. I sneak glances at Simon, watching his serious face as he checks his watch time and time again. I imagine what it would be like to lay down with him, and a thought that has been pushing its way into my brain can no longer be ignored. If Afia does not come back, can I take her place as the queen in all these men's hearts?

The thought is pushed aside as finally Klim staggers out of the forest. His face is pale and sweat patches are visible under the arms on his shirt. I run to him, Simon by my side, and we catch hold of his arms. He shakes us off roughly and glares angrily at me. He swears, a word offensive to my race, and I back away. It is like being with Knor all over again.

Simon speaks to him in a gentle, soothing tone, asking Klim what has happened. What has he seen? Klim turns his head away and, just before he vomits into the lake, I see tears start to fall from his eyes.

Chapter 25
Alex and Elian
Chernobyl, June 10th 2015

It is after midnight and Elian can't even think of going to bed. She sits by the window in the lounge, alternating between peering out at the dark landscape and stacking more logs on the fire. Klim and Sol have retired to their respective bedrooms, as has Alex. Yet again, Elian found she is sharing a room with him, amid apologies from Klim and offers from Alex to sleep on the couch, she waved them away, stating that she wasn't very tired yet anyway.

Now she sits alone, the three men sleeping soundly, leaving Elian with just her thoughts for company. She finds she has so much to think about, with her being here, amongst the buried bodies of her descendants, the murders and the unexpected bent cop angle. And then there's Alex. What of Alex? The source of so much consternation to her, a man she gave herself to, opened her home to, then hated with a fury that knew no bounds. And now . . . now her feelings are unknown, as are his regarding her.

Sighing, she looks out of the window again. It's quiet out here, no crickets chirping or dogs barking. She shudders as she remembers her encounter with the wolf. Are there more of his kind out there? Larger than they should be, just like the mushrooms that they passed during their brief time with the tour guide. And Sissy, is she out here somewhere? Did she desert Elian and make her way back home to the land she always pined for, just like Elian always suspected? And, if so, does she know that her niece is here? There are not many citizens of Chernobyl. News of strangers must spread quickly here.

Suddenly she wants to get out of this cottage and go down to the area where she knows Sissy and her family used to live. Because, really, aside from the blackmail and the money, that always what this trip was about for her, even if this is the first time she has admitted it to herself. Quietly, Elian slips her trainers on and let's herself out of the cottage. It's cooler out here, despite the warmth of the day. She goes down to the road, looks left and right, and decides to head east, away from the factory. From what she remembers, Sissy's home was one of the houses located further away from the nuclear plant. She scuffs her feet as she walks down the lane. Although there are no street lights, the moon is bright and it is not scary as she thought it might be. Rather, it is peaceful. The trees that border the road sway gently, the grass on the verge grows tall and lush and, as the sense of calm envelops her, Elian realises why Sissy loved it here so much.

Soon the road takes her down a narrow, winding trail, and there, at the bottom, a small cluster of cottages are nestled together. It is the end of the road. One of them must be the Bello's old place.

Seeing shadows and lights in a couple of the houses, Elian steps off the road and skirts around the back of the buildings.

She knows people live here, residents like Sol and Klim, but just how many is not known. She has read of a community of about twelve hundred people who stayed here after evacuation, and more recently she's read that there are now just over one hundred left. Of these, most are elderly women, the men having lost their lives to a combination of radiation-sparked illnesses and alcohol abuse. Yet younger people, like Klim and Sol, take care of the older ones. Although, her hosts are not really that young, they are in their fifties after all. The true story isn't known, not really. Just facts and figures that are reported in the press. But how can anyone really know the truth if they don't come here?

She moves around the side of the houses, feeling inexplicably sad as she looks at their gardens, so well tended and cared for, as though this is any town anywhere in the world. As she treads carefully, making sure to stay out of sight, she spots a figure sitting on the wrap-around porch of the smallest cottage. Elian squints in the darkness, trying to make out what they are doing.

With her eyes adjusted to the gloom, she can see the person is not doing very much of anything. Wrapped up in a thick Navajo blanket against the night chill, the woman – for Elian is sure that the petite frame is female – is simply gazing out across the landscape. Elian inches her way around the trees, heart thumping, and fists clenched as she strains to get a good look at the woman. The woman shifts in her chair, turns to pick up a pitcher of drink on the table by her side and, as she moves, her face is caught in the moonlight. Elian stifles a gasp, claps her hands to her mouth and feels unshed tears clogging her throat. She knows – her heart had surely known before her head did – the woman who sits on the porch in a stately manner, almost majestically, is Sissy.

When her breathing has steadied and she is certain that she is not going to cry out, she lowers her hands and watches her aunt. She wants to do nothing more than to run to her and throw herself into her arms, but her legs, as heavy as though they are cast in lead, hold her back. All she can think of, as she watches the woman who raised her, is that she walked out on Elian, never to return. Since that night she has wondered endlessly if Sissy would call, or get in contact from an internet café or library somewhere. People here have telephones, yet she never called, and she could have, at the very least to say that she was alive and unharmed. It is too much of a coincidence that, out of all the people in London, Alex picked her to come along as his translator, a role that he hasn't really had any use for, as Yuri, the tour guide, and both Klim and Sol speak perfectly good English.

Elian rubs at the spot between her brows. Her head is beginning to ache. Hopefully, she thinks, from the action and emotion of the last few days, and not the effects of radiation seeping into her system. She should go back to the cottage and try to sleep; but, as she looks at Sissy, still sitting on the porch, she knows she won't be going anywhere for a while.

*

Alex wakes with a start and looks over to the other side of the bed. There is no Elian in it and, going by the smooth, wrinkle-free sheets, she has not been here either. He sits up, presses the button that illuminates his TAG Heuer watch and scratches his head. He can't remember if he changed the time zone or not, so he digs around in his bag for his iPhone, which he knows changes automatically. It is one o'clock in the morning, and his watch is wrong.

He leans back against the pillow, but he feels wired and knows he won't be going back to sleep. Maybe he'll go and sit with Elian, she's probably feeling weirded out by everything. He knows he is. Hell, even if she doesn't need to talk, it wouldn't hurt to get things off *his* chest. He climbs out of bed and pulls on his jeans and hoodie, and goes in search of Elian.

It doesn't take long to discover she is not in the house, unless she is in either Sol or Klim's bedrooms. But, knowing Elian and her spikiness, that doesn't seem likely. Alex sits by the fire and pokes at the dying embers. The heavy weight of realisation dawns on him; she has gone out there, probably in search of her missing Aunt Sissy. He remembers the wolf, the way it was about to pounce at her, and he thinks of the serial killer, also out there, under cover of the wilderness.

"Shit," he mutters, glancing at the closed bedroom doors, wondering if he should wake Sol and Klim.

He decides against it, knowing that he is the only one to count on here. Zipping up his hoodie, he slips quietly from the house and into the cool night.

Never has he been in a place so uninhabited. All of Alex's life he has travelled to popular places filled with tourists and surrounded by other people. He has never done the whole wilderness trek or been off the beaten track. But now, as he stands here, in a town with only a handful of residents, he realises that if he can get past the slightly sinister feel, and welcome the peace and quiet, this could be a good place to be. But first, there are jobs to be done. Serial killers to figure out, corrupt police forces to deal with and, first and foremost, an errant Elian to locate.

It's not hard to guess which way Elian went, either to the left, which is back towards the factory from where they started their journey with Yuri, the guide, or right, past Klim's house and down the track. He chooses east, and knows from talking with Sol and Klim that the walk won't be long. Not far down the track, what could laughingly be called civilisation ends, and the wilderness begins. Two women pass him by and give him a strange look; small, dark eyes like raisins standing out against tanned, wrinkled skin. They are old, bent over, carrying a silver pail between them. They both wear wraps around their heads and he nods at them. Once he has passed them by he hears them whispering to each other. He wonders why they are out so late, although guesses that, here, time does not have the same meaning as in a civilised world.

As he walks down the road his eyes flick left and right. He tries to slow his shallow breathing, looking all the time for wolves and murderers. He is silently cursing Elian when he sees a movement by a tree, around the side of a small cluster of houses. Almost immediately after, he notices the figure on the porch, and that it is Elian crouched by the tree, watching. He darts off the road, round the back of the house and pauses fifty yards away from Elian. For a while he watches her watching the other woman, and he focuses his attention on the woman on the porch.

The moon comes out from behind a cloud, illuminating her for a moment, and he knows straight away that this must be Sissy. He groans inaudibly and puts his head in his hands, wondering what Elian must be feeling as she looks at the woman who deserted her. He turns his attention to Elian, feels desperately sorry for her as she kneels on the ground, drinking in the sight of the woman who had raised her. He blinks, Elian's shoulders are shaking, is she laughing? And then he realises; she is crying.

She doesn't want to show herself to Sissy, he understands that and he knows why. So, stealthily, but making enough noise to announce his presence, he comes up behind her. Elian turns at the rustling of the leaves underfoot and, before he even reaches out to her, she is in his arms.

He holds her tight, his own heart breaking a little as her body is wracked with silent sobs.

Chapter 26
Sissy

Chernobyl, Autumn 1986

I can't believe how my life has changed. My father is dead, buried in a zinc coffin surrounded by concrete in a graveyard in Russia. My mother might as well be dead. She returned to Pripyat after the funeral – which happened too fast for me to attend – and now she sits in the cottage, by the window, waiting . . . for who knows what?

My mother will tell me nothing about his death, nor will anybody else. They don't know that I already saw it, right after it happened. Therefore, I know that his final days were brutal and excruciating. I would do anything to take that away from him. I would take his pain into me if I could. As soon as he died he was buried, whisked away undercover like a criminal. He was put in the earth so fast that nobody could get to him in time to say goodbye.

Afia has not returned. I often think back to the day on the side of the lake, of what could have been if it were just me and Simon, my whimsical, childish fantasies and then the arrival of Klim, lurching out of the trees, vomiting into the water, refusing to look at us or speak to us about what had shaken him so. After what seemed like hours of pleading with him, Simon and I deposited Klim back at his house and watched him go inside. I've not seen Klim since. He won't answer the door to me.

I've not seen Simon anymore either. Once the government got their act together they started putting soldiers on in shifts. Two weeks on and then the next lot comes. To this day, we've not seen the same face more than once. Simon left a note for me the day he left. It didn't say very much, except he hoped I had some luck in finding Afia. He left a number, too, and an address at his home in Epping, England. I'll never need this information, but I've not thrown his address away.

I live in a kind of middle ground, a no-man's land. I have no company, nobody to talk to. Our family has been cut in half with the loss of my father and Afia. My mother talks to nobody, not even me, really, and she sees no one. Most of the residents of our town have left or are dead. Old Knor stayed, as did Klim, but I don't see them. I don't want to, anyway.

I want to see my father, but the memory of that night at the factory is too painful to think about right now. I went there and started to leave with him. If he hadn't had turned around to rescue his co-workers, would he be alive now? I wish he hadn't had seen those men that littered the roadside with their bleeding hearts and dead faces. Had there been nobody there, he may not have realised the severity of the situation. Had he realised that his eldest daughter would still be missing all these months later, he would have come home with me.

Hindsight is a wonderful thing.

On occasion, when the night sky turns milky grey, just before dawn, I leave the cottage and walk through my town. Sometimes I see the soldiers. I play at being Afia then, and the soldiers are mostly lonely. We might sit together and with skills honed over years of spying on my sister, I make them fall in love with me. But they are never content with the subtle flashes of skin that I have to offer them. They bat my hand away when all I want is to gently stroke their brow. They pant and groan and grasp with their needy, groping fingers until I have to run home.

I've become good at running. I'm fast, faster than anyone.

A lot of the time I sit on our side of the lake, looking over the water. I daydream of seeing Afia appear on the other side, and I send her silent messages telling her it's okay if she is living over there somewhere. She can stay there, if only she will appear and wave at me once, just so I know that she is alive. Constantly I wonder what Klim saw and why he seemed so angry. I have come to accept that there are some things I will never know.

My mother has heard from distant relatives today, a letter arrived all the way from Nairobi. It is a cousin who has heard of our plight here. The cousin cannot offer money; that is scarce, as it seems to be everywhere. But she can take me in; or, if mama would prefer, there are also relatives in the south east of England.

I read the letter aloud to mama and pause as I wonder what it would be like to live in Africa or England. Simon is in England, and I allow myself to daydream about emigrating there as his wife.

But then I look at my mother, broken shell that she is, and I know that, while she is still alive, I can't go anywhere.

They brought in people to survey the mess that was once the very epicentre of our existence. They sent photographers into the core and discovered the mass of the molten reactor. It had flowed like lava until it solidified and earned the nickname 'elephant's foot'. They say if you are exposed to the elephant's foot for three hundred seconds you have two days to live. How did they find that out? That's what I want to know. But it's not hard to figure, after all nobody seems to have seen these photographers again.

Once those in charge realised that repair wasn't an option, it became a case of damage limitation. Plan B is a sarcophagus, a giant steel and concrete arch which will entomb the radioactive remains of Reactor Four. If you can't fix it, hide it.

Who we talk to depends on the answer given to our questions. Some say the sarcophagus will last for one hundred years, others say the radiation will stay in our area for fifty thousand years, but we may be able to repopulate Chernobyl in six hundred years. The timescales are ludicrous; laughable. Our people take no notice.

So they remain, as do I. We go about our daily business of rising in the morning and making it through the day.

The men who stayed can't erase the things that they have seen, so they drink to forget.

Chapter 27
Alex and Elian
Chernobyl, June 10th 2015

Elian doesn't want to talk about spotting Sissy. Alex seems to understand, and for that she is grateful. He holds her for a long time, underneath the tree, and when he helps her to finally stand he doesn't let go of her. For that, she is also grateful.

They walk back to Klim's house in silence and Elian can't remember feeling this drained ever before. Not even in the days after Sissy left her did she feel like this.

"Are you okay to stay?" Alex asks her as they reach the cottage where they are staying. "I can take you back to Kiev. Put you on a plane back home, if you like."

It's a sweet offer, and kind of him. The more time she spends with Alex, the more she is coming to realise that he does have a heart after all. It's not all about him or money. And she considers it. It is a tempting offer, to go back home to London and carry on with her life and her work. She wouldn't have to be so paranoid all the time that someone is going to catch up with the lies that Sissy told. In fact, she doesn't even have to stay there now, not daring to go too far in case Sissy comes home. For Sissy isn't coming back, not ever.

The thought prompts a fresh batch of tears, which she swallows against as she angrily rubs her eyes with her jacket sleeve.

"I don't know, I don't want to make any decisions tonight, I don't want to think about her any more, not just yet," she replies. "What about you? The murders, I mean, what are you going to do?"

"I want to speak some guys back home, some contacts that I have. I need to know about this policeman, Arnja; and I need to know where the body of the victim is."

Elian listens to Alex, knowing her eyes are bugging out of her head at his words. This is serious, and Alex, though he could flee, is also serious about dealing with this crime.

At that moment she knows she will not return to London until this is all over. The girl who was in the grave couldn't cry for help. Alex can help and Elian will therefore help him however she can.

"We need to figure out a plan, we need to write down all of the known victims, the dates, other missing persons. We need to go to this grave." Elian lights up, stops and grabs Alex's sleeve. "DNA will still be there, traces of her hair or skin. Then you can get in contact with someone back home and get some more help, proper, *legal* help."

"And we need to do this before too many people realise we're here." Alex drops his voice, moves closer to Elian. "This is a small place, with few people, so we need to stay under the radar for as long as possible. That means no more midnight walks, at least not on your own."

"There won't be anything like that happening again," Elian snaps, ending that particular line of conversation. "I've seen all I need to now."

*

Later she sleeps. Klim's dog sits by her feet, regarding Alex with watchful eyes. Alex watches her for a while, still pumped up and unable to go to bed himself. He muses over her words, how she knows all she needs to now regarding her aunt. He knows it's not the end though. He knows that she is bound to confront her before they leave this place. But maybe, once she has, she can then move on with her life, live the way a nineteen-year-old should.

As the room lightens with the dawn, Alex accepts that there will be no chance of sleep now, so he pulls out his notebook and begins to write down everything he knows so far. When Klim and Sol wake he will talk to them about any gaps that he needs to fill in, and also get them to show him exactly where this grave was. Probably a job for Sol, thinks Alex. Seeing as Klim was put in the grave on the night that the police inspector's heavies came after him, it's likely that he won't want to go to that spot again.

Grabbing his phone, Alex taps out a quick email to his friend Luke, a forensic anthropologist with the Met.

Possible product coming your way, are you in a position to help? Most likely just standard DNA only.

It's unorthodox, but then most of this investigation is. And if it looks like they are getting in too deep, Alex promises himself that he'll pull the plug and turn the whole thing over to the proper authorities.

He doesn't want to though. Even though so far on this trip he has encountered some of the scariest moments of his life, he wants to stay, he wants justice.

A short while later Elian listens as the men huddle together. It is early, so early that the sun hasn't yet fully risen. A mist hovers over the land outside the window and Elian gives in to an involuntary shudder and moves closer to the trio.

"What's the plan?" she asks.

They look up at her and she raises her eyebrows. They have been squabbling, disagreeing about the trip to the grave that Alex wants to make.

"We need to go to where the body was buried, and we need to make it fast, before anyone else wakes up and sees us," replies Alex, looking pointedly at Klim.

Elian can understand why Klim might not want to go. Why dredge up the memories of being beaten and placed in the grave? Sol, on the other hand, is nodding in agreement to Alex.

"We don't all have to go," she says, being peace keeper. "Sol and Alex can go out there, Klim, I can stay with you."

They all look somewhat surprised at Elian's offer, and she can hardly blame them. After all, she and Klim can't really say they started off the best of friends, what with him following her back in London and turning up in Kiev. However, Elian is sure that he is holding back on something, and she relishes the chance of being alone with him.

*

Alex hesitates as he prepares to leave with Sol. He lingers at the door, watching Elian as she busies herself around the stove. Klim glares at Alex sullenly.

"You don't trust me. You think I'm going to do something to her?" Klim shouts suddenly, and Alex rears up.

"You don't even want to think about doing anything to her," Alex says softly, walking up to Klim so they are face to face.

Elian shoves her way in between them, putting her hand on Alex's chest and moving him away from Klim. Without knowing that he is going to, Alex grabs her small hand, squeezes it roughly in his and looks into her eyes. Her eyes are sparkling green emeralds and for a moment he is lost, unable to remember what he was going to say or even why he took her hand.

"I'll be fine with Klim," she whispers. "Go with Sol, do what you need to do and come back. We'll be fine, and you be careful."

Then Sol is on him, taking his arm and pulling him out of the door. Alex allows himself to be led away.

Instead of walking down the road that Alex took the previous night, Sol leads Alex around the back of the house and over to a small 125cc motorbike. Alex stares at the gleaming machine, all chrome, silver and orange. Repsol is plastered across it and it seems a fitting sight in this weird retro world that he has found himself.

"We're going on this?"

Sol nods solemnly. "It's fast and, if we're seen doing what we're about to do, we need to be fast."

As he talks he ties two shovels on either side, securing them with bungee cords. Alex can't take his eyes off them, knowing that they will be digging bodies up with those implements later.

As Alex climbs on the back and wraps his arms around Sol's stocky frame, he thinks about what they are about to do. Grave robbing, although if the body is not in the grave can it still be referred as this? As they roar off, Alex takes one hand from Sol's waist and pats his pocket, ensuring that he has the plastic bags ready for whatever – if anything – they should find at the grave site.

During the ride Alex had hoped to watch the route that they travel, in case he needs to come back to the site for any reason. But Sol's driving is fast and erratic, and his heads whips from left to right and sometimes all the way back, so he is looking over Alex's shoulder. Alex then finds himself watching the road ahead, which as a pillion passenger is not ideal. Finally, Sol turns off the road down a track that Alex would never have spotted and drives through the forest. Now that they are moving at a slower speed, Alex lifts his head and looks at his surroundings. He can see why it is called the Red Forest; the pines look as though they are in permanent autumnal state, rust red and dead, or, at the very least, dying.

Eventually Sol slows the bike right down and brings it to a stop. Alex climbs off and looks around. They are in a clearing surrounded by the red pine trees. Nearby he can hear a stream babbling, but can see no evidence of one. He watches as Sol walks around, scuffing at the ground, and Alex looks down. To the untrained eye this clearing would look like any other, but Alex *has* been trained, and he drops into a crouch to examine the ground at closer quarters.

"It's been disturbed here," says Alex, as Sol joins him. "Look, see how this earth here, this top layer, is looser, paler."

Sol nods, looking at Alex with a wondrous expression. "You're right; the grave was here, right where we are."

"How far did you dig down before you found her?"

"Not too deep, just about four feet."

Alex sits back on his heels and thinks. Four feet isn't very deep, not for any sort of grave.

"And when did you find this? How long ago?"

"Last year, at the end of last summer," replies Sol. "Why do you ask?"

"Because this top soil has been dug up a lot more recently than last summer," Alex says, as he rolls up his sleeves. "Come on, let's see what's buried here."

Chapter 28
Afia

1986

My name is Afia Bello and I am nineteen years old. Sometimes I tell myself that statement. It's like I have to remind myself who I am. Lately, it's easy to forget.

Did you ever feel like the world is not enough? I did. My world was never enough for me. It was quiet, peaceful and respectable. I craved excitement, thrills and danger. I wanted to travel the world, be in a girl group, become a movie star, all the idle daydreams of a normal teenage girl.

I was special, I knew that. My father told me often enough. The boys in my town made sure I was aware of my status. There was nobody like me.

It wasn't enough. But, until I met *him*, I didn't know exactly what it was I was seeking.

I first saw him in the forest. There were no words, or any need for them either. He looked dangerous and a little crazy, the way he stared at me. We were drawn to each other, like there was an invisible thread pulling us together. He pulled out his knife, he sliced my clothes until I was standing in front of him naked. It was the single most thrilling thing that had ever happened to me. He ran that knife over my skin, blunt side down, so I felt the cold steel. I don't know why, but I turned it over so it cut me. Something other than blood ran out. Something unexplainable, something inexplicable. Something beautiful.

I never felt as good as I did right at that moment.

Suddenly nothing else mattered except *him*. I had to see him. All the time I wanted to be with him. When I was at home with my family I would finger the scars on my stomach. My family, my hardworking mother and father and my little sister, would sit with me, each of them wasting their lives, working, working, working; worrying about what the boss thinks, the neighbours think, what the school teachers think. I was so smug. They knew nothing of what I had felt.

I returned to *him*, time and time again. I knew nothing of *him*. What he done for a living, for money? Where did he come from? What of his family? And you know what, it didn't matter.

All that mattered was *him*.

Chapter 29
Alex and Elian
Chernobyl, June 11th 2015

Alex had expected the unearthing of the grave to be an arduous task, but it is not as difficult as he had anticipated. The way that the soil came away easily, in loose crumbs, made him think that his suspicions were right; someone had been here recently.

When they'd dug a couple of feet down they paused. Sol pulls two bottles of water out of his bike pack.

"The girl, Elian, she's from here, right?" asks Sol.

"Not really, but her family were," Alex says, and pauses, looking over at his grave-digging companion. "Do you know them? Bello, was the surname. Sissy is Elian's aunt."

Sol nods, his face serious. "I know that Klim was close to them. He wanted to marry Afia, that's Sissy's sister. But she vanished, way back, before even I came here. Sometimes I wonder if she ended up like this." He jerks his head toward the half-dug grave, and there is a strange look on his face, almost of dislike.

"You mean at the hands of the same person? But that was thirty years ago, surely this hasn't been going on all that time?"

Sol shrugs, throws back more water and stands up, reaching for his shovel. Alex follows suit and, in grim silence, they get back to work.

"Do you know who Elian's parents are?" Alex huffs as he digs.

"No," replies Sol with a surprised expression. "Don't you? I mean, you are her boyfriend, right?"

Alex sidesteps Sol's assumption. "Sissy was her aunt, but she raised Elian. I don't think Elian ever knew her true parentage." He gives Sol a sideways glance. "Did you ever hear anything about it?"

Sol shrugs. "I was here later, after the family was all broken up. I didn't arrive until the winter of 1999."

"And you're happy here? I mean, you just live here, with Klim, never seeing anyone else? Don't the two of you ever want to go anywhere, take holidays?" Alex can't fathom the nomadic way of life.

"I've been back to England, just the one time for my father's funeral, just a couple of years ago actually. I go to Belarus for supplies, maybe a couple of times a year. Every April Klim goes off for a week, usually for the anniversary of the accident."

"Don't you go with him?"

Sol shakes his head and shrugs his shoulders. "Klim likes to be alone at that time."

Alex shuts up and digs on. He probably shouldn't even be discussing that matter with Sol. Elian's biological family is not why they are here, although . . . he can't help but feel that she is linked, somehow, to this mess. Whoever sent the original email suggested that he get to Elian and involve her in this. Remembering this point, Alex stops digging and looks up sharply.

"Who paid me to come here? Which one of you actually sent the first email along with the retainer?"

Sol sighs and sets down his shovel and reaches for his water bottle again. "Not me, if that's what you're asking. I just go along with whatever keeps Klim happy and out of trouble. I'm an outsider here, just like you."

There's a depth to Sol's words that Alex can just about pick up on, but can't make sense of. And, returning to the job at hand, he realises that he is questioning the wrong person. This grave digging isn't turning anything up either. The sun is completely up now and it promises to be another searing hot day. Not a day that Alex wants to waste digging a hole only to find nothing in it. He is about to suggest to Sol that they call it a day when his shovel meets resistance. He stops, eases the shovel up and then moves it cautiously down again. Once more it stops and Alex hears a definite crack. He takes his hands off the shovel and steps back.

"Sol, mate," he calls, his voice deceiving him and the demeanour he strives to give off, as it comes out small and tremulous. "I think I've found something."

*

Elian busies herself with making tea while Klim does anything he can think of not to sit and have a conversation with her. His old dog nuzzles her knees and absentmindedly she scratches behind its ears. The dog has taken a liking to her, and though she has never owned a pet, she finds she is rather fond of it too.

Klim is shredding old newspapers and rolling the pieces up in conical shapes, wedging them in next to the wood pile. Elian perseveres, does the washing up and then dries the plates and cups until all the crockery has been put away and Klim has no more paper to roll.

Their eyes meet, his are skittish, glancing away and then back at her. Her glare is defiant. Klim sighs and shuffles over to the table where he takes his seat and wraps his hands around the mug of already cooling tea.

"Did you know that Sissy is back here?" she asks, surprising herself as she hadn't planned on asking about her aunt.

"I'd heard," he replies drily.

"But you haven't spoken to her?"

"I've not spoken to Sissy Bello in almost thirty years," he says, his voice brittle.

She scratches her head, had presumed they were friends. Sissy had mentioned him, from time to time when she was in the mood for nostalgia.

"She made out we were friends, or more, perhaps?"

Elian thinks before responding. Had Sissy spoken about Klim like a friend? Yes, she's pretty sure she did. More than friends? Elian honestly can't remember, but she does recall a certain wistful tone when his name was mentioned. But hadn't Klim belonged to Sissy's sister before she vanished off the face of the earth?

"Why have you not spoken to her? And how long has she been back here, in Chernobyl?"

"She's been back a couple of years," Klim says, and pauses. "Two years, May 2013."

Elian is momentarily touched by the way Klim uses his fingers to count back the years. It is endearing, childlike almost. Then she realises what he has said.

"Three years, you mean."

He appears to think deeply, and then shakes his head. "No, it was two years ago. I only remember because it was practically the anniversary of Sol's father's death." He shrugs.

"Where was she then, for the year that she wasn't here and wasn't in London?" She is talking to herself, but Klim looks up at her.

"I gave up asking myself why that family does anything," he mutters.

Elian huffs out a breath, still wondering about the dates. There was nobody else in Aunt Sissy's life that she would have gone and spent a year with. All she had were Elian and Chernobyl, nothing else mattered.

Nothing, that is, except her sister. Of course, Afia, the epicentre of so much consternation throughout the years. She looks sharply up at Klim.

"Did anyone ever find out anything more about Afia? Was her body ever found?"

Klim winces. In fact, thinks Elian, he shrivels inside himself at the mention of Afia's name.

Elian holds her breath. For the briefest moment she feels that Klim is going to tell her everything that she has always needed to know. Because for all of Sissy's love that she lavished on Elian since she was a baby, Sissy never really told her niece anything of importance. Elian's history has always been shrouded in mystery.

She waits, but just as it appears that Klim might open up to her, something outside grabs his attention. A flash of colour passes the window in a blur and she and Klim hurry to the front door.

"It's Alex and Sol," she cries. "I didn't think they'd be back yet."

She hears the roar of the motorbike, a squeak as it brakes sharply, and the engine descends into silence as the ignition is switched off. Klim shuffles back to the kitchen with Elian and they wait expectantly.

"It's not both of them," says Klim, his mouth set in a grim line. "It's Sol, and he's on his own."

Sol is tripping over himself to get the words out and Elian leads him to the table.

"Where is Alex?" she asks impatiently.

"Back at the site." Sol takes the glass of water that Klim hands him and drinks it gratefully, before flicking his eyes over both of them, his gaze settling on Elian. "We found something."

"A body?" asks Klim, paling considerably.

"I think so. I didn't look too hard." Sol looks embarrassed. "Alex told me to come back here, he wants a small trowel, brushes, more plastic bags and gloves. Then I'm to take them back to him."

Elian watches as Klim does what is asked of him. He busies around, filling a rucksack with old plastic shopping bags and some dispensable gloves from under the kitchen sink. He orders Sol to the shed to bring back his set of gardening tools and some paint brushes if he can find any that are sealed. "If not, they should at least be clean," he yells as an afterthought.

Elian passes her hand over her face as it becomes clear what Alex's plan is. When the rucksack is packed and ready to be taken back to Alex, Elian picks it up and takes the map out of the front pocket.

"He's going to attempt to do the crime scene, isn't he?" She asks Sol, glaring at him defiantly, daring him to deny Alex's plan.

Sol exchanges a worried look with Klim. "I think so, but can he? He's not a police officer, or any sort of officer come to that, is he?"

"No, he's not an officer." Elian steps forward and plucks the keys to Sol's motorcycle from his hand. "Neither am I, but I'm pretty sure together we can do enough to nail the bastard who's responsible for this."

Chapter 30
Klim
1987

Klim can hardly believe that a whole year has passed since the accident. Sometimes it's like nothing has changed. The seasons roll around, he gets up in the morning and goes to bed at night. But then, suddenly, he will realise that he hasn't seen another living soul for over a week and it hits him like a thump in the chest. He could leave, go with the others who scattered themselves around the globe, but he knows he won't. This place is familiar, somewhere he had never planned on leaving, not even before the accident. Then there is *her*, the real reason for him staying here, buoyed by the hope that one day she might come back to him. He'll wait. Klim will wait forever if he has to.

He remembers the first time he saw her, when her family arrived and caused a stir in the village. She was, to his eyes, a queen. From her stature and aloof quality, it was as though she knew that she was something extremely unique and special, like a hummingbird or a rare treasure. As they grew and he admired her from afar, it came to a point when suddenly she was taking notice of him, and then the magic happened; he was allowed to adore her publicly. He thought they would be together forever, and even when he started hearing rumours about her with other young men, he dismissed it as envy. Then she told him herself, that she wanted to be with someone else. That night, he made love to her with all of his emotions etched plainly on his face, and when it was finished he was sure that she would see nobody would love her like he did. But she had left anyway.

It's hard to still love her, especially with the memory of the last time he saw her that lays low in a dark corner of his mind, only to rush at him, pulsating in its awfulness at unexpected moments.

That day, when he and Simon and Sissy had searched the land across the water for her, plays on his mind all the time. He still feels the excitement that he had felt when he quite accidentally stumbled upon the caravan on the edge of the woods. He had called out, but it was only when he knocked on the door that it had fallen open beneath his hand, allowing him to peer into the small interior. He was struck by how clean and tidy it was, he had not been expecting that. The curtains had been closed and the room was dim, but there was enough light to see the form of a woman huddled in the corner of the sofa. He moved closer, whispering her name. It was only when he was towering over her that she realised he was there. She had smiled, lazily, a corner of her mouth drooping and saliva bubbling between her full lips.

That she was naked was not the first thing that he noticed. It was the brown leather belt, a couple of shades lighter than her skin, buckled tight around her upper arm that he saw first. He saw the vein that bulged, blue and proud, and the needle that protruded from that vein and the dirty brown liquid, intermingling with a little blood in the plunger section.

As he had stood, horrified, she had tried to speak, but could form no words. Instead she had continued to smile, that terrible, horrible smile, and with the needle still hanging out of her arm she had shifted on the chair, opening her legs wide and beckoning him with her eyes.

He had backed up, knocked into the worktop and sent a pan tumbling into the sink. The noise bought him up sharp, broke the spell, and he had slammed out of the caravan, running back to the meeting point, not stopping until he reached the water's edge. Then, ignoring the cries of Sissy and the tentative words from Simon, he had vomited into the lake.

He couldn't speak to Sissy after that, still can't even a year later. Because all he sees, when he looks at Sissy, is her sister, Afia.

So now he spends most of his days alone in his house. A few times a week he calls on the other residents who stayed; the older ones who are too set in their ways to move on and start afresh. He has his dog, Jayne. Jayne is still a puppy really. His family only got her a couple of weeks before the nuclear blast. Klim remembers when his father brought her home and presented her to him. Klim named her Jayne straight away, after the British ice skater whom he became slightly obsessed with after watching the winning performance of the 1984 Sarajevo Olympics on the television. He is never totally alone, not with Jayne constantly by his side.

On occasion he goes across the water. The caravan has moved, but only a couple of miles further into the forest. Sometimes he sees her moving inside, the dim light inside casting her shadow over the windows. Sometimes he sees *him*, coming and going. She is still alive, one year on.

That's enough for Klim to know, for now.

Chapter 31
Alex and Elian
Chernobyl, June 11th 2015

Alex stands as he hears a motorbike approaching, and dusts off his jeans as the bike appears over the crest. As the bike swerves from left to right he frowns at Sol's erratic driving, and then as the machine comes to an abrupt stop he realises it is not Sol at all. She leaves the bike on the edge of the clearing, unloads it, and walks the hundred yards over to him.

"What are you doing?" He takes the bag that Elian hands to him and looks her up and down. "You shouldn't be here."

"Um, why?" Her eyes flash, no doubt daring him to come up with a reason why this is no place for a lady.

He backs down and kneels on the ground, removing the items that Sol and Klim have gathered for him. He surveys the haul, nods appreciatively and lines up the bags and the brushes.

"How did you even find me? I wouldn't have even seen the track from the main road."

"It took a couple of tries, but then I saw the wheel tracks the bike had made," she replied.

"Listen to me," he instructs. "I've pulled down those pine branches over there. If we hear anyone approaching, either by car or on foot, help me lay them over the grave, okay? If you saw the tyre tracks then someone else easily could. We'll figure out what happens after that if anyone turns up!"

His weak attempt at a joke falls flat and he watches her as she looks first at the dead pine branches, fanned out within easy reach, then her gaze lands on the grave. Bone, material and blood are clearly visible, but to her credit she hardly flinches. She straightens her shoulders and looks back at Alex.

"What can I do to help you?"

He nods, breathes out and plucking his iPhone from his pocket he puts it in her hands. "Take photos, constantly, every step of the way. There's plenty of memory so don't worry about how many shots you take, the more the better, okay?"

Alex kneels back at the graveside and can't quite believe what he is looking at. Sol was pretty sure that this was the same body they found last year, simply by going by the shreds of clothing that are still clinging to the form of the woman. She has disintegrated since the men originally found her. And she may have been moved as well, since Klim can't recall her being in the grave at the same time as him. Alex shudders, imagining what Klim must have felt when he awoke after the attack. It's everybody's worst nightmare.

Behind him he hears the sharp click every few seconds when Elian takes a shot. He can hear her breathing and he lets out a sigh and leans forward. "I'm not going to able to move her," he says. "She's . . . it's not going to work."

"What do you mean?" Elian asks, as she pauses and steps up to the grave.

"Oh God, she'll . . . break. This isn't an unconscious woman who I can pick up and move to safety." His tone is uncharacteristically sharp and he is immediately sorry.

"We can't do this," whispers Elian. "We absolutely cannot do this, it's got to be illegal, and it's certainly inhumane. This won't help anybody."

It's as though a fog has lifted as Alex rocks back on his heels and looks up at Elian. She is right, this is a crime scene, a *murder* scene, and he is not sure how he had even thought he could attempt at playing an anthropologist. His tools are makeshift and he has no right to be doing this. The victim deserves better, but there *is* nothing better, not in this town.

"I'm going to have to speak to some guys back home, back in England. We can't handle this on our own, it's too much. It's too dangerous." Alex stands up and slams the shovel into the ground. "It's over."

She looks relieved he notes as he looks over at her, and he can't blame her.

"Shall I cover her?" Elian asks in a small voice.

"No, I'll do that," he says kindly, and squeezes her shoulder as he walks past. "Thank you for helping."

"I'll pack these away, then load them on to the motorbike," she says. He thanks her as she collects up the shovels, bags and brushes and walks back to where she left the bike.

He turns back to the grave, bows his head and feels a rush of emotion. This is so much more than he ever conceived when he got that first email. All he thought about then was the thirty thousand euros. Now he is here, and it's so different to what he had anticipated. He sends a silent apology down to the girl, acknowledges that this is someone's daughter or wife. Deep down, so deep he can almost not think about it, he knows this trip is changing him. Or is Elian changing him? Weirdly he finds himself in an instant recalling his favourite movie, The Godfather. He thinks of the parts set in Corleone, Sicily, and the thunderbolt that hit Michael before it went disastrously wrong for him and even worse for Apolonia.

He is getting to his feet when he hears a noise out of keeping with his surroundings. It is high pitched, not quite a scream, but not far off either. It reverberates through the trees, disturbing a lone bird that launches itself into the air with a shriek to rival the one that Alex heard. Later, he will berate himself for taking so long to fit together the noise and the person, and when the puzzle piece clicks, he sprints away from the grave towards the motorcycle.

He can see where she had been, for the shovels and brushes are on the ground. The plastic bags are swept up in a breeze and they billow down the dirt track. The bike stands solitary, parked haphazardly, just the way she left it. But Elian is not there.

Elian has vanished.

And he thinks of Apolonia again, and a strangled cry works its way up from the pit of his stomach and erupts into a roar.

*

When Elian opens her eyes she immediately closes them again, as the glare of the sunlight is like a pitchfork in her brain. The world from her viewpoint is coloured red and her eyes sting. She realises it is blood and, from the pain in her temple, she works out that she has been hit on her head.

The second thing she realises is that she is moving and the world is upside down. Realising that she needs to look at her surroundings and figure out what has happened, she opens her eyes again. She can see the ground moving fast beneath her and a pair of legs striding with purpose in faded, dirty jeans. This is not Alex or even Sol or Klim, and she rears up, raising her hands to strike at the back of the stranger who is carrying

127

her over his shoulder. Her arms won't separate, however, and she brings her hands to her face to discover that her wrists are bound together. She bucks wildly, kicking out, realising that her ankles, too, are bound tightly.

She can scream though, her mouth is not gagged and with that being the only method of defence at her disposal she screams as loud as she can. Her view tilts as the land spins and suddenly she is falling, no – she is actually thrown, and her scream is knocked into silence as she lands painfully on the ground. Her assailant lunges down over her, covering her with his body and clamping his hand over her mouth. She coughs at the earthy taste of soil on his fingers and stares wide eyed at him.

"Do I need to tell you not to scream?" he asks. The Ukrainian words take too long for her to translate and he lets go of her face, shakes her and screams himself. "Do I need to tell you not to scream?"

She shakes her head frantically from side to side.

He nods, picks her back up and, slinging her back over his shoulder, he resumes walking. She hears a shout far away in the distance, someone – Alex – is roaring her name and tears spring to her eyes. Once again her assailant puts her roughly on the ground and he covers her body with his, his dirty hand again over her mouth. Elian can do nothing except listen to Alex fruitlessly shouting her name, and then his voice growing fainter as he moves further away from her. When Alex can no longer be heard she tenses herself, wondering if the man will pick her up and continue on his way to wherever he is headed. He doesn't move though, and when she feels him growing and stirring against her thigh she closes her eyes knowing exactly what is coming next.

*

Alex urges the motorbike on faster as he races back towards Klim's house. He thumps the handlebar with his hand, hard, and shouts into the wind as it whips the tears from his eyes. Rarely before in his life has he had reason to panic, being attached to nobody means he has never had cause to care about anyone, except maybe Selina, and never has she been involved in any sort of emergency or accident to make him feel helpless like this. But Elian, where did she go? Who snatched her within such close range to Alex. and how were they so stealthy that he never heard anything until she cried out?

When he speeds into Klim's drive he cuts the ignition, throws the bike down, the front wheel spinning. Sol comes out, followed by the dog. Sol's expression changes from mild intrigue to concern as Alex hurtles up the porch stairs. The dog, unused to people racing around, puts his ears down and skulks back inside.

"Elian's gone, that son of a bitch took her." Alex grabs Sol's arm as he swings through the door. "Klim! Where's Klim?"

"I'm here, what has happened?" Klim comes into the lounge, trailing his hand over the dog's head as he passes.

"We were packing up, we can't do anything there. So, she was loading the shovels on the bike. I heard her shout and then she was gone." Alex pulls his hands through his hair and turns to Klim. "We need to call the police, right now, because this just got really fucking serious."

Sol nods and moves back to the porch as Klim holds his hand up and blocks the door.

"We can't call the police, because this *involves* the police, we already told you that. And it's just now got serious? Because your friend is now in danger, it wasn't serious before, no?"

"That's not what I meant," Alex speaks through gritted teeth. "But this is too big for us, I realised that back at the gravesite. You should never have called me, you should have called the bloody FBI or something."

"Or maybe if you couldn't handle it you should have said, instead of taking our money." Klim jabs Alex in his chest and Sol moves between them.

"We will call other authorities. I'm sure Alex has contacts in England and they will handle this, professionally."

"Yes, I do. I'll call Luke. He can contact the Metropolitan Police, get them to speak to me here and send someone out." Alex reaches into his back pocket. As he does, his face pales noticeably. "My phone, Elian still has my phone."

"We will telephone it and Elian can tell us where she is!"

At his suggestion Alex throws a withering look in Klim's direction. "If he hears the phone he'll get rid of it and maybe her too."

"But if it is switched on, then the location can be traced, yes?" Sol looks hopefully between Klim and Alex. "By the GPS."

"Yes, yes," Alex cries, and grabs Sol's arm, pumping it up and down, wondering why he – the private investigator here – is not coming up with these answers. "I'll need to use your phone, telephone my contacts in England and get them on it."

"We don't have a phone, or the internet," Sol says quietly, his voice heavy with apology.

Alex clenches his teeth. "Then who does? Who in this Godforsaken place has any contact with the real fucking world?"

Sol and Klim exchange a look and turn as one back to Alex. "Sissy Bello has all the communication instruments, phone, electricity and internet. She has it all."

Alex has no time to think about it. That Elian was not ready for her aunt to know that she was here in Pripyat does not even come into the equation now. Elian's life hangs in the balance, and Alex will do all he can to get her back alive.

Chapter 32
Sissy

Watford, May 3rd 1996

It has been ten years since my life was destroyed. And, during that long, lonely decade, my world was painted grey and black, with the odd slash of blue. After the initial excitement of the nuclear explosion and the loss of Afia, Pripyat settled down and resumed a nomadic lifestyle with me in it.

We had letters on occasion talking about compensation. Mother would put them in the oven and then light the range; but one day I rescued one before she lit it. I didn't really understand what I read, but I arranged to get a passport, in case I was ever called upon to go to the Soviet Union for medical tests like the letter mentioned. And, finally, I was called, with a letter bearing an official seal and a plane ticket. But I never expected that, instead of Russia, I would end up here, in a bed and breakfast in Watford, on the outskirts of London.

I never told anybody that I had been summoned here. But, on the first day of May, I kissed my mother goodbye and came to England. She has no idea where I've gone, or why. She is so closed in on herself that I doubt she will notice that I'm not there anymore. Although we lived in the same house we had become strangers.

And now I am here, in a room painted a ghastly orange, with beige sheets on my single bed and a brown blanket. Optimistically I take it as a sign that my life is slowly getting better, going from black to brown. The bathroom and washing facilities are shared by all of the people who are renting a room here in this building. I sit on my brown bed and I wait for further instructions. For compensation and full medical care, this is certainly a strange way to go about things, even to me, who doesn't know very much.

The knock comes just as the sun comes out from behind the clouds, the promise of a lovely evening after a dreary, wet day.

It's a messenger boy, a local who is very young, dressed in baggy jeans and big, clumsy boots. Again, strange, but maybe that is how they work here; although I still don't know why I'm here, in London, rather than the Soviet or Kiev.

I'm directed into the centre of London and, as the letter I am presented with tells me it is twenty miles away, I am given a map and money. I follow the directions surprisingly well, taking a bus to Epping Underground, locating a tube that takes me to Oxford Circus, and then walking down Great Portland Street, then Langham Street, then I'm on the road I need, looking for Number 37, Flat 3. I'm so overwhelmed by my ability to follow maps and direction as I climb the three flights of stairs, that it doesn't strike me as odd that the door to Flat Number 3 is ajar. It is strange, however, that nobody appears to be in the flat. For the first time fear strikes me, growing as I hear a strange mewling noise coming from the rear of the flat. With my heart in my throat and, again, amazed at my bravery, I walk down the hallway. I look into each room as I pass; a lounge at the front with two large sash windows looking over Great Titchfield Street, a double bedroom with a large bed, a fitted wardrobe and a view from a single sash window over the tiled roofs beyond. Next is a bathroom, with antique fittings, but which look in a condition that suggests they are actually new. The last room is the kitchen. It is small, with fitted wooden work tops and a grand butler sink. There's just enough room for a chunky pine table and upon this table is the source of the noise. It's a baby, lying in a wicker cot, face scrunched up, squawking, and furiously waving tiny fists.

The note that I had read earlier now made sense, although nothing else did. I knew I had been lured here, not by the government with promises of medical compensation, but by someone else, a stranger. And as I stare at the baby I wonder, why me? Nobody even knows me, not really, certainly not well enough to place a baby in my care. And my sister's name comes to mind, for this child here has colour in it. It's not English or Ukrainian or Czech. All those little thoughts are all so fleeting, disappearing entirely as I reach in, pick it, no, *her*, up.

Lastly I think of my mother. And as I walk back through the apartment and stare out over London, I rub my face against the downy dark hair on the child's head.

Then I know. It is suddenly very clear. I won't see Pripyat again. I won't see my mother again.

And with this new life in my arms, and something worthwhile to do and be at last, it doesn't even matter.

Chapter 33
Alex and Elian
Chernobyl, June 11th 2015

When Elian opens her eyes she is assaulted by pain. Pain in her head, her legs, her whole body is stiff, cold and hurting.

She remembers instantly what had happened. She was snatched, practically under Alex's nose and carried over a man's shoulder like a sack of potatoes. Before she has even finished running the events through her mind a survival instinct kicks in. She sits up, forces her eyes to open wide and looks around the dark room, assessing her prison.

Cautiously she moves her arms, noting that her wrists are not bound, although at some point, judging by the red, tender skin, they have been. She moves her legs, runs her hands down them, her heart sinking as she finds a heavy metal cuff around her ankle. Her eyes adjust slowly to the gloom and she can make out shapes. The wall behind her seems thin against her back and carefully she turns around. The roof seems closer to her head than a normal house and following the curves of the room and ceiling she is pretty sure that she is in a caravan.

It's clean, too clean if anything, going by the lingering scent of bleach and disinfectant. She shivers suddenly, her imagination going into overdrive as she thinks about why this man would use so much bleach and disinfectant.

She stands and picking up the chain on her right leg she follows it from her ankle to see where it is fastened to. She finds an iron bar, fixed tight to the wall, and it is the glimpse of rusty brown stains that have not been cleaned that send her into a panic. A noise, almost a whimper, escapes from her and she yanks hard at the chain, but there is no give, nothing bends or suggests that it will come loose at all. Her voice rises to a scream as she chases the chain to the other end and yanking off her shoe, she drags the cuff downwards, to no avail.

The murderer has got her. She is held captive, chained like a dog. She screams loud and long, just like that time in the forest when Klim revealed himself and his gun. Only this time there is no Alex to wrap her in his arms and comfort her.

But here is someone; a shadow crosses the window and she sees the door open.

The man who fills the doorway is tall, neat, clean, handsome almost. But, despite his appearance, she knows it's the same man who took her. He holds something in his hand, black and smouldering and, weirdly, it looks like a horseshoe. He steps in, lets the door swing closed behind him and he walks slowly, but with purpose, over to her.

The silence is long as they study each other. His eyes are dark, black almost, and he is so close she can see his pupils as they widen so much they completely cover his irises. One hand goes to his belt and he undoes it. The snap of the buckle is like an electric shock as she realises what he is intending to do. Eyes shut she screams again, and there is a moment where nothing happens, so cautiously she opens her eyes. The horseshoe swings in a wide arc. It connects with her temple. Then, mercifully, there is nothing.

*

Alex stands on the porch and looks at Sissy's cottage. The house is shrouded in darkness, not even a candle flickers in the windows. He is alone, both Sol and Klim seeming very reluctant to go with him. They don't like to discuss Sissy, and Alex wonders why, but the truth of their past isn't high on his list of priorities.

He steps forward, knocks hard on the door and waits. A shadow passes across the front window and he knocks again.

"Sissy Bello," he calls. "My name is Alex, I'm here from England. I came with Elian."

There is an immediate noise, a scrabbling at the door. As Alex waits he is reminded of Elian's many locks and chains at the Fitzrovia flat. The memory tugs at him, but before he has time to process it the door in front of him is swung open and he is looking at Elian's mirror image, twenty years from now. It's not a bad sight.

"Sissy?" He steps forward and stops as she flinches backwards out of reach.

"Elian?" She peers round him, sees nothing but foliage and looks up at Alex.

"First, I must use your phone, I was told you have one. Then, I promise I'll tell you everything."

She must sense the urgency in his tone as she steps back and lets him pass.

"It's in there, in the lounge." Sissy's voice is rich, honeyed and Alex looks at her again as he hurries through the door. Her likeness to Elian really is uncanny.

He enters the lounge, stops short and looks around the room. It is ultra-modern, almost on a par with his office space at home. Modems click and whirr alongside a flat screen computer. He sees the telephone, a cordless, and he snatches it up, dials the number from memory and holds a finger up to Sissy to let her know he hasn't forgotten her.

"Luke Cosgrove." The voice that comes through the receiver is strong, clear as a bell and so welcome that Alex sags with relief.

"Luke, this is Alex."

"Man, where are you? What's with the email you sent, what's this about DNA? I've not got you on the books here for any jobs," Luke cuts in.

"This is very, very urgent and I need your help. Don't ask me too much yet. Hold on a second." Alex looks up as Sissy suddenly walks up to him.

"I'm going to let you talk in private, and I'll get us something to drink," she says, and he feels his eyes widen as she lays a hand on his arm. "I'll be in the kitchen when you're finished."

She walks briskly away, out of sight, and Alex breathes out. "Luke, this is a matter of life and death. I've not got much time, but I'm out in Chernobyl."

"Chernobyl! Alex, what . . ."

"Luke! Fuck, mate, please." Alex shouts, and he looks fearfully towards the door where Sissy has disappeared. "This is so fucking important," he whispers.

"I got it man, go on, talk."

"I'm in Chernobyl. I was hired privately and I brought someone with me to help as a translator. We're investigating some suspicious deaths in the area; it became clear that the person responsible was still around. The girl I'm here with, Elian, he . . . took her. He's got her, but *she's* got my phone, my mobile. I need you to trace it, Luke."

"All right, I want your location. Is it the number I've got for you? Have you got any apps for locating your phone on any other devices?"

"I'm in Pripyat, it's my same number and I've not got an app set up." Alex leans against the wall, thankful for the change in Luke's tone. He is in business mode now and, having worked with Luke many times in the past and counting him as a personal friend, Alex suddenly feels a burden lifted.

"All right," Luke murmurs, and Alex hears his pencil scratching at the other end of the phone. "I'm just writing some stuff, just logging in this . . . Pripyat . . . that one there. I've got the number you're calling from, are you staying there?"

"No, I'm just here using the phone. There's no technology where I'm staying. Listen, we can't go to the local police, there's this officer, Arnja, and he's corrupt, or he's got something to do with this. He's involved somehow, anyway. You need to stay away from them, but you need to get someone on his case."

"All right, got that. Got your iPhone number, Alex. Do me a favour and stay where you are for a while. I'll phone you back within the hour, okay?" Luke hangs up, abruptly, and Alex looks dumbly at the phone, the dead tone buzzing in his ear.

He knows he can count on Luke. The man has proved himself before, in every case he has taken on. Luke is thorough, precise and, to Alex's knowledge, has never made a mistake. Alex puts the phone back on the base. He taps at it with his forefinger, stares at it and then closes his eyes.

Elian, you hold on.

For the moment he has done all that he can and a wave of exhaustion sweeps over him. He wants to sit down, but the sound of someone clearing their throat startles him. He looks up to see Sissy standing in the doorway and he groans inwardly, he had almost forgotten about her.

"Are you finished with the telephone?"

"Yes," he says. "Thank you."

"So come through to the kitchen. I guess there's something you need to talk to me about." Her stare is fixed on him and suddenly he realises that the worst is yet to come.

Alex nods, takes a deep breath and follows Sissy into the kitchen.

He lays it all out bare as Sissy sits across the table and listens. She shows no emotion, not when he admits to going through Elian's personal papers, not when he tells her about Klim following her in London, not even when he tells Sissy about the wolf, the gun, the bodies. He frowns;

it's like being with Elian again. This woman is so closed off nothing can touch her inside. Anger flares inside him and he leans forward.

"This man, whoever has been killing people here, now he has Elian, too."

Sissy's expression doesn't waver. When the kettle boils on the stove she gets up, pours him a coffee and passes it over.

He sips at it, all the while waiting for the explosion that he is sure will come. It doesn't, and while Sissy sits in front of him, walls up all around her, the fury builds in Alex. But he can't leave, he needs the phone. And so they sit, silently.

Chapter 34
The Boy
1996

The boy has widened his net in order to ensnare his victims. Since the disaster there have been less people passing through Chernobyl and the immediate surrounding areas. The weeks straight after though were surprisingly fruitful. Many citizens left, tracking a path through the forest. Then, they came back. Sneaking in the moonlight, ghosts amongst the trees, their footfalls carpeted by the blanket of fallen pine needles. The boy got many people during that time and the confusion helped. Nobody knew where anybody was supposed to be. Then, towards the winter, there was nothing.

He started moving the caravan around the ten square kilometres of forest. He was satisfied with the people he found, a never-ending supply. Over ten years he watched the forest turn from the lush green, that it always had been, to the rusty red of today. It seemed fitting, like he was leaving a trail of blood in his wake, disguised as nature.

He has kept Afia with him. Glorious, ebony-skinned Queen Afia, the once strong, fearless, experimental Afia who in the last decade became subservient and submissive.

Russian Lev is still around, always to be found when the boy has something that he wants to buy. Their currency has changed; more often than not Lev pays the boy in heroin, of which he has a seemingly increasing supply.

In moments of lucidity, on days just like today, the boy sees the old Afia trying to break through. Her attitude, of which was once her main appeal to the boy, rises to the surface. The boy enjoys it when this happens, he takes advantage of it, until he feels that she is becoming close to independent, and he produces the syringe, searches amongst her mottled, damaged skin for a vein, injects for her, goes back to normal. Other than that he leaves her alone. He has come to realise that Afia will not go away, not now.

He wonders if she knows how he spends his time. He has never hidden it from her, never tried to conceal it. At first she was too into herself; then, as the time and the years passed by, she was too into the drugs.

The boy has become emboldened by just how much he has managed to get away with and he has started to keep his victims alive longer. It makes him proud, that he can restrain himself. It's like a test; his own personal challenge.

He is testing himself now; he has a young English man who appeared in one of the boy's pits one day. He has had him for a week, chained in one of the abandoned tunnels on the most westerly edge of the Red Forest. These tunnels are a whole new world for the boy. He approaches the tunnel now, whistling; he is almost happy today in his perfect world, knowing what is waiting for him.

The man is only in his early twenties, rich from old money and has never faced any sort of real problems. That's why he is here, travelling across desolate Europe on his family's pound. He was confused when he woke, this young man who is called Dale. He has done what every single one of the boy's victims has done, offered money. This offends the boy, the thought that money can buy anyone out of a spot of bother. Because money is the single most important thing in their world, as well as the one thing they never have to think about, they believe that everyone is the same.

The boy had laughed; cut Dale a little bit and then left him there. That was three days ago and since then the boy has not been back. This will be his first visit and he is excited to see what sort of condition young Dale will be in. He will be alive, after all his youth and healthy body will see to that. But he will be suffering through lack of food and water. The boy picks up his step in anticipation as the entrance to the tunnel comes into view.

He clears the branches away from the broken metal gate that hangs loosely on old, rusted hinges and eases his way into the narrow entrance. He snaps on his torch the beam lights up the green, damp walls. The boy runs his hand, almost lovingly, over the wet, slimy concrete. The tunnel has an aroma of rotten leaves and vegetation, along with a sickly sweet smell of faeces.

Dale is imprisoned about half a mile in. At the boy's estimation he is sitting underneath the old reactor, years of radiation seeping through the tunnel to fill his nostrils and lungs with deadly poison. The boy does not worry about this, after all, he has lived here for ten years and, apart from the occasional nosebleed, he has never noticed any detrimental effects on his own health.

With just the sound of his own footfall for company, the boy gets lost in his own thoughts. Eventually, he realises that he has walked for far longer than he should have. He stops abruptly and the tunnel is plunged into silence, only the sound of dripping water coming from afar.

He turns around and retraces his steps, all the while shining his torch on the left hand wall. The reflection of the chain glints silver and the boy breaks into a run. The metal hinge is here, attached firmly to the wall in two places. Two parallel chains running along the floor, blood spattered here and there from where he had cut Dale. The boy runs the torch beam along the chain, along the walls, along the floor. He kneels down and looks at the shackles. They have not been cut or sawn through. They have been unlocked. Somebody has had his keys and they have set Dale free.

The boy stands up and turns off his torch. He doesn't need to see anymore. He has seen enough.

Chapter 35
Alex and Elian
Chernobyl, June 12th 2015

It has been the longest day that Alex has ever known. And as the clock ticks over to midnight he is filled with dread. It is officially the second day of Elian's kidnap.

Sitting at Sissy's table he puts his head in his hands and lets out a groan. Is she still okay? Is she still alive, even? And where the fuck is Luke's telephone call?

As if by the power of thought, the bell of the telephone shrills through the house and Alex snaps his head up. Sissy, lost in a daze in front of him, nursing a cold coffee, opens her eyes wide.

Alex throws himself out of his chair, runs to the lounge and snatches up the phone.

"Hello? Luke?"

"It's me, man, I'm sorry it's taken so long to get back to you. It took hours for the call to connect. What's up with the phone lines there?"

"Uh, don't know," Alex clenches his fist. "Any news on the trace?"

"There's a phone mast in Belarus, one in Homel and Kiev. I've triangulated the GPS and I can narrow it down, but I can't give you a direct location."

Alex passes a hand across his face. "How much can you narrow it down by?"

Luke's pause tells Alex that he won't like his answer. "About a ten mile radius, and it's mostly forest. I'm sorry, Alex."

"All right," Alex replies with a jagged breath. "Email it to my address, maps, anything you can get your hands on. I'll access it here, and Luke?"

"Yes?"

"Keep working on that GPS. If you get anything, *anything* at all, ring me. I'm going to try and get another phone so I can be on the move. I'll let you know the number."

Alex softly replaces the receiver and turns to the doorway. Sissy stands there, her face as impassive as ever, and Alex feels another burst of anger towards her.

"We can narrow the location down to a ten mile radius, she's somewhere in a forest. Is that the forest over there?" Alex asks, his voice steely.

"Yes, the Red Forest," she replies, and offers nothing more.

"Do you know who might be doing this? Do you know about the murders that have been going on here for years?"

She shrugs, infuriating Alex further.

"Do you even care about Elian? I'm wondering, since you left her alone in London at sixteen years old. Now I come here and tell you that she is missing, in the hands of a serial killer, and I've got to say, lady, you don't seem to give a shit."

She flinches, turns her head away from him, but says nothing.

Alex gives up. There are more pressing matters at hand than the nothing-life of an old woman. "I need to borrow a mobile phone, do you have one?"

At this Sissy seems eager to help and she skirts around him, rummages around in the drawer of a large chest and hands him an old Nokia. He feels a stab deep in his chest, the memory of Elian handing her crappy old Nokia over to him. How long ago that seems now.

Sissy scribbles the mobile number down and hands it over to him, along with a charger. He picks up the land line and dials the mobile so he can store the number in the phone, then he texts Luke's phone from memory.

"I'm going now. If anyone calls your phone with any information you call me straight away, okay?"

Sissy nods.

With a sigh of annoyance he moves past her and opens her front door, pauses, feels the bile rise in his throat. "You make me sick."

It's a cheap, parting shot, but one he can't refrain from. And as he hurries down the steps and back along the lane, he wonders how the woman who raised Elian from birth can turn her back seemingly without a second thought.

*

Elian comes to with a gasp. There is so much pain that she doesn't know what to try and tend to first. Tentatively she touches her head. Her hand comes away sticky and she raises it to her face, peering in the gloomy room.

Before she can fully process the blood on her fingers, she realises, with a shiver, that she is naked from the waist down. As well as her head, there is stickiness on her thighs and she sobs out a breath. Her jeans are off, but caught around the chain on her ankle along with her underwear. She pulls them both back up, trying to ignore the pain between her legs, trying not to think about what he has done to her while she was unconscious.

How can I get out?

She sits up, looking around, noting that she is still in the caravan. The strange, horseshoe-like item is on the floor beside her and she shoots out a hand, picks it up and shoves it underneath her. She doesn't know what she's going to do with it, or if she will ever have an opportunity to use it, but just feeling the hard metal against her spine is something of a comfort.

She assesses her situation, trying to see, but failing miserably in the dull shade of the room. She can see the door, a chink of light shining through promising a fine day outside. There is a bolt on the inside which doesn't seem to be drawn across, there is a key hole and these windows, they appear flimsy and weak. But there is the chain, the shackle around her ankle, snaking along her body into the wall. There's nothing do be done with that.

Elian realises that she is thirsty, her mouth is parched and she clears her throat, wincing at how loud she sounds in the stillness of . . . wherever she is.

Where am I?

Pushing herself fully upright, Elian shakes her head at the dizziness that overcomes her and throws her legs over the side of the seat. Planting her feet on the floor she stands up. There is a stabbing pain low in her stomach, her head pounds and there is a dull ache between her legs.

Can't think about that, not yet.

She tries a few steps and walks unsupported down the caravan. The chain allows her to move just a couple of metres, the door frustratingly and tantalisingly just out of reach. A sudden gust of wind encircles the caravan and she moves back to the chair, sits down on the horseshoe.

I'm still alive.

She tells this to herself, first in her mind and then whispering the words. She is bruised and battered, but not yet broken. Right now that fact is very important, and she knows she needs to hold on to that.

For the moment she'll hold on, until she figures out what to do.

*

Alex sits in Klim's house, by the window, waiting for the Nokia to fully charge, but itching to get out there and search for Elian. Klim is packing three backpacks. Sol is complying with Klim's instructions to 'get this', 'fetch that'. Alex pets the dog's head. The dog has not left his side since he came back from Sissy's house. Maybe it's true that canines actually sense human emotion.

"Cute mutt," says Alex. "What's his name?"

Klim smiles, pauses in his packing. "She's a girl. Her name's Jayne."

"Jayne," Alex repeats. "How old is she?"

Klim stiffens, before resuming packing. "She's named after Torvill and Dean, the skaters, you know? I got her just after the 1984 Olympics."

Alex visibly blanches, is sure that Klim can see him working out the mathematics in his head. "That would make her thirty-one years old, Klim!"

"Yes, so?" Klim's tone is defensive, and Alex reckons it's not the first time someone has expressed disbelief at his old dog's age. "I look after her very well."

"It's the fucking radiation," Sol announces, as he comes into the lounge carrying an armful of supplies for their planned forest search.

Klim tuts and shakes his head. Alex gathers that this is a conversation that they've had many times before.

"Radiation, huh," Alex says as he stands up, eyeing Jayne warily now. "So, are we set?"

In response, Klim slings a bag at Alex, who catches it and puts it on his back. "There's a torch, water, jacket, maps. Don't forget your phone."

Alex unplugs the mobile, fingering the numbers, itching to dial his own iPhone but knowing that could be a death sentence for Elian.

Has his phone been discovered? Even now are the filthy hands of the killer wandering over his keypad, searching through photographs and messages? Or are his hands somewhere else, touching Ellie, hurting Ellie?

"Jesus," he whispers, as a chill runs through him, and then, to the others, "Let's get on with it."

As Klim says goodbye to Jayne, there is a small sound on the porch. Shuffling, reluctant footsteps, and then a slight knock at the door.

Alex lurches forward, swings the door open, hoping against hope that it is Elian, escaped, come home.

"Sissy." He is aware that he sighed in disappointment, but also surprise that she has come here after his words to her earlier.

She steps forward, into the light, and Alex notes that she avoids the curious stare from Sol and the disgusted look that Klim throws her way.

"Have you heard something?" Hope surges again, but diminishes as Sissy shakes her head.

"I want to help," she starts, and then shakes her head. "I *need* to help you find her."

"You weren't so eager earlier," Alex challenges her. "What's changed?"

Alex looks on in astonishment as Sissy screws her eyes up and drops her chin to her chest. "Because this is my fault, it's all my fault," she sobs openly now, and quick as lightening she grabs Alex's arm. "And I think I know how we can find her."

Chapter 36
Afia
1995

I remember the time that I walked out of Pripyat, never to return. We had met up on the riverbank. It was a cold night and we huddled inside one of the shelters that fishermen sometimes used. In the distance the smoke clouded the moon and I knew then that our small home town was destroyed.

I was elated. I'd wanted out of Pripyat for so long, ever since we'd come here, to this small, backwoods town. I was more than this town could ever be. My parents never understood my desire for more, and they'd never let me go. I couldn't defy them by leaving. When the opportunity presented itself, on that cold night in April, I took my chance.

We sat close, but not touching, until he rolled over and looked at me.

"What is this?" He touched my red suit, the one I'd had mail ordered in.

"It came from England," I said proudly.

"It is shit," he replied, and produced his hunting knife.

Then he proceeded to slice it away from my body. I was under his spell. I felt it when he cut me, here and there, and I encouraged it with my small moans. My pantsuit was ruined, but I had other clothes. When I was meeting him I'd learned to take a change of clothes with me. Ruefully I said goodbye to my suit. As I scrunched it up in a plastic bag I had in my handbag, I said goodbye to a little piece of myself along with it.

He made me bleed.

I wanted him to.

It was a spell.

Oh what fairy tales I believed in back then, twisted and dirty though they were! I played along with them. I was the whore. I didn't know what he was, so closed was he. Maybe that was the appeal of it. I craved the danger of the unknown.

Later, I craved something else, and I became the heroin's whore.

I'm not a prisoner here, at least, I'm not bound by any physical means. Although the craving for my drug is certainly physical at times. But I choose to stay here, although, that too doesn't really feel like a choice either.

So I spend my days in the solitude of the Red Forest. I do nothing except sleep. I eat when I remember, and I think a lot of what my life once was, when I was the belle of the ball, and I dream about what my life could have been.

Lately I dream about the child that grows inside me. At least, I think it's growing. It doesn't move much and I'm hardly showing. I barely know I'm pregnant. My monthly cycle stopped around five years ago when I got so skinny and unhealthy. I know it's there though. Those people I read about when he is in a generous mood and brings me back magazines, them who feign ignorance and say they had no idea they were pregnant, they're lying. If I know, in the state that I'm in, they surely do.

I've cut down on the H in recent weeks, in order to prepare. It's not enough to reverse the damage caused, to either one of us, but I'm trying my best.

I won't keep this child, if it lives, because who knows what sort of state it will be in, what with our radiation-filled land and my own addiction. But, if it is alive, I need to work out what to do. I can't let him get his hands on it. He thinks I don't know what he does, with tiny babies and their parents, but I'm not as wacko as he thinks. I know exactly what he does, and my child won't begin its life being sold to a Russian baby racketeer.

I need to find a home for it so it can start afresh. Somewhere far away from this shit hole. My only problem is finding someone to help me, someone who will care about an innocent child, but who doesn't care about me and will leave me alone. I don't want it living here, even if it is with its own family, because the family won't stop looking for me and, when it's old enough and learns of its heritage, it might try and find me too. No, it mustn't be in Chernobyl or even Kiev or a neighbouring city. It needs to be far, far away.

And then it hits me. These people that he takes and kills, I bet they would do anything in exchange for their freedom.

The seed has been planted.

I know what I need to do.

Chapter 37
Alex and Elian
Chernobyl, June 12th 2015

"What do you mean you know where she is?" Alex fires at Sissy.

Sissy shakes her head and glares across the room at Klim. "I didn't say I knew where she was, I said I know how we can find her. What I meant is, I think he can tell us where she is." She lifts a quivering hand and points to Klim. Alex and Sol turn to face him.

"She's fucking crazy," protests Klim. "She always has been."

"I'm not crazy!" Sissy's sudden scream pierces the otherwise quiet room.

"Yes you are, you were always mad. I wouldn't be surprised if all this was something to do with you and your miserable . . ."

"Hey!" Alex lets out a nervous laugh. "Come on, you guys, Elian is what matters at the moment, right?"

Sissy and Klim drop their gaze to the floor and look abashed.

"Right, Sissy, why do you think Klim knows where Elian is?"

It takes an age for Sissy to speak again, and when she does her voice is so quiet that Alex has to lean in to hear her.

"When we looked for my sister, a long time ago now, we were all there, all three of us searched for her." She looks up, flicking her stare between Sol and Klim, as if daring them to defy her. "We split up, and when he came back something had happened. He'd seen her, I know it. I've always known it."

"Hold on," Alex says, confused. "All three of you searched for her? Sol, you said you never knew Sissy. Back at the grave, you said you came here after Sissy's sister vanished. You came here later."

There is a silence. Nobody wants to talk now. Alex looks at each of them in turn and, finally, it's Sol who speaks up.

"I was here, but I wasn't me back then." He pauses, his eyes landing on Sissy, and Alex can't understand the look that passes between them. "I came here directly after the accident in eighty-six, but I wasn't called Sol. My name was Simon."

Alex moves backwards until his legs hit the chair and he sinks into it.

Looking at the group in front of him and the strange lives they lead makes him realise that this town, this deserted place, holds so many secrets and lies, and it seems that Elian is at the centre of it all.

*

When Elian wakes up there is an unknown face looming over her. He is white, this guy, but talking in Ukrainian. She pushes the fear aside as realisation strikes that they don't know she can understand them.

"I'm not interested in this," says the newcomer. "Not for sale, but look at it. That's a fine woman, look at it."

The man who snatched her, the one who raped her, comes into view, both men now scrutinising her. She moves back into the chair, pushing herself into the material.

"You can use it, Lev." He shrugs, uninterested, and moves out of Elian's sight.

"Isn't she . . . she's gotta be a relation of your woman?" The one called Lev looks with intrigue down at Elian. "She's a nigger!"

Elian grimaces and turns around to face the wall. She can't stand to watch them as they discuss her as though she is a cut of meat. It's been a long time since she was called a nigger. And who is he talking about, which woman? Sissy?

She doesn't have time to think about his words further, as Lev misconstrues her turning around as compliance, and he reaches forward, puts his strong hands around her stomach. It is like a switch has been turned on, Elian can't take another sexual attack and she throws her arm out, elbowing Lev in his ribs. Scrabbling beneath her she picks up the horseshoe and aims it over her shoulder. By the hiss from his clenched teeth she knows she got him, but it's not enough, so she fights on, kicking with her feet and flailing her arms. Lev struggles to grab her wrists and then she sees the other one approaching, arm raised and the last thing she sees is his fist coming fast towards her face.

Later, she is alone again, and she knows that she has probably been kept alive until he tires of her. She shifts around, pats down her body to check for damage. She is clothed, but unsure if either of the men had sex with her. With pain upon pain, it's difficult to tell if there are new wounds and bruises. She can't see the horseshoe anymore and imagines it's been confiscated. She roots around in the pocket of her jeans, seeking a tissue or something to wipe at the crusted blood on her face. Her pockets are empty. But, as she searches, she recalls Alex giving her his iPhone, telling her to take photos of the poor dead woman, just before she was knocked out and snatched. Where is it? Where was it when she was taken? *Think, Elian!*

She massages her temples. She can't remember if she put the phone in her jeans or her jacket, or even if she packed it in the motorbike bags along with the shovels. Or did she hand it back to Alex? And then, as she drops her hands and looks around the small caravan, she sees it, Alex's sleek silver iPhone, just sitting there in the small kitchen area. Ignoring the pain that seems to radiate into all the parts of her body she jumps up and lunges towards the phone. The chain leaves her a couple of feet short and, frantically, for who knows when he will next appear, she looks around for a tool to use to sweep the mobile towards her. There is nothing lying around, this caravan is bare of all the usual household items. She looks at the chair she has been sitting on, reaches over and tugs at the long cushion that makes up the back part. It comes away easily and she moves as far forward as the chain will allow, holds the cushion out in front of her. Then she gives herself a silent instruction to handle the bulky item with care, not to get so overwrought that she ends up pushing the iPhone over the other side of the worktop where she would never be able to reach it.

She can feel the sweat dripping down between her shoulder blades as she places the long cushion on the worktop and hooks the phone towards herself. With a final sweep the mobile flies off the top and lands at her feet.

Oh, please don't have run out of battery!

She sends a silent prayer and then a quick 'thank you' as it tells her there is 45 per cent left. Having never used an iPhone she wastes precious minutes trying to navigate through it and then she is on the call screen. She has hit a wall. Who does she ring, the police? The 999 emergency number wouldn't work here.

Jesus, ring anybody!

She breathes deep, sees the button which says contacts and then a list comes up. Alison, Anna, another Alison… it's Alex's black book and she lets out a cry of frustration.

Calm it, move on. What was the name of his friend, the one who worked with the police, the one who was willing to look at the DNA?

She can't remember, but his aunt pops into her mind and she knows that she is called Selina. She scrolls down, faster now, getting to the S names. Sarah, Sara, Sabrina...Selina! She presses the little telephone symbol and then it's ringing and then... an answer phone.

It's not a disaster, she thinks as she starts to speak in a low voice. "My name is Elian, we met . . . once. I was with Alex, your nephew, in Pripyat. I was snatched and I'm sure it's by the same man whose crimes Alex is investigating. I don't know where I am, I'm in a caravan and it seems to be in a forest."

Elian kneels on the seat and peers out of the window as she talks. "I don't think it's far from where we were staying, but please . . . I have to get out of here."

Elian's voice breaks and, even though nobody is at the other end of the phone, she doesn't want to hang up.

Will this voicemail be the last time anyone hears her voice? Reluctantly, she presses the little red phone symbol and ends the call.

Chapter 38
Sissy

Late Summer 1996

I'm the happiest I have ever been. I have never, ever, felt this way before. For the first time in my life I have a purpose, and it's not to search for my missing sister or take care of my ailing mother. Now, I'm the mother.

We've had a perfect summer, Elian and I. That's what I named her, Elian.

That day, the first real day of summer 1996, I waited for a long time for someone to come back to the apartment and tell me it's been a terrible mistake and take her away from me. But nobody did, and in my arms she stayed. We sat in the window seat, looking out over bustling London all day. Then, she started to gripe. She was hungry, and I had no idea what to feed her. Before I allowed the panic to set in I placed her in her tiny Moses basket and explored the flat. I discovered that whoever had left Elian here for me had also left everything that a new baby could possibly want. In the bedroom cupboard were bottles, steam-cleaning equipment, formula, clothes, nappies, a basin, even a pram. I was so very relieved, for I wasn't ready to go out and face the world yet, bulk buying for this unexpected baby. Which led me to another question, what would I do for money? The well-stocked apartment had enough for the two of us for a week or so, but what about after that? Would I have to get a job? Who would look after the baby? Or was this just a temporary measure; was I nothing but a short-term babysitter?

I made myself mix Elian's milk. I fed her then changed her nappy before I allowed myself to panic. I worried for a while and then, like a whirlwind, I spun through the apartment, tearing it apart, looking for something that would tell me exactly what was going on.

When night fell, I found it. Or rather, *he* found me.

The doorbell sounded and I froze. At first, I didn't even know what it was. Some sort of alarm? It buzzed again and it was only by the blinking of a light by the front door that I realised what it must be. The light that was flickering seemed to be a button, so I pressed it.

"Hello?" A tinny voice came through making me jump and I stepped back, away from the door. "Miss S Bello?"

That was my name!

"Hello?"

"Who is it?" I asked, softly.

"I'm David Lattimer, I'm from Lattimer and Finch Solicitors, just here to sort out your paperwork for the flat, Miss Bello."

I had no idea what he was talking about, but I had to make a split decision, and I chose to let him in.

I watched as he spread out lots of papers on the table in the lounge. "Now, this apartment, it's paid for in full. You are mortgage free. There is a monthly allowance that will go in this bank account." Mr Lattimer slides a separate pile of paper over to me, among it a cheque book and a little card. "This is ongoing, there is no end date. So, your deeds, just sign here, and here."

I signed everything that he put in front of me, all the while expecting him to realise the mistake he had made. He gave me more keys, keys to the downstairs door, more for the apartment front door. He laid down lists of instructions: where to put my rubbish, where to apply for a parking permit, communal parts of this building. Lastly, he produced a form.

"Have you decided on a name for the child?" He asked, peering at me over half-moon glasses.

"Uh, I call her . . . Her name is Elian."

"Write it here, please," he instructed, and made a little 'x' on the paper.

I write her name down and he reads it out aloud. He pronounced it 'Elaine', but I didn't correct him, as long as it was written correctly.

He flicked through many more files in his briefcase, muttered to himself and then produced the paper he had searched for with a flourish.

"And Gold is the surname," he stated. "Should that be G-O-U-L-D, do you think? Is she Jewish?"

And I saw the little tie clip he was wearing, silver with a small gold star of David in the middle and I understood, this man, the one here right now who is giving me a whole new life, he was Jewish. And so I replied that, yes, my baby girl was Jewish too.

He announced that we were done. He shook my hand, pumping it up and down, and after he had packed his briefcase he made to leave.

"Wait," I had cried. "Tell me, please, who is doing all of this for us?"

Impatiently he glanced at his watch, then the briefcase was opened again, more digging around, more files came back out. "Ah, yes. This is on behalf of the Ukrainian and Russian Governments. This is compensation for the after effects of the 1986 nuclear disaster for residents based in, but not confined to Pripyat, Chernobyl. Hah."

He barked a short laugh at the end of his speech, winked at me and then Mr Lattimer went on his way, still smiling and emitting the occasional chortle as he left the apartment and went down the stairs.

I ran to the window, peeped out until I saw him come out of the front door. There was a man waiting for him across the road, a man I'd never seen before. He was young, maybe in his early twenties, with sandy hair and a slim build. Mr Lattimer walked over to him, arm outstretched, presumably for a handshake. But the young man ignored his hand and wrapped his arms around Mr Lattimer instead. They conversed for a minute and then they did shake hands, preparing to part ways. Mr Lattimer strode up the street, coming from the direction I'd walked from that morning. The sandy haired man stood for a moment longer, then he raised his head, seeking something out, seeking me out, I'm sure. Our eyes met, he nodded, half raised his hand in a wave, and then, he too went off down the road in the opposite direction to Mr Lattimer.

I often thought about Mr Lattimer's strange laugh after he told me where all the money was coming from and what it meant. I analysed it a lot over the weeks and the more I thought about it the more it seemed to me like his laugh was one of disbelief. Like who would be so stupid to fall for this story?

And, the sandy haired man, what part did he play in everything I had been given? These questions and more beside – like where did Elian come from – kept me awake for many nights during that summer.

Eventually though, Elian and I relaxed a little. I began taking her out in her pram and nobody looked at us, nobody at all. I discovered something else on our travels, there were people here with skin like me! Others, too, Italian, Asian, Pakistani, Spanish, the accents and languages all blended in.

I didn't go out of my way to make friends, for although Elian and I had all the papers and passports and licences that we needed, I was sure that our presence here in England wasn't totally legal. There were still too many unanswered questions for me to feel comfortable with too much exposure. But, I was happy, Elian was thriving, and three months later we are building a life here.

Our life is simple. Our monthly allowance is enough, but not overly extravagant, so we live within our means. Often, I think about Mr Lattimer and the stranger who waited out on the street that night. I wonder what they thought about our sudden appearance, or if they even think about me anymore. I wonder who the sandy haired man is. I wonder if I'll ever see either of them again.

Chapter 39

Alex

Chernobyl, June 13th 2015

Between the four of them they search the forest for hours. Sissy and Alex join up and Klim and Sol go off on their own.

As they walk, Alex fires questions at Sissy about her past, how Elian came to be with her, who Elian's mother is, why did Sol lie and who was Simon? As expected, she refuses to answer. Elian and Sissy, with their distrustful nature and paranoia, could be one and the same person.

"How well do you know this forest, Sissy?"

This one, it seems, she is happy to reply to. "Like the back of my hand. It's not changed since I was a child. Well, nothing has changed except the colour. But I know the forest well. Why?"

Alex throws his hands up in a gesture of frustration. "It seems endless, limitless. And if this maniac has been killing women for years and burying their bodies, then I'm guessing he knows it as well as you do."

Sissy is quiet and he watches her as she walked slightly ahead of him, swinging her torch from side to side.

It is nearing daybreak when they come full circle and meet up with Klim and Sol. With tight lips and a downcast expression, Alex doesn't have to ask if they found anything.

"Let's go back," says Alex, "and hope that Luke has got some better news for us on the GPS."

Despondent, they walk in silence back towards Pripyat.

"I'll go check my emails, you two get some sleep," Alex says to Klim and Sol. "We can start again later."

Once inside Sissy's house, Alex heads straight to the lounge. He's sure Luke has no further news for him, after all, he would have phoned or texted on the Nokia. Still, he's unable to sit and do nothing and he knows sleep would evade him, so he fires up Sissy's computer. While he is waiting for it to load he casts a glance behind him, making sure he is alone, and he flicks through the paperwork littering Sissy's desk. There's a cheque book, which strikes him as odd, seeing as there is hardly a local bank nearby. He leafs through the stub, looks at the amounts and the notes that Sissy has made. A memory tries to break through, but then the computer screen blinks into life and he puts the chequebook aside and logs into his email. Nothing of any interest, in fact, no new ones at all, except from Selina. He almost skips past it. But, feeling a sudden pang for his own family, he clicks on it. Seconds later, he shouts for Sissy.

She hurries through, holding a coffee pot, and looks at him questioningly.

"Elian's alive!" he shouts, and standing up he covers the ground between the two of them, picking Sissy up and spinning her around.

"How? Did she call?" Sissy's eyes are big and round, reminding Alex of a frightened owl.

"She called my aunt, out of all the people on my phone she found Selina and left a message on her voicemail." Alex feels revitalised and smiles as he dials his own home number from Sissy's landline. "Clever girl, Ellie."

The telephone is answered immediately, as though Selina was sitting on it. "Alex, is that you?"

"Yes, yes, thank God." Alex flicks a finger at the coffee pot and then gives Sissy a thumbs up. "Aunty, tell me what Elian said, every word please."

As Selina relays the message, word for word, having written it down verbatim earlier, Alex scribbles it down on an envelope that he finds on the desk.

"A forest, the red forest." Alex spins the chair around and looks out of the window at the black night. "We're so close . . ."

"Alex, tell me what is going on. Who has that poor girl?"

"Listen, I'm going to email you back with Luke's number. I really need you to speak to him, the more people we have helping the better," Alex says. "Will you do that?"

"Of course, I'll do anything you need. Should I ring her back on your mobile?"

"No!" Alex's voice is louder than he intended, and he grimaces. "If he hears the phone ringing, who knows what he'll do?"

"Well let's hope she's got the good sense to hide the phone," replies Selina. "What should I do if she rings again?"

"Stay by your phone. If she rings tell her I'm coming for her." Alex pauses and swallows, as an unexpected lump comes into his throat. "Tell her . . . tell her I love her."

He hangs up before Selina can make any comment at *that* remark and, as Sissy comes back into the room, he gratefully accepts the mug of coffee that she hands him.

"Where is she? What did she say?" Sissy asks.

"Elian left a message on my aunt's voicemail, she's somewhere in the Red Forest, just out there," Alex replies, downing the coffee in a few mouth-scalding gulps. "Sissy, do you really think Klim saw something, that day when you were all searching for your sister?"

Sissy nods eagerly. "I know he did. I don't know what it was. After that he never spoke to me again."

"Never?" Alex is disbelieving.

"Not until today." Sissy shrugs.

A flare of anger surges within Alex at the thought of Klim keeping something from them, anything that could help right now. "Come on," he barks at Sissy. "We're going back to Klim's house."

Sissy has to run to keep up with him as he stalks down the lane, but he doesn't slow down. In all fairness to her, Alex thinks, she doesn't ask him to either.

He doesn't knock when he gets to Klim's cottage, but barges through the door, coming up short at the sight of Klim, staring into the fire, and Sol, his arms wrapped around Klim's waist. It is not the stance of friends, the thought runs through Alex's mind, but he shakes it away, nothing must dissuade him from Elian.

The two men break apart as Sissy enters behind Alex. Klim steps forward, an expectant look on his face.

"Elian used my phone to leave a message for my aunt," he snaps at Klim, knowing that his words are short and sharp, but past caring. "We know she's in the forest somewhere. She thinks she's in a caravan. But, what I need to know is what you know about where someone might live out there in that forest, Klim."

Klim's face has drained of colour and he steadies himself against the fireplace and casts an undecipherable look at Sol. "Caravan?" He whispers.

"You know of a caravan, in the forest?" Alex breathes slowly, trying his best not to sound angry, not to make Klim flee. *Tread carefully*, he tells himself.

159

Klim looks at Sol and then back to Alex, all but ignoring Sissy. Sissy steps forward and Alex holds his breath, prays that she won't antagonise her old enemy.

"The past is just that," she says, and her words are soft and breathy, reminding Alex of Elian more than ever. "Afia is in the past, none of that matters anymore. Elian is here, she's our present, our future. Tell us Klim, tell us if you know where the caravan is."

Klim sighs heavily and moves to sit down by the window. He peels back the net curtain, looks out and then lets it drop.

"You're right, Sissy. I did see . . . that day, when we were all together, I saw . . . something."

His mouth sets in a line and, for a horrible moment, Alex thinks that Klim is about to cry. He sits down opposite him and is about to speak when Klim carries on talking. And his words chill Alex, along with the way he talks, as though nobody else is in the room.

"I found the caravan, and it looked new. I thought it was some people camping, foreigners or something, people who didn't know what had gone on with the accident. Then I walked right up to it and realised it wasn't new at all. I went in, it wasn't locked or anything. I just walked right in and . . ." Klim tails off, clears his throat. "I was struck by how *clean* it was, unnaturally clean, really. And she was there, sitting on the bench, naked. Afia."

He stops again, looks at them, his face twisting into bitterness as his gaze lands on Sissy.

Alex looks over at Sissy, wondering how she is going to react, but she does nothing at all except stare back at Klim.

"She was a wreck. She sat there, with nothing on, with a needle hanging out of her arm. She offered herself to me, she opened her legs and offered herself to me!" Klim is shouting now, half out of his chair, all of his anger directed at Sissy. "And you made me look for her, you made me see what she had become!"

"I didn't!" Sissy exclaims. "You wanted to come. You turned up here wanting to help look for her." Sissy looks to Sol for help. "You were here, you know the truth."

Sol shrugs uncomfortably and Alex realises this is not the first time Sol has heard this story. He has known all along.

"Are you saying she was on drugs? Yet you left her there. You found her all that time ago and you never brought her home?" Sissy's anger is slow at coming, but when it does the small room is suddenly filled with fury.

"She didn't want to come home, she was right where she wanted to be," Klim yells back at Sissy. "She was never kidnapped or murdered, she ran away, just like she said. She ran away to be with him and she stayed there and she's still there now."

Alex steps in, pushes Klim's shoulder firmly to reseat him, but Sissy is behind him, leaning over, still shouting at Klim.

"What do you mean she's still there? When did you last see her? How can you keep this from me, all this time, my family, my . . ." Sissy tails off and sinks into a crouch on the floor. "We thought she was dead, my mother died thinking her eldest daughter had been murdered."

"I didn't tell you because she made me sick. I loved her. I still love her, but I'd rather she was dead than living like that."

There is a long silence and Alex shoots a look at Sol. Sol shrugs and retreats into the kitchen.

"When did you last see her? Do you still visit her? Is she still alive?"

"I've not seen her since the summer of 1995, August, actually." Klim's response is clipped and short, and he looks Sissy in the eye. "It was either her or me. I couldn't live like it anymore. So, I never saw her again."

Sissy is not calm, Alex can see that she is struggling. She covers her face with her hands and is silent for a long time before looking up at Klim.

"1995 huh?" Sissy stands up and walks to the door before turning back. "That was really the last time you saw her?"

Klim shrugs, looking away from Sissy and biting his lip.

"So you see her in 1995 and then forget her, never see her again," Sissy spits and comes back to stand in front of Klim. "You bastard."

Klim looks at Alex and back at Sissy as though he is missing something. "So, what? I wasted years on her, she was never coming back to me. Why should I live the rest of my life torturing myself?"

Sissy slaps him, the sharp noise resounding in the room. Sol and Alex flinch as though it were them that she hit.

"Because that last time you saw her, that last time you *used* her, you son of a bitch, before you walked away from her for good, you got her pregnant!"

Chapter 40
Simon (Sol)
1987 – 1999

The army is not the life that Simon wants for himself. In fact, when he left school he wanted to go to Amsterdam and start a life there. If that wasn't possible, then he wanted to study poetry and English literature at a university in England. When Simon finally got up the courage to tentatively mention his plans, his father quashed them.

It would have been the end of it, had Simon not started going to the Admiral Duncan pub. He didn't know it was a gay bar then, he simply enjoyed the company and the friends that he made there. It was his father, yet again, who put a stop to it by enrolling Simon in the British Army.

Simon, along with his mother, lived a life of peace to ensure that they didn't upset the head of their household. So, into the forces Simon went.

Chernobyl was his first call of duty, straight after his passing-out parade. From the moment he was stationed there he knew that he would love it. Once he looked past the ruined lives and the tragedy itself, the solitude, the lack of people, the general sombre attitude of the few remaining residents suited him more than he would have ever thought possible. He met Sissy. Strange Sissy Bello, another misfit, who didn't seem to want anything from him except his help in finding her missing sister. Then he met Klim Karpik, another solitary man, close to Simon's own age, wanting nothing at all from Simon, and barely even speaking to him on the odd occasion that all three of them were together.

It was the day that the three of them went over the river to search for Afia that changed Simon's perspective on life.

Sissy changed, as though a switch had been flicked. She was looking at him differently, the way that his father would *want* a woman to look at Simon. (Although not a black, his father wouldn't like that.) And then, when Klim came staggering out of the woods, tears streaking his handsome face, Simon began to look at *him* differently, and he knew he had found the answer to the question that it seemed his father already knew.

This wasn't a war and Simon's brief stint in Chernobyl drove home the fact that he could never go to war. He wanted peace, and the tranquillity that he found in Chernobyl was everything Simon knew he would ever need to be truly happy. But all too soon he was sent home. Once they realised that the health threat was very real, the soldiers were not allowed to be there for more than a few weeks at a time.

Back home, Simon found a backbone that he never knew that he possessed. With his meagre army earnings, he left his home and moved to a tiny flat in Old Compton Street and resumed his patronage at the Admiral Duncan. In 1990 he took a job in an independent book store and, in the summer, he met Brian Edwards, an architect who Simon slipped into a comfortable, happy coupling with. At times Simon was so happy that he was frightened, causing many a late night discussion with Brian.

"Nothing this good can last forever, surely?" Simon would whisper in the darkness of their bedroom.

"Nothing lasts forever anyway," Brian would reply in his philosophical way.

Brian even talked Simon's parents around, flirting with his mother; his manliness and total lack of camp exterior meant that even Simon's father could stand to be around him.

Simon had just begun to accept that, yes, this really could last forever, when the unthinkable happened.

While Simon and Brian enjoyed a pre-dinner drink in their favourite haunt, just yards from their home, a bomb exploded. Simon had stepped outside for a cigarette, a habit that Brian abhorred; therefore he never smoked around him. It was a decision born out of courtesy that no doubt saved his life. Brian was caught in the epicentre of the blast and wasn't so lucky.

It was the 30th April, at the end of a century, and just as the majority was starting to accept the way that Simon, Brian and so many others had chosen to live. Simon would see in the New Year, the new decade and the new century without Brian.

He walked through the summer of 1999 in a daze, in a fog. He couldn't see through it, not even with the kind words from his parents and friends. And, it was a chance sighting of a familiar face who, unknowingly, transformed his life for what would be the second time.

He was sitting in Regents Park, far away from Old Compton Street and the Admiral Duncan and Soho. It was sometime around November and it was cold. Even wearing his thick parker coat, Simon was freezing. He knew that he should go home. But, on the other hand, he had nothing to go home for so on the bench he stayed, watching the happy couples as they walked by, nobody looking at him or giving him a second glance.

And then someone else walked past, a woman with a small child and, just as Simon saw them, it started to snow.

The little girl was enraptured by the flakes, calling out to her adult companion as if she'd not seen them.

"Mummy Sissy! Look at this snow!" The girl stopped and raised her face to the grey sky, a huge smile on her pretty face.

It was the name that jolted Simon. Took him back to another place and another time, and he looked up and over at the woman.

He knew instantly it was the Sissy that he had known all those years ago when he was in the army, when he was a straight man, before she had unwittingly played a part in changing the direction of his life. He almost stood up, nearly called out to her, but he took a moment, watched her, and realised that she was not as confident and carefree as the little girl who accompanied her, the one who called her 'mummy'.

He watched her walk past and then, at a safe distance and not knowing why, he followed her. They walked out of the park, down Great Portland Street and Bolsover Street. A rush of people came out of a bar and by the time he was on the corner of Great Titchfield Street he was just in time to see Sissy and her daughter going into one of the apartment buildings. He walked past, slowing down as he went past the entrance, and as the winter sun dipped below the buildings he made his way back to his flat.

*

It was surprisingly easy to leave his life behind, and he credited that in part to Sissy. He knew nothing of her story, of how she had come to leave Pripyat and live here in London. He knew nothing of her daughter, if she had a husband, if her sister was ever found. He didn't need to, all he needed were the feelings that Sissy had stirred up inside him, a sudden realisation that he could live again. It wouldn't be the life he had planned and experienced in part with Brian, but it would still be life.

It was easy to get in to Chernobyl and once he was on the outskirts, the forest and the neighbourhood all came flooding back to him. He went to

Sissy's old house, looked around the exterior, and finally peered through the window. The inside was deserted, almost empty of furniture; the few remaining pieces that were left were covered in sheets. Simon let himself in, made himself at home.

He had been there for a couple of weeks before he left again. The tinned goods that had been in the pantry were almost gone and Simon was so cold, having not dared light a fire, that he knew he had to show himself.

He went to Klim's cottage, just down the road, and, apart from being overgrown, the lane that he walked down was no different to the way it had been over a decade ago. He got up to the porch before he saw any sign of life and, even then, it wasn't Klim that he happened upon, rather the unmistakable sound of a safety catch being released on a rifle. Then, with cold metal resting on his temple, Simon had swivelled his eyes to his right, meeting the cold glare of Klim.

"It's me, I'm not here to cause trouble," Simon said, and immediately felt foolish. Sure, he remembered Klim, but what on earth had made him think that this man would recall him?

"Who are you?" Klim's voice was gruff, his vocal chords no doubt not used much in this abandoned wilderness.

"Simon, I'm Simon. I was here back in 1986. I helped you and Sissy look for her sister."

Finally the gun lowered and Simon had breathed out heavily, not even aware that he had been holding his breath.

"What are you doing here?" Klim prodded Simon slightly with the barrel of the gun in his stomach and with that one, single, slightly aggressive act, all of the emotions that Simon had been holding in over the last few months came out and he had grabbed the gun, placed the muzzle under his chin and stared Klim in the eye.

"I thought I came here for a new life," gasped Simon. "But maybe this is as good an action as any."

They stood in a strange stalemate for a long time. Simon's eyes were filled with unshed tears; Klim's held a look of puzzlement. It was the dog who broke the trance. As they stood there, unmoving, a large, slow-moving Labrador came slowly up between the two men. Still nobody moved and, eventually, after looking from Klim to Simon, and back again, the dog pushed its snout into Simon's palm and let out a tiny whine.

Klim lowered his gun. The tears spilled over on to Simon's cheeks and he slid down to sit on the porch floor. The dog moved closer and Simon found his arms encircling the dog's sturdy body. He leaned forward, crying into the dog's neck.

Later, when the tears finally subsided and they were sitting in Klim's warm lounge, Simon gratefully took the glass of whisky and shook his head.

"I'm sorry, really," apologised Simon. "I don't even really know why I came here." He barked out a nervous laugh and threw back the drink, the alcohol burning a harsh but welcome path down his throat.

Klim's response was to sling a blanket at Simon and tell him to let the dog out before he went to sleep.

After that night, Simon never left.

It took a while before they counted themselves as friends. Klim seemed to sense that Simon needed peace in his recovery period, and Simon was happy just to spend time alongside someone who was equally quiet as he. Simon knew he was more than halfway towards the new life he craved when his name was changed by Klim. It was accidental, as so many life-altering events are, when Klim started shortening Simon's name to Si. In his accent, it sounded more like Sol, and so it remained.

On Christmas Day they worked all the way through from sunrise to nightfall, chopping wood, while Jayne the dog wandered through the yard, snuffling the leaves. After dinner they pulled their chairs up to the fire, Jayne snoozing between them, and shared a bottle of brandy.

"Did they ever find that girl? Afia, I think her name was," asked Simon.

Klim, glass halfway to his mouth, stopped and turned to him. "You remember that?"

"Of course, I never forgot it," replied Simon. "Well, it kind of went to the back of my mind, you know, like things do. But then, just before I came here, I saw the sister, Sissy, in London and . . ."

"What do you mean, you saw her? Where? Who was she with?" Klim butted in, leaning close to Simon, his eyes ablaze with some emotion that Simon couldn't fathom.

"Uh, Regents Park. She walked past me, she didn't see me. She was with her daughter."

Klim held his hand up as though stopping Simon from talking, even though he had finished. "We don't talk about her, or her sister. Not here, not in this house."

It reminded Simon of his first night when Klim had stood on the porch with his gun pointed at Simon's throat. He left it and, to stop Klim from brooding, he had told him all about Brian and the nail bomb that had killed him.

Klim had listened intently, and when he had finished talking he had nodded and, in an uncharacteristic gesture, had patted Simon's hand.

He spoke no words; there was no need for any.

It was New Year's Eve when Klim had spoken about Afia again. They were back in what Simon was coming to think of as their spot, in front of the fire with Jayne between them.

"I did find Afia. I found her that day that we all looked for her together. And I went back again, I went back so many times, year after year."

Simon felt himself pale. "You found her body? Did you bury her?"

Klim laughs, a harsh sound in the quiet room. "She wasn't dead, although she might as well have been." And he went on to tell Simon of Afia's drug addiction and self-imposed solitude.

"And, she was my drug. I kept going back, all the while thinking, one day, she would wake up and realise what her life had become and she would come home with me. And she never did, and so I had to stop."

"So she was there of her own accord, she wasn't kidnapped? Did you ever meet the man who she left you for?"

Klim threw back the rest of his drink and shook his head. "No, I never saw him, not up close anyway. It got to the point where I realised I'd missed the best part of my life. I'd lost my youth, all for her. I can't leave here, I need to stay because I can't . . . I just can't leave. But I have to live a different life, for my own sanity."

And Simon got it, he totally understood what Klim was saying. If Afia came back, Klim would take her in and give the rest of his life to her. Much the way that Simon would if, by some twisted miracle of fate, Brian should turn up, resurrected and alive. In the meantime both would settle for second best, a friendship born out of misery. And with that, as an unspoken promise, Simon became Sol, Klim let him in and life changed again.

Chapter 41
Elian
Chernobyl, June 14th 2015

Elian sits alone, fiddling with the shackle on her ankle. She has scraped a lot of skin away and her fingers are slippery with blood. There's no way that she can free herself from the chain, not unless . . . No! She shakes her head, droplets of sweat flying around her head. And, anyway, without a knife or saw, that's not an option anyway.

She looks at the iPhone by her side, bites her lip as she sees the battery is down to nine per cent. The battery bar is now glowing red, warning her that she is in danger of losing her lifeline. Did Selina pick up the message? Why hasn't she called her back? She kneels up on the bench, looking out of the window at the black night. She wishes she could see a landmark, anything, no matter how small, that would give her a clue to tell someone where she was. This forest is huge; she knew that anyway from the stories Sissy used to tell her.

Her gaze lands back on the phone and she picks it up, slides the bar across and looks at the many icons that come up. This phone can do anything, everything, she knows that much from hearing the guys at the office talk about it. Surely it can help her in more ways that just allowing her to make a phone call. She presses the button marked 'extras' and sees an option for a compass. Could that help? Tracking and navigating are not something that Elian knows much about. Surely a compass is simply used to know what direction one is heading in? She opens it anyway and the screen comes up with a circle and a request for her to tilt the screen to calibrate it. She does as it asks, lets the little red dot spin all the way around the wheel and then, once it has loaded, she sees an actual compass symbol pop up. It informs her that she is facing north and then flashes up 19 degrees. She doesn't understand it. She knows that, at any point, she could be killed. The direction she is facing while she is murdered really doesn't matter.

She goes back to the phone book, scrolls through the list of mostly women's names and then, just as she is about to give up and save the battery, she happens upon the name Luke. Luke! That's the friend that Alex was going to send the DNA to. Now she has the name, she can't believe she forgot it. She presses the call symbol just as the battery gives her a warning that it is now on four per cent.

Come on, come on, please!

Then, she hears a voice at the other end.

"Luke, is that . . ."

She doesn't understand what has happened, except for a burning at the side of her head and a silver flash as the iPhone flies across the room. Darkness, as a shadow falls over her and she can't believe she didn't hear him come in, didn't see him pass the window even. She tastes blood, as a flurry of fists connect with her face and then the blood is gushing in her mouth, down her throat, and she coughs frantically, trying to clear her lungs. She turns, smashing her hands on the window and then she is moving backwards, pain spiking through her as she is pulled along the floor. She shrieks as the chain cuts into her ankle and he moves back to the wall, unfastens it with a key that hangs around his neck and then he's back at her head, dragging both her and the chain towards the door. The phone is still lit up and she screams as loud as she can, her hands and arms flailing as she tries to reach for it. More pain as he grabs her hair and drags her, stamping on the phone as he walks past. She is winded as her body is lumped down the three steps from the caravan. He lets go of her for a moment and, despite the pain, she flips herself over onto her front, scrabbles desperately at the soil and then he has picked her up as though she is weightless. Over his shoulder she sees the caravan growing smaller as they move further away from it.

Soon there is nothing but the occasional scrape of leaves and tree branches and the sound of her laboured breathing. Elian closes her eyes and feels the welcoming darkness of sleep. Then a thought occurs to her that if, by some slim chance, she got out of this then she should really know where she is. And she recalls everything that she has ever heard about people being in this sort of situation.

"Tell me your name," she gasps. "I'm Elian, that's my name, my family came from this area, but this is the first time I've ever been here. Were you born here? Are your family still living here?"

She is rambling on, but he hasn't even broken his stride, and she struggles against him, pushing at his firm shoulders with her hands. "Let me down, I can walk. I'll walk with you."

He stops and lowers her to the ground. Her feet find the forest beneath her and she sways, fighting to steady herself.

"Listen," she says. "You don't have to."

She is cut off again, but not by his fist. His head cracks against her face and she staggers backwards only to be jerked forward again by his large, meaty paw that grips her upper arm.

When he slings her over his shoulder and resumes walking; this time she doesn't fight back.

There is a gap, a worrying one, as Elian realises that they are undercover, walking down a long corridor. She doesn't remember going into a building, or a door opening, and she wonders if she blacked out. It wouldn't be a surprise, she reckons, going by the ache in the front of her skull, and the pain radiates down her neck and shoulders, branching off into her arms and legs. She wonders if anything is fractured; nobody can be hit that hard and not suffer some lasting effect from it. Before she has time to ponder further her view tilts and she finds herself sitting with her back against a damp, concrete wall. It is pitch black. He doesn't even have a torch and the fact that he doesn't need one tells her how well he must know this place.

There is a scratching noise, a strong sudden smell of sulphur and then the corridor blooms into light as he touches the match to an oil lamp near her feet.

Her gaze falls on her jeans and she is sickened by the red stains that adorn them. Her arms are crusted in mud and leaves and more blood, and she risks a look up at him.

"Won't you talk to me?" she whispers.

In response he picks up the oil lamp and holds it close to her face, so near that she can feel the heat radiating from it. She shies away, shuffling back until the wall impedes her from moving further.

He is looking at the rest of her now, his eyes moving greedily over her body, lingering on her midsection and the blood encrusted jeans. She stares at his face, trying to memorise it. It's a normal face, more than normal. She can tell that, in his youth, he was handsome. His age is impossible to gauge. His body is firm and toned, muscles rippling beneath his shirt, but his face is lined and grey streaks his otherwise dark hair. His skin is dark, but gypsy-like rather than mixed race like her, the sort of skin one acquires after working outside for many years.

"I'm going to enjoy you." His voice is low and his words chill her to the bone.

He moves away and Elian breathes out, reprieve, even temporary, is enough for now.

Out of the glow of the lamp she can't see him, but she feels a tug at her ankle and hears the chink of the chain. She stays very still as he reattaches her and then, without another glance her way he walks away down the corridor, taking the lamp with him.

She watches the light swinging against his legs, growing smaller as he gets further away, until it vanishes altogether, leaving her alone in the pitch dark.

She hears another scratching, similar to the one when he struck the match, but this is ongoing. The sound multiplies, gets nearer, and then she feels something nudging against her leg. Then it is on her, scrabbling at her tender flesh where there is a gap between her jeans and her top. She punches at it, realises it is a rat and knows that where there's one . . .

Chapter 42
The Boy
June 14th 2015

The girl is on his mind as he packs up the caravan and prepares to move it. He fingers the silver mobile phone in his pocket and pulls it out, studies it. He has seen these before; he has taken a few off previous victims. He was foolish, leaving it here for her to use. Although he didn't think she would use it, he had deliberately left it out of her reach. He had been playing with her but, to his surprise, she had played him right back.

He knows how the technological devices of today work; he has a keen mind and absorbs all the information that he can on all of the different machines from tomorrow's world. It can be traced, but not any longer, because it is switched off and the little card inside it has been destroyed. But he doesn't know how far along the process whoever she had called had got. Or even if that was the first time she had used it. If it was sometime during the previous hours that he had left her alone, then someone could be on their way right now. His whole life's work could come undone in an instant, and he is not ready for that.

But, all is not lost. He will simply move on, the way he has been moving around this forest for the last thirty years. He thinks briefly of Afia, and wonders where she is. He hasn't seen her for a while, a couple of weeks at least, but she knows where to find him if he moves the caravan on. In the three decades that she has been by his side, she knows the coordinates of where the next resting place will be. Even with her brain addled and her body wrecked, she always manages to locate him. So sure is he of her loyalty and relentless need for the brown drug, it never crosses his mind that she will ever move on.

He links the tow bar to the battered old Volvo car and shifts both car and caravan ten feet to the edge of the clearing. Then he goes back and, on his hands and knees, he scours the area where the caravan has stood, ensuring nothing, not even the tiniest drop of blood, remains. He is nothing if not meticulous.

As he works he thinks about the girl again. She is familiar, somehow, but he can't put his finger on why, exactly. It's not her skin colour reminding him of his constant companion, Afia, for this young girl's skin is different, lighter. He thinks of her telling him her name, asking questions about him, his family; like that would change her outcome.

Putting thoughts of her aside, he stands up, brushes off his trousers. With one more critical stare he appraises the clearing. Happy that no trace of him will be found, he gets back in the Volvo and drives off between the trees to his next port of call.

Chapter 43

Alex

Chernobyl, June 14th 2015

Sissy is stalking around the lounge; the only sound is her footsteps. Klim sits in the chair, starring into the middle distance. Sol is motionless in the kitchen, his eyes downcast. Alex can tell that Klim is reeling from Sissy's accusation, if the truth be told Alex isn't sure what to make of it himself.

"Sissy, are you talking about Elian?" Alex asks, his eyes never leaving Sissy as she paces like a caged tiger.

"That can't be!" Klim speaks up and looks from Sissy to Sol and back again. "She's been living out there with him, whoever the fuck he is, and what of Elian? She's your daughter, Sissy!"

Sissy spits out a laugh, turns away from Klim and picking up Elian's discarded jumper she wraps it around herself.

"Isn't she?"

Nobody answers Klim, so Alex speaks up. "Sissy was called to England in 1996. She thought that she was sent there by the Russian Government, to get compensation for her family for the nuclear fallout. But that letter was a fake, someone wanted to get her to England. Whoever it was sent her to a flat in London, where, instead of compensation, she was handed a new-born baby. That baby was Elian. The flat was paid up, and the two of them stayed there until Sissy came back here three years ago."

Sissy, Klim and Sol stare at him.

"How do you know all this?" Sissy shouts.

"It's my job, and I'm also being paid to come here and find out who is killing the population off, one by one. And I also want to know which one of you hired me to come here." Alex looks sharply at all three of them, but nobody speaks up.

"Klim, you told me you were in London, stalking Ellie because you wanted to make sure that I followed through and came here. But, I don't think it was you who paid me, was it?"

Klim gapes, reminding Alex of an absurd goldfish, but Alex senses he has finally grasped the right lead, and by taking hold of that all of the threads start to unravel.

"It was Afia, wasn't it? She even signed her email with her own initials, though they were back to front, surname first, just like I saw in Sissy's chequebook at her own house. Where did she get the money, Klim? 1995 wasn't the last time you really saw her, was it?"

Klim leans back in his chair and closes his eyes. He starts to speak, but a sob erupts from him and he leans forward, burying his face in his hands.

Sol gasps dramatically and, though he has kept quiet so far, now he comes into the lounge and brandishes his beer bottle at Klim.

"Every year, every April, you still see her. I knew I was right!"

Sissy comes to stand beside Sol, arms folded. "I thought she was dead. All this time you let me believe that, you really are a bastard."

"Hey, come on," Sol, still with his voice raised, turns to Sissy. "You knew she wasn't dead, I told you myself!"

Klim stands up, towering over the both of them and holds his hand up. "When did you tell her that?"

Sol looks abashed, as though he had forgotten Klim was there. "Back in London, when I bumped in to her."

"When you went home for your father's funeral?"

Sol slumps down in the chair that Klim has recently vacated and shrugs.

"But you didn't tell me you'd seen her." Klim pauses and the silence is loaded.

"You're not the only one with secrets, Klim," retorts Sol, as he gets up and stalks back to the kitchen.

There is a buzzing noise and music, strangely retro, fills the room. Alex realises, belatedly, it's the Nokia phone that Sissy leant him. He leaps on it, accepts the call and puts the phone to his ear.

"Hello?"

"Al, its Luke, I've got some more information for you."

"Yes?" Alex holds his hand up for silence from the others, even though they are already listening intently.

"She activated the compass on your iPhone, it set up the location service and I've got the exact GPS." Luke is breathless and Alex punches the air.

"That's great news, spell it out to me, I'll write it down, then text me too," instructs Alex, making a writing motion in Sol's direction.

Sol nods and brings a pad and pencil over and Alex jots down the coordinates and Luke's directions.

"There's more, she, uh, she called me, Alex. It didn't sound good."

The elation he felt a moment before drains out of him and Alex leans against the kitchen counter. "What do you mean?"

"I was on the phone for less than ten seconds, she said my name, then there was an almighty bang and then . . ." Luke tails off, clears his throat before finishing his words in a rush. "Then she was screaming and then I got cut off."

"Fuck." Alex picks up the paper with the location Luke had given him and passes them across to Klim. "Does this look familiar? Is it where you thought the caravan was?"

Klim shakes his head, barely looking at the paper. "It moves all the time, and I don't meet her there. I never look for the caravan now. When I see Afia we meet . . . somewhere else."

"Luke, I've got to go, use this number if you find anything else. Did you put anyone on to the police officer, Arnja?"

"Yeah, we've got men coming in from Kiev. So listen, stay put. Let them handle it from here."

Alex hangs up and looks at the others.

"Come on, grab your torches, we're going back out there."

And, not waiting for a reply or even to see if they are following, Alex slams his way out of the house and heads for the forest.

Chapter 44
Afia
1996

I go down to the tunnels each day to see if there is anything new inside. When I'm at the caravan he doesn't bring them inside, but I knew there must be somewhere that he carried on with his work, unnoticed and unimpeded. So I followed him, thinking that he must know I was there, this man who is so at one with the forest that he hears the wildlife before it's got to within half a mile of us. But I must have got so good at walking in the shadows, miles away from the flamboyant, showy girl I used to be, he never heard me at all.

And I never knew about these tunnels before. There's no obvious entrance, simply a trapdoor in the ground, covered over by leaves and soil and forest debris. I wait patiently while he is down there and I think of the days that I used to scale a tree and sit above him, some childish perverted pleasure at observing him unseen. I could barely climb a flight of stairs these days, with the heaviness in my stomach, let alone a tree. I sit away from the tunnel and, to pass the time, I look down at my belly. It's not very big, this child will not be very well nourished, but I can tell it is there. He can't tell, not anymore, even though he still fucks me, he doesn't know every inch of my flesh and my soul like he used to.

Sometimes I think about walking away. I know my family is gone, my father is dead, and even though my mother is technically still alive she's not really living. I know I could walk right back into Klim's arms, but what would that be like? It would simply be swapping one prison for another; and he wouldn't want me to live the way I've gotten used to living. I can't walk out of here on my own.

A grating noise interrupts my reverie and I peer over the mound that I'm using to conceal myself. It's *him*, closing the trapdoor. The wood has swollen with the rain we've had this year and eventually he uses his foot, slamming it down on the trapdoor. I wait until he has vanished into the forest and then, to be on the safe side, I wait another ten minutes. Then I make my way carefully over and force my way down into the tunnel.

I flick on the torch that I'm happy I had the foresight to bring and shine it around. The tunnel isn't very wide and as I make my way through I have to stoop slightly to stop my head grazing on the roof. I walk for a long time before the tunnel suddenly widens a little and my torch reflects the motionless figure of a man. He doesn't move, not even when I walk right up to him. For a terrible moment I think he is dead, and I worry, not for him, but for me, as I'm running out of time. He blinks, finally, and I let out a great sigh of relief as he slowly turns his head to look at me.

His face is drawn and pale and he has a black eye that looks very painful. I allow my eyes to travel over the rest of his body and, apart from torn clothes and a few blood stains, he looks okay.

Now, I don't know what to do. Although my plan had been to find someone that I can use, I didn't really think past that.

"Can you walk?" I ask him, flinching as my voice echoes around the tunnel.

"I don't know," he says, seeming shocked. "Do I need to?"

Oh God, he has given up. I can't have that, I need a fighter, someone who might have lost their physical strength, but not their mental vigour.

I kneel awkwardly down in front of him and, reaching forward, I go through the pockets of his cargo trousers. As I search him intimately he doesn't move, he just watches me. I find a wallet and I flip it open, pull out his driver licence and hold it up to my torch. His name is Dale Sinclair and he is English. I put the licence in my own pocket and turn my attention back to the wallet. As well as the usual bank cards and coins, there are an awful lot of *karbovanet* notes, more money that I've ever seen in one single time. I've picked the right person. I smile, but he mistakes my glee for greed and he pushes the wallet towards me and turns his head back to the wall.

"Dale Sinclair," I say, tasting his name on my lips. "How much will you pay for your freedom, Dale?"

I see him come back to life before my eyes. He is wary, not fully trusting of me and I can't blame him for that. It will take a long time before this young man trusts anyone again, if ever. He is on death row, he has accepted his death. He did not expect a last minute reprieve, especially not from someone like me.

But I have to ensure that he knows the very important part he has to play and, in a low voice, I tell him what will become of him if he doesn't place his trust in me. I tell him what *he* will do to him, what he has done to countless others. I can tell by the look in his eyes, why have I let this happen? Why did I not *do* something? And I want to tell him that I know in a way I'm as guilty as *he* is. Even though none of them died at my command, I still have their blood on my hands. I've asked myself the same question over the years, never really finding an answer. I don't think I cared enough, about the innocent souls. What were they to me? Nothing, that's what.

He is looking at me distastefully now and I grab his hand and roughly put it on my stomach. At precisely the right moment, the baby kicks. His eyes, wide now, meet mine. This baby hasn't really kicked much and not as firmly as just then. I fall back, leaving his hand hovering in mid-air.

"What do you say, Dale Sinclair?" I ask. "Shall we help each other?"

He is eager now, twisting his body around the chain that shackles him as he attempts to stand up. I put my hand on his arm, push down as if I can contain his excitement.

I explain to him then that we have to bide our time, until this child is born Dale can't take it. When he does take it, he needs to make sure that it is okay, that it is with someone who will help it. It hits me then, the logistical problems of this. I fall back and think, lost in a plan that I can barely hold on to.

"I've got a lot of money." Dale's voice breaks the silence. "Really, it is a ridiculous amount, limitless, really." He looks embarrassed almost and I nearly laugh.

"I'm only twenty-five. I'm taking a year out before I start work at Canary Wharf. I don't need to make more money, but it's in my blood. In a few years I'll be working on Wall Street. I'll give up my money and all my ambition to get out of here, I swear it."

"Yes," I reply, after observing him for a while. "I believe you would."

I stand, patting my pocket where his driver licence sits. "I'll come back, Dale. I promise. You hold on, you hear me?"

Then I leave, almost running back down the tunnel and bursting out in the fresh forest air. I lean over, hands on my knees as a sharp pain flashes like a bolt of lightning across my stomach. I stuff my sleeve in my mouth and look back at the trapdoor. I have to close it, cover it, conceal it. I stagger back, brushing the leaves and stones over the entrance. As I finish, something is released in me and as I feel the wetness soak my thighs and trousers, I know that Dale won't have to hold on for very long at all.

Chapter 45
Elian
Chernobyl, June 15th 2015

Elian fights to keep her eyes open. Her arms hurt from hitting out every time a rat comes near and she knows now what true exhaustion feels like. She has fastened her trouser leg on the right side into the shackle and her left leg into her sock. She stands up so the rodents cannot climb over her, but still they persist and she kicks out her feet, pain shooting through her every time she moves one of her limbs.

He has been back since he put her here. Wordlessly he raped her, holding her face down with one hand, while the other punched at her head and shoulders repeatedly. More chilling than his attack, however, were the words that he spoke in her ear.

"I know who you are now . . ." he breathed in between thrusts. "You were born here. She gave you up. I never gave it much thought until now . . . I never wanted a child. But, here you are . . . And isn't this just insane?" His voice thunders staccato as he reaches his climax. "This. Is. Just. How. It. Should. Be."

He had climbed off her, leaving her shuddering on the floor, his words ringing in her ears. Down the tunnel he went and she was sure she heard him laughing. With her face pressed into the damp floor she had thought over his words. What was he saying? That he, that vile specimen, is her . . . father? Her eyes watered and, without warning, she vomited, the putrid water hitting the concrete and splashing back at her. She hasn't reacted. She was way past that. She cried then, not caring if he heard her, if he came back even. She lay her head back down, gasping, sobbing that now not only was she physically hurt but mentally mortally wounded at the same time. The rats had forced her to her feet eventually and she had pulled her jeans up and tucked the bottoms in so the rats kept away. The act of rearranging herself, of concentrating on that was a blessing to stop the torrid thoughts of what had just happened and, more importantly, what had been said.

She has lost track of how long she has been standing and she falls back against the wall, leaning against the wall, tipping her head back to try and catch the drips of water that fall gently down from the ceiling. Her mouth is parched and she is concentrating so hard that she almost misses the soft approaching footfall. A swinging light is coming down the passage and Elian stands up straight, wraps the chain around her fist, preparing to fight. As the person comes into view Elian steps forward into the light.

It's not him, and there's a second of relief before Elian realises that it may be his friend, Lev. But as the person steps up to Elian the chain falls from her fingers and speaks quietly.

"Sissy?"

"What?" The woman holds the lamp up and scrutinises Elian.

"Who are you?" Elian's voice is loud, shrill, and she steps back against the wall, twists the chain around her hand again.

"What did you call me?" This woman's voice is harsh, brutal and Elian shrinks back even further.

Elian looks the woman up and down, trying – and failing – to assess if she is a threat or not. "I thought you were . . . someone else. Who are you?" Elian's head pounds and she rubs a hand over her temple, wishing she could think clearly through the fog that is hanging over her brain.

"Who are *you*?" The woman puts her face to Elian's, her eyes glint dark in the dim light, and there is a look of fury on her thin face.

"My name is Elian Gould, I was here with my . . . friend. I've been kidnapped, will you help me?" Elian shakes her head helplessly, this woman doesn't even look like she can help herself, let alone anyone else. "Can you get some help? I'll tell you my friend's name, its Alex Harvey, he's staying in Pripyat with Klim and Sol. My aunt – hey!"

Elian's words end in a scream as the mysterious woman grabs her shoulders, digging her bony fingers in Elian's tender skin.

"What did you say your name was?" The woman's face is wild now, her tone piercing up and down the tunnel.

"I . . . I'm Elian, I was here with . . ."

The woman puts her finger to her lips in a gesture of silence and Elian falls quiet. For several long moments they regard each other.

"Do you know who I am?" The thin, scruffy woman asks and her voice is husky with some emotion that Elian can't place.

She is about to reply in the negative, for Elian has never seen this woman before. But slowly, much slower than how her mind usually works, the cogs start to whirl.

"Are you Afia?" There is a touch of incredulity to her voice and the other woman, Afia, grins, showing missing teeth in what was once a lovely face.

"My golden girl," Afia whispers, and brings her face up to touch Elian's face.

Elian shies away from Afia's dirty fingers, but Afia keeps on coming. Elian feels tears running down her face, hot, scalding tears, and all of a sudden she knows it's not because of kidnap, or the subsequent attacks or even the predicament she is in. It's because what she has suspected all along, about the mysterious Afia, is true.

"Are you my . . ." But she can't say the words. She can't call this wreck of a woman her mother. She pushes Afia's hand away and slides down the wall, sitting in a crouch.

"My pot of gold," Afia murmurs, but there is an edge to her voice and she crouches down in front of Elian. "Why are you here? I saved you, I sent you all the way to England. Why are you here? Why are you still here?"

Then Afia folds into herself, sobs wracking her chest as she wraps her arms around her knees and rocks back and forth.

"Do you have a key?" Elian asks through gritted teeth as she swallows her own tears down.

It's as though Afia doesn't even hear her as she tilts back her head and shouts, her voice bouncing off the walls. Elian shakes the chain, smashing it on the concrete floor.

"Can you get me out of here?" She is shouting too now, not caring if he is coming back down the corridor and hears her.

Afia stops crying and rubs her face. "I already got you out of here, you were never supposed to come back." Her arms fly out and she grabs Elian's arms.

"I don't want to be here," Elian cries, as she rattles her chain again. "Look at me, look at what he's done to me! You think this is it, the bruises? You think he stopped at that?"

Afia falls back and her hand flies to her mouth. "What?"

Elian buries her head in her arms and closes her eyes. Suddenly she can't shout or fight any longer. She flaps her hand at Afia and takes a deep breath. Let him come back, let it all be finished. Now she has admitted to herself the extent of the damage that has been done to her, she wants it to be over.

As if by willpower alone, she drifts off to another place and, when she opens her eyes, the tunnel is shrouded in darkness and Afia has vanished.

Elian wonders if she was ever there at all.

Chapter 46
Sol
2012

The letter arrived way too late for Sol to attend his father's funeral, but he knew he had to go back to England anyway, at the very least to pay his respects and visit with his mother. When he raised the subject, however, Klim was surprisingly unsupportive. It led to their first real fight in the fourteen years that they had lived together.

"Why do you need to go?" asked Klim, an uncharacteristic whine in his tone.

"He was my father," exclaimed Sol.

"But he's gone."

"But my mother's still here," rallied Sol. "She has nobody now, I have to see her."

The fight went back and forth long into the night. Klim wearing Sol down almost to the point of him deciding not to go after all.

"I don't know why you hold on to the past, it's not coming back, Sol," grumbled Klim, as they got ready to turn in.

That was the remark that did it for Sol. For, despite Klim's assurance that he hadn't seen Afia in over a decade, Sol suspected that wasn't true at all. And as Sol was pretty sure it only happened once a year he was prepared to let it go. But when it turned in to one rule for one . . .

"I don't think you're one to talk about letting the past go, do you?" Sol's tone was mild, but his words were loaded.

"What's that supposed to mean?" fired back Klim.

Sol left it there. But the fight had played on his mind and followed him all the way to Gatwick and beyond.

He drifted through the days, made sure his mother was going to be okay, that her finances were in order and she didn't have any money worries. On the plane he'd had an insane idea to bring her back to Pripyat. But, on seeing her interact with her neighbours and surrounded by her church group, he was at peace with leaving her to go back to the place he called home.

It was an impromptu, last minute detour to the Admiral Duncan that stirred everything up. Memories came back at Sol, thoughts that he hadn't really allowed himself to think, and after the Admiral Duncan he had found himself wandering down Great Titchfield Street, and stood outside the door where he had last seen Sissy Bello. He had an urge to knock, to tell her how she had changed his life without even knowing it. When the door suddenly opened, Sol wasn't prepared for Sissy to be standing there.

He froze, and then said a quiet 'hello'. In return Sissy gave him a polite smile.

"Good morning," she said, and walked down the stairs and proceeded down the street.

He nodded to himself. Of course she wouldn't recognise him. They spent a few days together under extreme circumstances over a quarter of a century ago. He watched her go, pleased that she had done well for herself, and was about to head back to the underground when she stopped suddenly and turned, seemingly to scrutinise him.

He smiled awkwardly and then laughed out loud as her eyes widened.

"Simon?"

"Yeah," he said, still smiling, and covered the distance between them.

"Simon! I . . . I can't believe it." She clasped a hand to her chest and shook her head.

"Look at you, all grown up!" He grinned foolishly, ridiculously happy. "Do you have time for a coffee maybe, before I head off for the airport?"

She didn't want to, he could see that much. But she was polite and accepted.

He let her lead and they stopped at a traditional English café just a few hundred yards from her house.

"I almost didn't recognise you," she said, as they sat facing each other in the greasy spoon. "You've changed so much."

"It's been a long time," he agreed. "You look great, by the way. England suits you."

And she did look great, poised and smart. She looked well-heeled and well to do.

"It was hard, at first, but you know, it's a great place." Sissy laughed nervously. "Of course you know, this is your home."

He smiled uncomfortably and didn't correct her, although he wasn't sure why.

"I saw you before, here, about thirteen years ago." He gave a little shrug. "I wasn't in a very good place back then, kind of wish I'd spoken to you though."

She didn't offer a comment, but smiled and looked down at her mug of tea. "So you said you were going to the airport, where are you off to?"

He wrapped his hands around his own tea, holding on to his mug as if to brace himself. "I'm going home," he said, lightly.

"Oh, and where is home?"

He took a deep breath and looked up, meeting her eyes. "Chernobyl, Pripyat, in fact."

"Oh?" Her smile was fixed in place, but her expression was one of disbelief.

He waved his hand, uttered a short laugh. "It was strange really, I went back in 1999 and . . . I stayed there."

"Where are you living out there?"

He reddened, as he remembered breaking into her old house and squatting there for a week. No need for her to know *that* little bit of information.

"Do you remember Klim? Klim Karpik? I live with him now."

"I remember him," she smiled, but it was cold.

His blush deepened, of course she remembered him; what with the three of them searching for her missing sister. Still, she must have been relieved to find out Afia was alive, even if she was a drug addict.

"So do you ever hear from your sister? Afia, wasn't it?" He asked, taking a sip of his now-lukewarm tea and grimacing.

"Sorry?"

"Your sister; Klim told me he doesn't see her anymore, but I don't believe him. I don't know why he can't tell me. I'd understand, you know?" Suddenly it didn't seem right, talking about Klim to Sissy, and by the look of horror on her face she felt the same.

"I'm sorry." He shook his head, drained his tea and stood up. "You've probably got things to do. I should go too if I'm going to catch that plane."

"Sorry? Oh, yes . . ." she tailed off.

"Sissy, you take care."

Clearly she wasn't going to stand up, so he leaned over, hugging her awkwardly before releasing her. "See you."

He exited quickly, shoving his hands in his pockets, never dreaming that their meeting again would be so strange and uncomfortable, wishing he'd never walked down her street. As he walked past the window he glanced back.

She hadn't moved. She hadn't watched him go. She sat at the table, staring at the wall, looking like she'd seen a ghost.

She looked haunted.

Sol shivered, pulled his collar up around his ears and let out a sigh. He couldn't wait to get home.

Chapter 47
Alex
Chernobyl, June 15th 2015

"So, Sol let it slip to you, that he suspected Afia was alive and Klim was visiting her?" Alex asks Sissy as they walk along, Jayne trotting beside them.

"Yes," she replies, throwing the comment over her shoulder as she marches determinedly ahead. "I had to come back, I needed to find out it was true."

"But you came back to Chernobyl only two years ago, but you left London in 2012. Where were you for that year, Sissy?"

"I was everywhere, all over the place. I wanted to find the man who gave Elian and I the London apartment and the allowance every month. I wanted to know his connection to Elian's parents, and I thought . . ."

"You thought what?" Alex prompted.

"I thought if he'd helped us all those years, he might be able to help me finally find Afia. He's obviously got the money and the resources," she replied.

"Why didn't you just ask Klim, Sol had told you he was seeing her?"

"Do you think Klim would tell me anything? He hates me. He's only confessed now because you worked it out." Sissy shouts out the last part of her sentence but Klim, up ahead, doesn't react.

"Christ, what a fucking mess," mutters Alex. "So did you track down this mystery man?"

Sissy shakes her head. "No, he's untraceable. So I came back to Pripyat. I thought I could follow *him* when he went to meet her." She gestures towards Klim. "And last year I did, all the way to Belarus, but I lost him."

"And you, Klim," calls Alex. "All these years you've been meeting with Afia, sleeping with her, and you never told Sissy, or Sol, for that matter?"

"Afia didn't want anyone knowing where she was. She was happy. She felt like she had escaped," Klim shoots back. "You don't know what her life was like, she was oppressed, her parents were way too strict."

"They've been fucking dead for years!" exclaims Sissy. "And what right do you have to make a decision like that?"

"It was Afia's choice," replies Klim, through gritted teeth. "And she made it."

"And you never thought that Elian was your child, even after your liaisons with Afia, even though the dates worked out?" Alex asked Klim.

"Of course Elian is not my child. I only saw her mother a few times, she was with *him* every single day, and . . ." Klim tails off and sighs. "What with the radiation and everything, I don't think it works anyway."

Alex suppresses a laugh, humour bubbling up inside him even though it's not funny in the slightest.

"For what it's worth, I presumed you knew she was alive," Sol says quietly to Sissy. "I didn't mean to hurt you."

Sissy nods grudgingly, and then comes to a stop as Klim, up ahead, holds his hand up.

"We're here."

Alex looks around the clearing, shining his torch round the perimeter. There doesn't look like there has been any activity here recently, but he knows the killer would be smart enough to cover his tracks.

"If a caravan had been here we'd know," says Klim desolately.

Alex shines the beam of his torch higher and turns in a slow circle. "Look," he says, moving the beam side to side. "Look at those trees, the branches have been snapped and if I'm correct I'd say that's just about the right height for a caravan to pass through."

As one they move closer and peer up at the branches.

"I think he's right," Sol breathes, looking at Alex with something close to wonderment.

Another thought strikes Alex and he whistles for the dog. Jayne lollops over to him.

"Sissy, take off Elian's coat," he instructs, and as she passes it to him he shows it to the dog, shoves it in Jayne's face. "Find Ellie, go on, Jayne, good dog, find Ellie."

Klim snorts. "She's not a sniffer dog. She . . ." He breaks off, his eyes widening as Jayne puts her nose to the ground and tracks around the clearing.

The dog pauses, nose to the ground, one paw raised slightly, and then, with a single yap, she bounds off into the forest.

"Come on!" Alex shouts, and with a rejuvenated energy they race off in the direction that Jayne went.

After about a quarter mile Jayne slows down and the others stay close to her, shining their torches all around, all of them unnaturally quiet.

Finally, when the moon is at its highest point and the air is at its coldest, Jayne stops, emits a single low bark and sits down.

Alex steps up to the dog, strokes her and looks around. "There's nothing here."

The other three kick at the ground, shine their torches up into the treetops and finally the torches are dropped in a collective weary motion to their sides.

Sissy sits down heavily, breathing hard and Klim and Sol sink to the ground.

"We're never going to find her," whispers Sissy, brushing unstoppable tears from her eyes.

"Wait," Sol's voice is loud in the moonlight and he pulls himself into a crouch and brushes at the floor. "Wait just a second . . ."

They all see it as it appears, as the leaves are brushed aside and the outline of a trapdoor is revealed.

They pounce, pulling at it, not expecting it to open so quickly and falling back on to the carpeted pine needled ground. A corridor opens up to them and, without so much of a glance of agreement, they pile in, Alex first, and he is running as fast as he's ever ran before to find her.

At some point Sissy overtakes him and Alex laughs out loud, remembering the night they had chased Klim and how Elian had sprinted into the lead and he laughs, because he *knows* it's going to be okay, they're going to find her down here and she's going to be scared and cold, but she's going to be all right . . .

He almost collides with Sissy and he grabs a hold of her, righting himself and wondering why she stopped so suddenly.

"She's not here," she says.

"How do you know?" Alex is perplexed, and he shines his light down the corridor, seeing that they have what seems likes miles left to search. "We're not even close to the end of the tunnel yet."

Klim and Sol pull up beside them, Jayne lagging behind, panting heavily.

And then, by the light of all four torches, Alex can see why Sissy had stopped at this point. In her hands she holds a chain, fastened at one end to the wall, the other crudely hacked off. Broken pieces of the chain are littering the concrete floor.

"She was here, though." Sissy's voice breaks in a sob.

Alex shines his torch on the wall and suddenly he can't breathe. He wonders why it didn't hit him sooner, the combined stench of vomit, faeces and old, dried blood.

He steps closer, feeling like he could vomit too, as he forces himself to look at the evidence of past souls that have been imprisoned here, and he thinks that this can't be all Elian, for, if it is, if all of this came from inside her, then she's surely dead.

Chapter 48
The Boy

He traipses along the tunnel, not noticing the smell or the damp or the rats that dive into the shadows. He never notices these things now and, if he does, he doesn't give them a second thought. This is his life, the way his life always has been. His world is the blood and the need for it, and the desire to pound his dick into some nameless, faceless piece of flesh. The cutting of the skin is the build up to his release and his relief, and it doesn't matter that it is wrong or bad or wicked.

It is simply what he needs and he is unstoppable and invincible. Or so he thinks.

As he stops at the point where he has set up his holding area he holds up the lamp and casts the dull glow over the chain that is no longer containing anyone. He pats his chest, feels the reassuring outline of the padlock key that hangs on a cord around his neck. He takes it out from under his shirt and looks at it, then back again at the empty space in front of him. He stoops down and picks up the chain, runs his hands down to the end and sees where it has been sawn off.

Where did she get a saw?

The boy breathes in and exhales slowly. He drops the chain and it lands with a clang on the concrete. Then he sees it, a flash of red on the wall to his left. He lifts the lamp, moves it across the wall. In red letters, written in blood, is a message to him.

'Fuck you.'

He swallows and grips the handle of the lamp so hard that it snaps in his fist.

He has been here before.

*

He walked down the tunnel, hurried his step a little bit. He had held off long enough, he had tested himself and he passed the test and now it's time for his reward. He was looking forward to his prize, young Dale's tender, English flesh. He had thought about it for a while, salivating over the thought of how *clean* Dale would taste. For, let's face it, most of the people who pass through his traps are not renowned for taking care of themselves. Dale was everything he wanted: clean, healthy blood.

194

But Dale wasn't there. The chain had not been broken, the padlock sat on the end of it; the shackle intact, but unlocked.

That was when the boy had started wearing the key around his neck. And yet, somehow, almost twenty years later, the same thing has happened again.

*

The boy bites his knuckles, licking absent-mindedly as beads of blood burst through his skin.

There is only one person who can be responsible for this. And that's the same person who did it to him twenty years ago.

Afia.

Chapter 49
Klim

London, June 2015

It is the first time that Klim has ever been out of Chernobyl. He has a passport; everyone who was affected by the 1986 nuclear fallout has a passport, because afterwards, and for many years, there was talk of leaving. But nothing ever came of it and, until now, there was never a good enough reason to leave.

As he leaves the plane and steps into Gatwick Airport, he knows this will be the first and last time that he will ever visit this city, indeed this whole country.

The Underground is even worse. It is crowded, noisy and it stinks. To his surprise he has no problems following the different coloured lines on the map and figuring whether to go east or west at the different exits, but it is the time of day when everyone leaves work and the trains are packed wall to wall with hot bodies. At first, he tries to apologise whenever he knocks into someone or steps on their toes, but he soon catches on that nobody else seems to do this. Nobody talks to each other either, they all stare at their phones and they all wear earphones. He guesses they are listening to music, but it can't be very good going by the absence of expression on their faces. They look like robots and he frowns to himself.

He follows the white-walled tunnels when he gets off the train, turns a corner when he sees an exit sign and lets out a cry as a great wind batters him in the face. He grabs his hat, flattens himself against the cool tile wall and looks around at his fellow passengers. They seem nonplussed by the rush of air and so, feeling foolish, he carries on walking.

He is happy to get out from beneath the earth and up into the air. London is hot and although the streets and pathways are busy, they are not so tightly packed together like they were in the trains. His map serves him no purpose up here, so he buys a different one, a larger one, called an A to Z. He spots a green area over the road and joins a group of people waiting to cross and is relieved when he finds it is indeed a park, with much more space, and a man selling cool drinks from underneath an umbrella. He gathers all of the change from his pocket, requests a lemonade and holds his hand open, palm up, and lets the vendor pick the coins out himself.

With his drink and new map, Klim retreats to a bench and begins to study the A to Z. He wonders if this is the same part that Sol sat in when he saw Sissy all those years ago. Maybe even the same bench.

It is mid-morning the following day when Klim decides to try his luck at the offices of this detective he has been told about. He gets on the train again and is pleased to find the carriage is almost empty. He sits down, the first time he has sat on a train, and then realises that his neighbouring passenger has stiffened. He glances around the train, wondering what sort of faux pas he has made now. He remains seated, feeling the heat radiating off him, wishes he had not worn his leather jacket today. He cracks his knuckles nervously and scratches at his head underneath his hat. When he feels a thin trail of sweat trickle down between his shoulder blades he can stand it no longer, and as the train slows to a stop he jumps off, not even taking notice of where he is.

It takes Klim a full day to get back out there and he is very aware now that he is wasting time and money. He needs to speed things up, so he goes directly to the office address that he was given. He curses when he gets there, for there is no handy café or public house opposite. It is a small street, full of bookstores and antique shops, and he can only browse for so long before he becomes an object of suspicion. He is standing outside the detective's office building, pretending to study the map, when a man comes out of the entrance. Klim looks him up and down, and is about to dismiss him when an older woman swings the door open and calls his name. Klim looks up, feels a strange thrill run through him and, after a brief exchange, Alex the detective walks confidently down the little street.

Klim stays a good way behind him, keeping in his mind that, if this man is a detective, he will surely notice anyone who follows him; but the guy, Alex, seems not to take any notice of anybody. He checks out his own reflection in shop windows, a move which Klim sneers at.

Finally, Alex the detective stops and greets two people outside a café. He sits with them, passes something over to the older chap that he is with and then he does a classic double take. Klim follows Alex's line of sight and sees a young woman hurrying down the road towards them.

Klim puts his head down and moves speedily across the other side of the road, ducks into a small supermarket and peers through the window. He puts his hand under his jacket and presses hard on his chest. Be still, my beating heart, he thinks as he stares and stares and stares.

It is Afia. Or it *was* her, thirty years ago. Slim, utterly beautiful and . . . spunky, he sees now, as this young woman converses animatedly with Alex.

The youngsters part and Klim sees the girl marching off up the road. After a beat and another exchange of words with the couple at the table, Alex follows her. Klim consults his map, looks at the alleyways that run off this road and wonders if he can come out ahead of these two. He leaves the shop, sprints off down a lane and comes out on another main road. He thinks he sees her up ahead and he speeds up, not knowing if he is following the right person. Should he be tailing Alex instead?

He swears under his breath, directing his frustration at the person who put him here doing this horrible job that he is not cut out for, and then realises he is directly behind her. He falls back, swerves around a cluster of people and darts across the road, even though the little man on the pole is still red.

There is a park in front of him, and he slips in through the gate, loops around the path, now totally lost. He casts a glance behind him and then sees her, somehow he has got in front of her, and it shoots home the fact that he really is not a detective, to wind up ahead of the person he is supposed to be following. He pauses, stands by a tree and hopes she will pass him by. She looks upset and he gets it now, this is Sissy's kid and he studies her from afar with interest. She looks so young, this girl; yet Sissy is back in Pripyat, has been for ages, so who is taking care of her daughter?

Klim darts back around the tree as the girl looks up and seems to stare directly at him. He risks a glance back and now she is moving in the other direction, practically running now, and the guy is there, Alex the detective, and Sissy's girl is furious, lunging at him with her handbag.

Klim heaves a great sigh. He is weary and he wants to go home. And while the girl berates the detective, Klim wonders why on earth he ever agreed to this and, with a shake of his head, he gives up and slips quickly, but quietly, away.

Chapter 50
Elian
Chernobyl, June 15th 2015

Elian is running, galloping effortlessly. It shouldn't be this easy with my injuries, she thinks, and almost without realising she slows to a stop and turns around in a circle. She is surrounded by the dead trees of the Red Forest and nothing, not even the night time creatures, makes a sound.

Am I dreaming, or dead?

She concentrates and realises she can't remember how she came to be here, in the forest. The last thing she remembers is sitting on the concrete floor in the underground tunnel, unsure of whether Afia had been there or if that had been a figment of her imagination.

Like this is, right now.

Trying to keep a hold of her methodical sense of order, Elian brings her hand up to her face and rubs her temple. It hurts; it actually hurts like hell, which would suggest she is neither sleeping nor dead.

A twig snaps somewhere behind her, launching her into a run again, and this time she doesn't think about it, she just sprints, head down, eyes on the ground in front of her through the forest.

The sky is still ink black when she stumbles out onto the lane. Keeping to the verge, she jogs along until Klim's house is in sight. Klim's old dog is resting on the porch, his nose on his paws, watchful yet obviously sleepy. His ears prick up when she wearily climbs the steps and she pats his head, wanting nothing more than to lie down with the dog and pull its warm body close to her, but she can't do that, she can't leave herself exposed out here on the porch. She spots that the door is ajar, and fearfully she has a sudden thought, what if *he* got Klim and Sol and Alex too? The house is empty, apart from Jayne, and Elian makes her way over to the dying fire, pokes at the embers and hefts another log onto it. She should go to Sissy's house, really. Their past and her aunt's betrayal shouldn't matter, for if anyone can take care of her now it is Sissy. But she can't face the walk, even though it's just down the road. She doesn't think her body can take it. Bone tired, but unable to sit, she wanders into the bathroom, catches sight of her reflection in the mirror over the sink. She gasps audibly and leans closer to the mirror.

Her face is a pallid grey, blood is crusted around her hairline and her left eye is bruised and swollen. Looking down at herself she lets out a whimper. Her jeans are torn and her thighs feel tender and tight with dried blood. She pulls reams of toilet tissue off the roll, dampens it and scrubs half-heartedly at her face. Something falls on to the floor with a small chinking sound and she looks down to see fragments of silver chain links that had been caught up in her jeans. She shakes her leg and a vague memory comes back, someone leaning over her and sawing with a tiny hacksaw. Backing away from the mirror she glances at the bath. She needs to have one, she needs to feel clean again, but the practical side of her brain, the bit of her mind that seems like it's only half working, tells her to wait for the police. They can collect evidence off her, fluids and skin from where she might have scratched *him*. A tiny sob collects in her throat, as a flashback of him pounding into her, assaulting her, ripping and tearing at her insides, and made all the worse for who she actually now knows him to be.

A sharp bark from the lounge and footsteps on the porch make her head snap up. Elian stuffs the paper tissue in her pocket and leans against the bath with relief, it's the others. Finally she's not alone, they can look after her, tell her what to do now.

She pushes herself off the bath, runs through the hallway and into the lounge, already feeling tears welling up.

But the man who stands outside on the porch and fills the doorway is not Klim, Sol or Alex. She has never seen this man, this big, angry-looking, and sweating man. She knows instantly that it must be Fat Arnja. She skids to a stop, using the doorframe to brake, and he looks over at her, his dark eyes piercing right through her.

A vision of the shallow grave flashes through her mind, along with the fact that this man knew what was happening to the poor victims in his vicinity.

"You!" His voice booms out around the room and he marches to her. "You come here, you stir up all the trouble! We don't like people coming here, we don't need more people here."

It doesn't occur to Elian to be frightened of this man. This overweight, unhealthy-looking man does not give off a vibe like the one that took her, nor the Russian one who tried to attack her, and she is in Klim's house.

She feels safe being here. So she speaks up, her tone berating the corrupt policeman.

"Is that why you kill tourists that you happen upon?" Elian spits out the words and, for a mere moment, he seems affronted, hurt even.

"I kill nobody!" Arnja grabs her arm, pressing against her already bruised skin and she yelps.

"You don't stop it though, you know who does it and you don't stop them, what sort of policeman are you?"

"This is my town. I say what can and can't happen here, and you and your little friend have arrived and now the police are here, police from Russia and police from the United Kingdom and everything has been ruined." He tries to pull her towards the door and with her free arm Elian clings to the doorframe.

His words ring in her ears, the police are here, so Selina must have called them, or Luke or Alex. But where *is* Alex? She screams out, her thoughts cut dead as Arnja leans forward and bites down on her fingers that hang on to the wall.

"Leverage, that's what you are now. Come on." He puffs as he tugs on her arm, then changes tactics as he removes the gun from his holster and aims it at her. "I won't kill you girl, but I'll fucking shoot your kneecaps out and I'll fucking carry you." As if to prove his words he aims the gun at Jayne who is darting around their feet, yapping.

"No, I'll come," Elian shrieks, pushing his arm down so the gun points to the floor.

Now she is frightened, and she should have been before. This man might be heavy and fat, but he is bigger than her and he has a gun. She has nothing to defend herself.

As they move towards the door Elian pulls a bit of bloodied tissue out of her pocket and drops it on the floor. He seems to relax as she walks with him and she hopes that they are not going far, praying that the trail of toilet tissue that she discards won't blow away, and won't run out. But it does when they come to the end of the lane and, concealed between the trees, she sees an old Land Rover. He lets go of her for a brief moment while he fumbles with his keys and, without even planning it, she drops to the floor, wriggles under the car, out the other side and wraps her arms around herself as she rolls the few feet down the embankment. She hears a shout and in a crouch she runs into the woods, trying to keep low, zigzagging through the dead trees. A gunshot blasts out and to her it sounds like it is just behind her. And, for the second time in less than an hour, she is sprinting through the forest, running as though her life depends on it.

When Elian reaches the stream she hesitates, glances behind and when she can neither see nor hear anyone she crouches down, scuffs at the bank with her shoes and then backtracks, wrapping her arms around the trunk of a large tree and hauling herself up. Nearer the top it still has some foliage and she squats on the apex of two branches, keeping as small as she can. It seems like hours later, but is in fact only minutes, when Arnja crashes through the trees, followed by another man. Elian squints down from above and recognises him as the Russian, the one who called her a nigger.

"Why did you let her go?" The Russian asks Arnja in a nasally whine.

Arnja turns and clouts him around the ear. "Shut it, Russian Lev. Do you think I did it on purpose? The important thing is that we find her."

"It's all coming apart anyway," Lev replies, rubbing his head. "I've been thinking about leaving all this for a while."

Arnja sniggers and looks disdainfully at Lev. "Where the fuck would you go?"

"There's this place, in Holland, in The Hague, actually. It's only half an hour from Amsterdam, right next to the sea. I've been there a few times and I'm thinking of relocating for good. Do you know how many whores get knocked up in Amsterdam? And half of them are so strung out they'd do anything to get rid of an unwanted problem. There's a tourist trade there, which is more than can be said for this dump."

Elian listens intently, all the while praying that they won't look up and see her.

"Fuck your fantasies, get over there and find that girl!" Arnja points a finger across the stream and Lev eyes it warily.

"Just do it," hisses Arnja.

In a flurry of swear words, Lev splashes across the stream and once on the other side he turns back to Arnja.

"I'm out, I'm packed and I'm ready to go. This just isn't for me anymore, I'm out of here." With his chin held high, but still a glint of fear in his face, Lev nods once, turns tail and disappears through the trees on the other side.

Elian breathes a silent thank you that there's only one left and she looks down at Arnja. Instead of leaving, however, he brushes down a fallen branch and sits down. Pulling a pack of cigarettes out of his pocket he lights one up and exhales a plume of smoke. The barrel of his gun glints from the holster and he fingers it absentmindedly.

In her tree, Elian watches the cigarette smoke swirl around her before disappearing in the black sky. She clings on to the branch, closes her eyes, and hopes that Alex, or indeed anyone who is not on Arnja's side, will find her soon.

Chapter 51
Afia
2015

We meet in the News Café, directly opposite the British Embassy. It's always the same place, although the name and owners have changed many times over the years. One year, they were renovating and I simply sat on a bench outside and we had our annual meeting there.

Every year I arrive the day before Klim. He thinks that he is special, that he's my only reason for making this journey. He is wrong. I go to my safety deposit box, remove a year's worth of reports sent to me by Mr Lattimer and I hole up in my hotel room. Along with a bottle of *Putinka* Russian vodka, I drink in the updates on my daughter. Mr Lattimer does his job very well and without sentimentality. No photographs were one of my stipulations and he has always complied with my instructions. Naturally I lament my life and what it has become. I get roaring drunk and I swear that, this time, I'm leaving with Klim tomorrow.

But, I never do.

And, he never asks me to.

I know I could go with him, but I also know that he is a very proud man. He would accept me, but he would never proposition me.

I always keep my reports well hidden if he comes back to my hotel room. I know him well enough that if he knew there had ever been a baby, and that I'd give it away, he would kill me. He would put his rough, big hands around my scrawny neck and he would choke the life out of me.

We have a love/hate sort of relationship.

This time when I meet him in the cafe he is distracted, on edge. Usually when we meet he is stoic, hard faced and stony. I wheedle it out of him, eventually, and he tells me they found more bodies, that the murderer is still out there, threatening their lives and their security. I listen sympathetically, never letting on that I know that I've always known. He tells me that they went to Arnja, the fat bastard police chief. I act shocked when he tells me of Arnja's reaction, but inside my heart beats faster. That Arnja is more dangerous than the actual killer. I know that *he* has only one goal, to slaughter and satisfy himself for a while. Arnja, on the other hand, is sly and greedy. Money rules his heart and his head. I wonder what's it in for Arnja, wads of *Hryvnia*, I'm sure, and it must be coming from Russian Lev's side, for my boy has no money. He has no need for it.

We return to my hotel after lunch. We fuck perfunctorily and then he tries to talk to me about the track marks on my arms and my feet. I fuck him again to shut him up.

Later, he tells me that Sissy has come back to Pripyat, for good it seems. I knew she was there last April, but not that she had put down roots. This piece of news does make me sit up and pay attention. For, if my sister has come back, has she brought my daughter with her, my little pot of gold at the end of the rainbow? I'm flustered and trying not to show it. My girl can't come here, not with *him* around seeking new flesh to devour for himself. *He* was the reason I moved her across to England in the first place.

I lay naked on the bed, thinking back to the reports I read from Mr Lattimer. Was Sissy mentioned in them? I couldn't remember. I didn't think so, but then I wasn't looking for a mention of her; my girl was all I directed Mr Lattimer to report on.

When Klim has gone I do something I've never done before, I book the room for an extra night. I use the hotel computer and eventually I find a hidden gem. My girl's boss is also a private investigator. I look him up, this Alex Harvey. There's not much about him personally, but there's one picture and his handsomeness takes my breath away. He is older, which is good; it means he is wiser. Going by the image he is money orientated, which is also good. I set up a new email address and, posing as a client, I draft a message to him. I stand my retainer at seventy-five thousand hryvnia and, almost as an afterthought, I point him in the direction of one of his employees at the magazine. I give her surname and obstinately I write it the way I always intended it to be written. He is an investigator. He'll find her if he is as good as his website proclaims.

I like the sound of this man, this Alex. I like that he is stable and hopefully single and able to offer a young lady a good life. I don't know what my daughter looks like, but if it is anything like me at her age, then he would be lucky to have her. She will be fucking stunning; a showstopper. A head turner.

And if she is here, or is thinking of coming here, then things in Pripyat need to change. For my girl I will sacrifice *him*. I will have *him* caught and I will make the place safe again.

I find Klim again, purely by chance in the saloon a couple of streets away. He is staying another night to take supplies back to Pripyat. By unspoken agreement we retire to his room together and later, stretching languidly, I roll over to face him.

"Would you do something for me?"

He turns his head and looks at me through half-lidded eyes. There's a strange look in them, a queer mixture of love and distaste.

"You know I will," he replies gruffly.

So I tell him about the private investigator who works with Sissy's 'daughter', and I ask Klim to go to London and make sure the detective comes here.

He looks up at the ceiling and closes his eyes. "You're mad," he says.

"I paid him already," I tell him.

His eyes are still closed. "Jesus Christ," I hear him mutter, as he turns over and switches off the light.

I smile to myself in the darkness. Klim will go to London.

He will do anything for me.

Chapter 52
Alex
Chernobyl, June 16th 2015

As they congregate at the entrance of the tunnels Alex looks at his watch. It's well past midnight, now the 16th June. It has been five days since Elian was snatched.

A noise, deep in the heart of the forest makes them all start. It was a scream. Maybe it was a bird or a fox, a wolf, a human? Alex shivers, looks around and realises that the dog isn't with them.

"Where's Jayne?" he asks, looking at Klim.

Klim shrugs. "Who knows, probably back at home by now. That fucking tunnel is bad enough to send anyone on their way." He pales as he speaks, and Alex knows that all of them are imagining Elian down there.

"Back to the house, then," instructs Alex. "We'll meet up with the police. We'll tell them what we know about Elian. We can bring them back here, it'll be getting light in a few hours. They'll have their own dogs."

"The police?" Sissy speaks up, and Alex clenches his fists at her nervous tone.

"Yes, the police, Sissy. They will have specialist equipment; it'll be in their hands to locate Elian. Or is that not what you want? Are you still fucking panicking about the stunt you think you pulled all those years ago? Is your crime more important than finding her?"

"No! Of course not," shouts Sissy, affronted.

Alex flaps his hand in her direction, dismissing her, and starts the walk back to Klim's cottage. He doesn't say that the chances are very high that, if they find Ellie now, it will more likely than not be her dead body anyway. Christ, it hurts to think it, there's no way he can say it out loud.

It is with a heavy silence hanging over the four of them that they reach the cottage and wearily climb the steps. Jayne is outside on the porch, not in her usual slumbering state, but sitting upright; alert and excitable.

Alex walks in and heads straight over to the kitchen area. He grabs the open bottle of vodka and swallows a few mouthfuls down, hoping now not for good news, but simply to become numb. He can't see her when she's found, he doesn't want to see that beautiful body broken and bruised.

"Hey, what's this?"

Alex looks around the kitchen counter, sees Sol stooped over something on the floor and he walks over to him, still clutching the vodka bottle.

"Did someone hurt themselves?" Sol holds up the bloodied tissue between his thumb and forefinger, showing it to the others who have gathered around.

Alex thinks back to the last time they were in here. He remembers Klim and Sissy arguing, but doesn't think anyone was actually hurt, not enough to spill blood anyway. He straightens up, looks down the hallway that leads to the bedrooms and the bathroom. He goes into the bathroom, pushes the door open with his foot and looks in.

"She's been here!" he shouts. "Elian was here!"

He looks at the mud that has fallen from someone's shoes on the lino and the red and brown smudges on the edge of the bath.

"How do you know it was Elian?" Sissy pushes her way into the bathroom, taking in the scene, before glancing hopefully at Alex.

Alex drops to his knees and collects up a little pile of silver. He holds it in her palm, shows it to Sissy.

"She cut the chain off her ankle," he says, and deposits the chain links back on the floor, rubbing his hands together. "But where is she now?"

"There are more tissues!" A shout comes from outside and, as one, Sissy, Klim and Alex run out to where Sol stands on the porch.

They stare at it, the white paper standing out in the darkness. A thought catches in Alex's mind, and he looks around at the land beyond the house. Across the lane something else shows up against the undergrowth and he runs over, his weariness gone, on the trail again. The trail that Elian has left for them.

Silently the others join him and, slowly, they work their way down the lane, casting their eyes left and right, looking for the breadcrumbs, whilst Alex congratulates Elian in his head.

Soon enough they reach the end of the road and they come up short as they find a seemingly abandoned car.

"It's Arnja's," confirms Klim, as they peer inside the vehicle.

"I can't find any more paper," calls Sol. "What now?"

Before Alex can answer a rumbling noise becomes apparent from the other end of the lane and headlights glow in the distance.

"Get down," says Alex, and they move to the other side of the abandoned car, crouching behind it.

"It's the police!" cries Klim. "It's the real ones, not Fat Arnja."

Alex hurries out in front of the three-car convoy and waves his arms. Around a dozen men spill out of the car and Alex draws them close, gesturing to Klim to join him. Alex talks fast, pausing impatiently as Klim translates.

When they have brought the police up to date, the men that have gathered are off and moving, past the car, down the bank and fanning out military style as they walk back in to the Red Forest. They don't use torches, they don't speak to each other and they move completely without sound through the undergrowth. If any one of them sees something of interest they make a small motion with their hands, one that is immediately understood by their fellow comrades.

"They're like machines, the British Army was nothing like this," whispers Sol to Alex, and Alex nods back, lost in his admiration for these police-soldiers.

After about a mile the men at the most northerly point come to a standstill. In formation, everyone else comes to a stop. Alex, bringing up the rear, cranes his head. All he can see is a strange sort of sign language going on up ahead. Then, as they silently draw their weapons, he moves as quietly as he can around the perimeter and up to the front.

He opens his arms wide at the guy who seems to be in charge, silently asking with his eyes what is going on.

The man looks back at him, mimes smoking a cigarette, and as he faces forward again Alex realises that the pungent smell of tobacco is heavy in the night air. They start to move again, the other men spreading out even more, planning to surround whoever it is who is out here, Alex realises. He stays close to the one in charge, stopping again when everyone else does and he covers his chest, sure that his heart beat must surely be heard in this deathly silence.

The man next to Alex barks, it's the only way that Alex can describe it, for it wasn't a single word or a shout, but the command is barked. As one, the dozen policemen flick the tactical lights on their weapons on and exposed is a large man, sitting lazily on a log, smoking a cigarette.

"Arnja!" Alex hears Klim say the man's name and he looks over at the heavyset guy, unable to believe that this unhealthy, overweight specimen is a police chief.

Arnja, cigarette stuck to his bottom lip, blinks rapidly at the twelve lights that shine in his eyes. His lower half shifts, as though he has tried to stand, but he can't without supporting himself. Arnja plants his hands on either side of him and this time he manages to push himself to a standing position. He looks from left to right, assessing his sticky situation, and slowly raises his hands.

The man next to Alex says something and, in the light from the guns, Alex sees Arnja's face drain of all colour. He wonders what was said to provoke such a reaction. Alex turns his head to look for Klim or Sissy but, as he does, the one in charge barks again. Alex swings his head round, sees that Arnja has turned and is covering the ground, breaking through the only part that is not covered by the police. He attempts to leap the stream, but the man beside Alex says something, an order is given. Alex knows that, even though he doesn't understand the words, and then, as the fat man jumps, the bullets of twelve rifles punch through his jacket into Arnja's back.

There is silence and once the smoke has cleared the police venture forward. None too gently they grasp his clothes and drag him out of the stream. With a viciousness borne out of years of warfare, the man in charge aimed a kick at Arnja's inert head before spitting on him. Sissy, Sol and Klim come up behind Alex and stare down at the dead man.

"But there's still no sign of Elian," moans Sissy, and covers her face.

As Sissy speaks, there is a flurry from above, and the sound of a branch cracking. The twelve men reconvene, swivel and aim their weapons up in the sky. Sissy cries out at the sudden movement and Alex pulls her back beyond the line of police, shielding his eyes as he squints up into the treetops. At first he thinks it is a body up there, spread-eagled across a branch. Then it moves, splintering more branches. He sees a pair of legs dropping down, searching sightlessly for a foothold and it is with a lump in his throat that he recognises the Converse trainers.

"No guns," he snaps, transferring Sissy to a soldier and moving around the men. "That's our girl, that's the one that he snatched."

The men cast a side eye at their leader, unwilling to lower their arms on Alex's command. Alex shouts over to Klim, tells him to tell the men that this is not an enemy. Klim rushes up and translates and, with a miniscule gesture, the guns are finally put away.

Sixteen pairs of eyes watch Elian's slow progress down the tree truck. When she is within reach, two of the policemen come forward and lift her safely down to the ground, before stepping back to their place in line. She leans against the truck of the tree, eyeing the crowd that are silently watching her. Alex shrinks back at the sight of her. Uncomfortably he notes the blood that stains her lower limbs and he wonders what was done to her. Deep down, he knows. She hasn't simply been imprisoned or even just beaten. He does not dare go to her because, if he does, he knows *he* will break down, and that she doesn't need. But nobody else is claiming her, not even Sissy, the only woman in the group and the one whose touch Elian would probably accept. So he steps forward, locking eyes with her and reaching his hand out. For a second he thinks she is going to fall into his arms, the way she is supposed to; but, at the last minute, her hand flies out and she catches his wrist, holding tightly to it.

"Let's go, yeah?" Her tone is low and quiet and he sees a glint of something in her eyes, something unimaginable, something terrifying.

He nods and then Sissy is there, wrapping her arms around her niece, covering her from the gaze of the onlookers, pulling her away from Alex and all of the other men. Protectively, she holds on to Elian as they make the final walk back to the cottage.

Chapter 53
Afia and The Boy
At the end

She sits by the river side, watching the clear water flowing out of the forest. It has quite a force to it today, almost tidal, and she imagines that it is flushing all of the bad out of the Red Forest, all of the death and poison and decay and taking it downstream, depositing it eventually in the sea. It's with a cleansing feeling that Afia sits on the bank and, as the sun rises over the concrete wilderness beyond the forest, she senses that not only is it a new day, but the start of something new altogether.

As she waits, Afia tries to imagine a future outside of Chernobyl and the Red Forest. She has enjoyed her tastes of freedom on her visits to Belarus. Nobody looks at her, and on her brief time in the city she feels that she blends in. Much the way that she imagines Sissy did upon her move to London. Or maybe she can stay here, especially if Sissy is back and has taken over the family home. After all, visiting the city once a year is one thing, but being out there, all alone, that might be too much, too soon. Something tugs inside her chest and she grabs the front of her shirt and massages her collar bone, pressing it back down, burying it deep inside, hiding away the fleeting thought that came of the possibility of spending time with Elian . . . No, that can't be done! The child is an adult now, raised by Sissy and nothing to do with her, Afia, really.

You saved her though, she tells herself with a small, self-satisfied smile. She allows herself that much, and a little more besides as she leans back, looks up at the sky, and runs through a replay in her head.

Afia had been truly frightened, maybe for the first time in her life when she returned to the tunnel and began using the little hacksaw on the chain that bound her daughter to the bowels of hell. When she had freed her, she had thought Elian was dead already, as the girl wasn't moving or even paying any attention to Afia. But she could see the rise and fall of her chest and her emerald eyes flickering behind half closed lids. So she had dragged Elian down the tunnel by her wrists, heaving her up through the trapdoor and forcing her upright. The cool night air did little to revive the girl though, and when Afia had turned her in the direction of the lane and pushed, Afia bit down on her clenched fist with frustration as Elian had slumped, face down, among the pine needles. Afia had watched her for a while and then she hung her head and sat beside her daughter. This would be the first and last time they would meet, she didn't want Elian's memories to be of her birth mother, shouting and prodding her, roughly making her run away, even if she were making her run for her life. So she sat beside her, stroking Elian's hair that was so much like her own used to be. With her fingertips she traced the outline of Elian's cheekbones, touched her lips and, when Elian's eyes finally fully opened, Afia pulled her over so her head rested in Afia's lap. She let a few tears fall, saw them through blurred vision as they splashed on to Elian's cheek, the cool moisture waking her drowsy daughter. This time when she helped Elian to her feet she managed to stay there, and Afia pushed her, very gently this time. Elian had staggered a few steps, leant on a tree and then seemed to gather momentum as she pushed away with her hands, and with a final backwards glance she began to run.

She stood for a long time, there in the darkness. Even when she could no longer see Elian through the trees, still she stood, swaying slightly, an unidentifiable feeling sweeping through her. She was gone, really gone this time, and she wouldn't come back. With a sigh, Afia went down to the riverside to wait.

*

The sun is fully up in the sky and promising a hot day when he arrives. She can hear his gentle footfall behind her, but she doesn't turn around. After a minute he comes to sit beside her and she shuffles closer to him, close enough to lean her head on his shoulder if she wanted to, but she doesn't.

They sit a long time together like that, reminding Afia of the night back in 1986 when they sat on another riverbank; her, full of the magic and optimism of youth, planning a future of adventure and passion. He, as always, dark and brooding, just like now.

"You set her free, didn't you?" He asks.

"Yes."

"And she was . . ."

"Yes," she replies, simply.

Out of the corner of her eye she sees him nodding, as though she has confirmed something he long suspected, something that has never been mentioned before.

He moves suddenly, lunging at her, locking his arm around her neck and pulling her close. To an observer it may seem like a passionate embrace, but to Afia it is a deadly one. With frantic movements she grapples beneath her, her fingers searching underneath the flowing, summery dress that she has put on today. Finally she finds what she is looking for, she grabs at it, raises her hand and brings it down sharply to thud between his shoulder blades.

She pulls back and looks at him. His mouth is a perfect 'o' and Afia closes her eyes so she doesn't have to see him. But he's not done it seems, as he locks the hand that is holding her, even tighter. She struggles against him, pushing at his hard chest. With his free hand he grabs her arm, spinning his cord necklace around her wrist and tugging it tight. Afia thrashes, but, even now, even at the end of his life his strength is immense. A tiny red bubble forms at the corner of his mouth and he smiles, showing his perfect white teeth and he holds her even tighter, even closer.

"You and me, always you and me," he murmurs, and as his life blood ebbs away he stands with a roar, bringing her with him and steps off the bank into the river.

As they are dragged under he goes first. She sees his face, his eyes remain open, but the light goes out and she plants her feet on his body and pushes against him with all she's got. His arm, that was around her neck, is released and for a moment they bob up to the surface and she gasps, half water, half air, before his dead weight pulls them down again.

She can no longer feel her hand, the one that is tightly bound in the cord, and she raises her arm with a vague idea of pulling the necklace over his head. But, his upper half is tilted back at an awkward angle and still they are sinking ever downwards. With her eyes wide open she looks up and the sun seems so very far away now.

Her lungs are burning, bubbles rising in front of her eyes as she struggles with the cord and now, right at the end, finally she knows, like so many others before her, what it is to be imprisoned by Niko.

Chapter 54
Alex

Chernobyl, June 16th 2015

Klim's cottage is too small for a dozen police officers, not to mention the medics and the forensic team, as well as the two representatives who have turned up from the Met.

Alex hangs around on the porch with Sol and Klim for a while, watching the officers traipse in and out.

"I'm going to Sissy's cottage, send some emails," he says eventually. "I'll be back in a little while."

As he strolls down the lane he can't help but reflect on how different it seems out here now that it is a safe place to be, except for the fact that the actual killer is still out there of course. Alex stops walking as he contemplates this. It's not over, though Elian is safe and alive; the killer is still out there, somewhere.

But the chain has been broken, Alex consoles himself. Fat Arnja the protector is dead and now the police – the *real* police – are on the case. And, Elian is alive. Just that one word – alive – is enough for Alex.

At Sissy's cottage Alex helps himself to a coffee and sits down at the desk. For a reason that he can't fully explain, he can't face talking to Luke so he fires him off an email, thanking him for his help and promising to catch up with him as soon as he is back in England.

He does ring Selina though, both out of a sense of duty and knowing she will be going out of her mind with worry. His suspicions are confirmed when she answers the telephone and, upon hearing his voice, she promptly bursts into tears.

"I'm all right," he assures her. "And so is Elian."

"Thank God she's unharmed," she breathes in reply, when she has got her crying more or less under control.

Alex hesitates, "Not exactly unharmed." Then he is stuck for words and there is a long silence.

"Alex, are you there?"

"Yeah, sorry," he swallows. "I've not really had a chance to talk to her, the police are with her now. She was . . . attacked."

He can't bring himself to say the word 'raped', or even think about it too much.

"Just come home and bring that poor girl with you," she instructs.

Alex is distracted with something going on outside. "Hold on," he says, and with the cordless phone he walks to the window and looks out.

More police are out there now, spreading out into the forest again and there is another group, moving down the lane, some of them talking urgently into walkie talkies.

"Aunty, I have to go." He bids her a hurried goodbye, hangs up the telephone and jogs back down the lane to Klim's house.

Amongst the crowd Alex spots Sol's ashen face and he shoulders his way through to him.

"What's happening?"

"They found more bodies," replies Sol.

"More? You mean different to the one we dug up?"

Sol grimaces, "Yeah."

Alex looks around the room. "Where's Elian?"

"In there." Sol nods towards Klim's bedroom, "With Sissy and a doctor."

The head police officer, the one who led the siege against Arnja in the forest, stalks past and Alex shoots a hand out.

"Hey, what's your name, man?" Alex demands.

"Gruber," he replies, fixing Alex with a withering look until he removes his hand.

And Gruber is German, realises Alex. It makes sense, the way they conduct themselves, how they had moved through the forest, stalking like machines.

"You are the media?" Gruber asks disdainfully.

"No. Christ, no," laughs Alex nervously. "I work with the police in London. My colleague, Luke, called you in on my behalf." It's not the total truth, but not an outright lie either, reasons Alex. "They're saying you found more bodies."

"Yes, we need identification, but we are pretty sure the man is the one responsible for the kidnap of the young woman." Gruber begins to walk away and then he stops and turns back. "The young woman, did she come here with anyone else, besides you?"

"No, why?"

Gruber shrugs. "I thought there might be a connection between her and one of the victims. No matter."

Gruber goes, pushing through the crowd, leaving Alex staring after him. A shiver, as cold as ice, runs through him, and suddenly he knows exactly who one of the victims is.

Chapter 55
Sissy
Chernobyl, June 16th 2015

I feel like I'm back in 1986 and Sol is taking me to the makeshift morgue to identify my sister's body. Only this time a man called Gruber is taking me, although Sol is here too.

I think back an hour in time, when all I was concerned about was Elian's well-being, only half listening as the big German man droned on about new victims that had been found. I didn't pay much attention until I heard him use the words 'African origin'.

This time we are not going to a makeshift mortuary. We are travelling to the one in Donetsk, by helicopter.

Things really have changed in the last thirty years.

Panic is sifting through my stomach like waves on the sea and I try to stifle them by telling myself the last time I went to a morgue to identify her body, it wasn't her.

Is it possible for it to happen twice? Am I really that lucky? Is *she*? I doubt it.

"I'll come in with you," says Sol, as we circle lower and lower, coming in to land.

He's not asking, but I nod my consent anyway.

I turn my thoughts to Sol, or Simon, as I still think of him. I wonder what he feels about this. He has never laid eyes on Afia, yet she has been at the centre of his life for so long. I don't know quite what his relationship is with Klim, but I don't judge it, whatever it is. Comfort and love can come to us in so many different ways. I know that as much as anyone. *My* love and *my* comfort ended up being Elian, a little being who was delivered to me by God-knows-who and landed on my doorstep. She saved me from a life of chasing men for attention and living for my sister's return. If it hadn't have been for her, I don't know where I would have ended up. It's funny really, my comfort could have been Sol or Klim, if either of them had let me. If either of them had wanted me.

The blades of the chopper are still turning as Sol climbs out first and turns to me, holding out his hand. I ignore it, and hold on to the sides of the doors as I awkwardly clamber out. Holding on to my coat we move quickly across the landing site towards a small building, with Gruber leading the way.

Inside the building there is a clinical scent of cleanliness, yet I still recall the smell of death and decay from the last morgue I went to. The corridor is brightly lit and Gruber checks a note on his clipboard and stops at a door. He opens it and ushers Sol and I in.

The room is lined with lockers and I can't see any bodies awaiting our perusal. Gruber strides over to one of the lockers, opens the door and pulls out a long tray. Now I see where the bodies are kept.

Sol and I walk over and I can feel the chill from inside the lockers. I let out an involuntary shiver and, as Gruber reaches for the sheet, Sol takes my hand. This time, I accept his support.

When the cover is pulled back I think for a moment that I *was* lucky twice, this is not my sister. This aged, lined, tired-looking woman can't be my sister. But then I realise that it was thirty years ago that I last saw her, and if I look in the mirror, I too am aged, lined and tired. But my ageing is the natural process, this woman is ravaged and not simply by time.

I don't realise that I am leaning against Sol until his arm comes around my shoulder and he holds me upright.

"Is this Afia?" he whispers to me.

I close my eyes and she is in my mind, strutting around, the peacock, the talk of the town, the movie star, the superstar. And she could have been a superstar. But, instead, she chose the route of heroin addict, a fact that is confirmed when I open my eyes and see the evidence of so many years of abuse up and down her arms. Tiny bruises connect the dots. Not only on her arms either, I note, as my gaze travels down to her bare feet. She is so thin. Always she was dieting and trying to exude the appearance of runway models, but this skinny woman is not model thin, she is emaciated. Her mouth is slightly open and I rake my eyes over her face, noting that her remaining teeth are tiny stumps in her head.

"How did she . . . die?" I ask Gruber.

"She drowned," he replies, in his matter of fact manner. "I believe that she killed the other victim that we found, there were stab wounds to his spine. From the scene it looks like she mortally wounded him, there was a struggle and they ended up in the water. Do you see these marks?" He lifts up her right wrist and it moves stiffly.

I peer closer and see the indentations in her hand and wrist.

"He was wearing a leather strap around his neck, her arm was tangled up in it, so when he went under the water she went with him."

I can feel Sol stiffening beside me, no doubt disapproving of Gruber's vivid and graphic explanation. But I don't mind, I need the full picture to carry in my mind, so I can finally start to move on.

"Who was he?"

Gruber shrugs. "We don't know. There was no identification, he's not known to any of the police. The only people that knew his true identity are now dead."

"Can I see him?" I ask, before I've even thought it through.

"Sissy, really, I don't think it's a good idea," blusters Sol.

Gruber looks over at me, interested for the first time.

He checks his clipboard again and looks at the numbers on the locker doors. The other victim, the one who my sister killed, is right next door to her. He opens it up, pulls the tray out and folds down the sheet.

This man has not aged a day. His face is still the same as the first time I saw it, when he had my sister up against a tree and roughly violated her. I can't believe it. I can't believe that she spent thirty years of her life with this cruel monster, when she could have chosen Klim. What was wrong with her? Is this the same man that kidnapped Elian and killed all those other women? Did she know all this time what he was doing? Did she find out about Elian and finally snap? Was *she* the one that set Elian free?

There are so many questions. Elian will be able to answer some of them, but some will remain unanswered for eternity.

I've seen enough.

"That's my sister," I say, and nodded over to her. "And that man is called Niko."

Gruber scribbles on his notepaper and covers both Niko and Afia over with a sheet. I nod to Sol that I'm ready to leave and he leads me to the door. Before we exit I turn back to Gruber.

"Just one more thing, put that fucking monster somewhere else, I don't want him next to her."

And Sol and I leave the morgue.

Chapter 56
Elian

Chernobyl and then London 2015

Elian sits opposite Sissy in Klim's lounge. The three men have discreetly vanished, but Elian knows they won't be far away.

"It's like a puzzle where lots of pieces are missing," Sissy speaks up suddenly. "It seems that way to me, so it must to you too."

Elian nods and takes a deep breath in, then exhales slowly.

"You can ask me anything and I'll tell you," continues Sissy.

Elian knows that Sissy wants to hear her say the same words, but she can't. There are some things that she doesn't want to talk about yet, maybe never. Perhaps one day, but all she wants to do is return to London and think about what to do next.

"And you're going to stay here?" Elian asks.

Sissy smiles, but it is bittersweet, heartbreaking really. "I'll stay here for now."

There is nothing more to say, even though nothing much has been said at all. Elian rises carefully from her chair, still feeling the bruises and the cracked ribs with every movement, every breath.

In time they will heal. She wishes the same could be said for the rest of her.

Sol, Klim and Alex are hanging around on the porch, Jayne sitting by Klim's feet, tongue lolling and looking up at her master. It is the dog that Elian says goodbye to first.

She kneels down and wraps her arms around Jayne, marvelling again at the story she has been told of how the dog tracked her to the tunnel. "Good girl," she whispers, and sneaks a biscuit out of her pocket. Jayne takes it happily and responds with a lick to Elian's face. The others laugh lightly.

Next Elian hugs Sol, and he grips her back, tighter than she is comfortable with. She knows his story too, of how when he was a much younger man, no more than a boy really, he tried to find Afia for Sissy and Klim. He didn't succeed with that, back then, but she hopes that the fact he helped find her makes up for it a little.

She moves on to Klim and their embrace is a little more sedate. She still doesn't know what to make of Klim. He is serious, stoic and more removed than Sol or Sissy, even more so since her rescue. She is about to move away when he pulls her back and speaks quietly in her ear.

"I'd like to talk to you, when you're ready."

She nods hesitantly, not knowing what on earth the two of them would ever have to talk about. But, it would be rude to say such a thing, so she summons a smile from somewhere for him.

And then Sissy is there, in front of Elian, holding on to her shoulders, closer than Elian likes, and her tone and expression are frantic.

"If you want me to come to London I'll be there, straight away, you've got my phone number, my email. Promise me I'll see you again?"

Elian stares at her. Sissy is upset that Elian is leaving. She is scared and worried and she is feeling all of the emotions that Elian herself felt when Sissy upped and walked away three years ago. But she can't say that, there is so much that she can't say. She knows, months and years down the line, the behaviour of these people is going to eat her up, just the way that the heroin ate Afia. That's another thing she can't say, so she simply pulls Sissy into a hug and holds her tight for a moment.

"I'll see you again, Sissy," she says, and turns around. "I'll see all of you very soon."

She is pleased with how light hearted her words sounded, for that was how she intended them, even though she is feeling anything *but* light hearted.

Then it is just her and Alex, walking over to the mini-van where dreadlocked Yuri awaits them. It feels rather surreal to Elian as she climbs in and moves to the very back of the van. From the fragments that she remembers over the last week or so, not once did she imagine she would be getting back in this tour bus and leaving.

Alex deposits their bags in and sits up front with Yuri. Elian allows herself a smile. Alex will field Yuri's questions, batting them away from her so she doesn't have to answer.

*

The trip home seems to take no time at all, probably because Elian sleeps most of the time, only waking when they have to move from bus to plane and from plane to Gatwick Airport.

"You're coming back to mine, right?" Alex says as they stand out the front of the terminal.

Elian is about to protest, but senses that Alex is having none of it. So, she nods her agreement. A cab is hailed. Elian promptly falls asleep again, and when she wakes her head is resting on Alex's shoulder and they are outside his house.

She stands in the porch, waiting patiently while Alex pays the driver, when suddenly the front door is opened, and Selina is there and pulling Elian in to the hallway.

"Oh, boy, am I glad to see you," Selina pulls Elian close.

Elian pats her back in a somewhat awkward manner, and then she stiffens. There is something about this woman's embrace, something that tells Elian that she has been worried, that she actually cares, and before she knows it is going to happen, Elian's eyes are streaming and violent sobs are shaking her small frame. Suddenly she can't even stand anymore, and Selina allows her to sink to the floor, the older woman still holding her and they sit there, in the hallway, Selina doing nothing but making clucking noises, shrouding Elian in warmth, and simply being there. Then Alex is there, holding their bags and, through her blurred vision, Elian can see him watching them both. His mouth is working and for a moment she thinks he will climb right on in there with her and Selina. But he edges past them and leaves Elian with Selina, a heap in the hallway.

*

Elian wakes and outside the window she can see it is dark. There is a lamp switched on beside the bed that she is in and a glass of water. She can't remember going to bed. In fact she doesn't recall anything in between Selina greeting her at the door and now. There are gaps in her memory, not just of today, but also of events that happened in the last few weeks. Fragments occur, flashbacks of a tunnel, of chains, of a forest and a cabin. Or was it a caravan or a cottage? She acknowledges that they are not so much gaps as roaring chasms, great quarries of darkness, and it is the dark bits that scare her more than what she does recall.

After a few days she goes out on her own, wanting to be away from the well meaning, but suffocating, care of Selina and Alex. She finds her Oyster card in her bag and travels to Oxford Street, wondering if she should be concerned that she had to study the tube map. She thinks that the route is one she should know, but can't say for sure.

The flat in Great Titchfield Street is familiar. She knows instantly that everything is where it should be, nothing strange here. It is a relief to be home and she flops on to the sofa, puts her feet up and looks around. All of her life she has worried about being here, more because of what Sissy didn't say rather than what she did. But she has been assured that she has nothing to be concerned about, that a man – a stranger – put her and Sissy here and looked after them for something that someone else did for him. Elian lets out a groan and rubs her head, everything is so confusing. It's hard to think straight. She wonders if it is because she is tired, but something tells her that she shouldn't be tired, she has been sleeping for days now. Rather than go to sleep yet again, she stands up and unpacks her small bag, putting everything in its place. With that job done she wanders back into the lounge, peers through the blinds and blinks in surprise as she sees Alex running down the street towards her flat. She moves to the hall, buzzes him in as soon as he rings, and then he's hurrying up the stairs. She can hear him breathing heavily before he turns the last corner to her landing.

"Still no fitter," he laughs as he leans against the banister.

She joins in his laughter, thrilled that she remembers an incident where she made a retort about his fitness. Even though she is laughing, she knows she shouldn't be so happy to remember something that only happened a week ago, but it seems like a step forward.

"Come in," she invites, and holds the door open for him.

She is so happy that he is here. She had wondered if, now her official job was done, he might not want to know her anymore. And of all the things that Elian is unsure of, spending time with Alex Harvey is not one of them. Her heart leaps as he walks past her into the lounge, wondering what he is going to say. Maybe he'll take her out for dinner. She recalls the meal they had in Kiev, just the two of them.

"I was worried about you, you went off without telling anyone," he says as he sits down in the chair she has recently vacated.

She frowns, sure that she told Selina that she was going out.

"You need to go for a check up, Ellie." Alex's tone is gentle now and she looks at him, startled.

"Why?"

He shifts uncomfortably. "The doctor in Pripyat said you must visit your GP when you get home, they need to check that your ribs are healing and the . . . tests that they need to do."

"Tests?" Elian is genuinely confused and she stands in the doorway, gripping the frame as she stares at Alex.

"Ellie, do you remember what happened to you, back in Chernobyl?"

She shrugs and looks away. Yes, she knows someone, that man . . . Niko, took her. He was mentally unhinged, he was cruel and yet she was saved. But somehow, that doesn't seem to be what Alex wants to hear, so she says nothing.

Alex rests his chin in his hand and looks out of the window for a long time. She starts to feel a bit silly standing there, holding the doorframe, and she clears her throat.

"Would you like a cup of tea?"

Then, suddenly, he turns and stalks towards her, takes a hold of her waist and she flinches away from him. He grabs the bottom of her T-shirt, lifts it up and she wants to scream, but she's frozen, her mind and her mouth not able to stop him. But he is not venturing further, with her shirt up around her breasts he moves her into the bedroom, makes her look at herself in the mirrored wardrobe door.

She gasps at the ugly green bruises that cover her ribs. Something skitters into her mind and then, frustratingly, is gone again.

"What tests?" She asks again, her voice dull this time.

It takes so long for him to answer that she moves away from him, pulls down her shirt and sits on the end of the bed.

"The doctor in Pripyat, he said you'll need to go to the doctor here, they will refer you to a clinic, just to be sure . . ."

"WHAT TESTS?" she shouts it this time, furious at him and at herself for not grasping what he is talking about.

"HIV, and STDs . . ." Alex tails off. Elian hears his voice break.

Sitting on the bed Elian can see her reflection in the mirror. She stares at herself; she can't stand to look at him.

"Ellie, do you understand?" He is back, sitting beside her, chirping in her ear like an annoying insect.

She flaps her hand at him, stands up and walks to the bedroom window.

"Yes, I remember," she lies. "I'll arrange it now, I'll sort it out. Would you mind leaving now?"

"Ellie," he breathes her name, and in response she forces a smile on her face.

It is false. Fake.

"I'll meet you back at your house." Her voice is jovial, her cheeks in pain from the pretence. "I'll be back in time for dinner."

He goes. Finally he leaves and she crouches underneath the large sash window in the lounge, making sure he is not hanging around outside.

She doesn't have time to fall apart, if she doesn't turn up at his house he'll come back, so she needs to move fast.

She grabs a rucksack, a large one off the top shelf of the wardrobe, packs everything she has just put away. She adds a few more things, not registering what she is packing, very aware of the time and that she needs to leave now.

At the front door she pauses, looks around. The home that was so dear and familiar only an hour ago is now cold and empty.

Hoisting the bag on her back she hurries down the stairs, out of the front door, and heads back towards the Underground.

With no clear direction in mind, Elian finds herself getting off the tube at Tufnell Park. Walking down Fortess Road she sees an internet café and, nearby, a newsagent. In the newsagent she buys a notebook and moves on to the café.

Finding a spare seat and terminal she pulls out her notebook and, almost frantically, she starts to write down everything that she can recall from her recent memory. As she scribbles as much as she can in chronological order, more scenes come back to her. She inserts names and places, smells and tastes.

And then, when she puts her pen down, a conversation comes back to her.

There's this place in The Hague, it's only half an hour from Amsterdam, right next to the sea.

She picks up her pen and writes it down verbatim, before she can forget it. Then she reads it again.

Who said that? Was it a conversation that she was part of?

Russian Lev.

The two words whisper through her mind and, like a trigger being pulled, a whole new train of memories is set in motion.

He was part of it, all of it, he was in with Arnja, with that Niko. He had packed his bags, was planning to start a new life in Holland, in a town by the sea, and he called her a nigger. For some reason, despite everything else that was done to her, his words stung.

And, she doesn't think she even mentioned him to the authorities back in Chernobyl, this Russian Lev.

There's a light in Elian's eyes. More than a light, it's a fire.

Slamming her notebook closed she stands up and reaches for her bag. A plot is slowly taking form in her brain. Her plans have changed.

Chapter 57
Alex

London 2015

Relief rushes through Alex as he opens the door to find Elian on the doorstep. He wants to say so much, but he settles for, "You're just in time for dinner."

It is just the two of them, with Alex having persuaded Selina to leave them on their own for the evening. They eat a risotto, which Alex made, and Elian finishes hers so quickly that he wonders if she remembered to eat at all today.

When they have both finished, Alex clears the plates and comes back to the table with a brown envelope. It has Elian's name on it and he passes it across to her.

He watches her open it carefully and pull out the neat bundle of notes that total seven thousand five hundred euros. She nods as she flicks through it, and then puts it back in the envelope and mumbles a polite thank you to him.

"It was thirty thousand, in total, but the remainder was to be paid, well, after we finished. Obviously we're not going to get that, now . . ." Alex tails off.

She knows Afia is dead. She knows Afia can't pay now. She doesn't care about the money, and she knows Alex knows that. Inwardly he curses himself for his clumsy words.

He busies himself putting the kettle on, but it's really an excuse so she doesn't see his face. He had thought, when he gave her the money . . . he's not actually sure what he thought. He didn't expect her to take it straight away, although God knows she more than earned it. And fear clutches at his chest; now that she has her monetary fee, is it over? Was that all she was waiting for? He curses under his breath again, wishes he had held it back a bit longer, purely for selfish reasons; because, if she is broke, then she has to stay with him.

But she is not broke, she still has a job at *Edge*, if she wants it, and her home situation has not changed. The flat is hers, clear and free of any mortgage.

"Alex, is it okay if I use your computer?" Her voice brings him back to the present and he starts, turns around and smiles at her.

"Of course, do you need any help with anything in particular?" He keeps his tone purposefully light.

"No, I just want to check in with Sissy," she replies. "I don't feel ready to call her, but I'd like to email her."

"Of course, come on, I'll log you in and leave you to it."

He settles her in his room, comes back with a cup of tea for her and puts it on the desk. She smiles up at him, clutching on to a notebook and he retreats back to the kitchen and sits at the table brooding. She had smiled at him, but it hadn't reached her eyes. They were dull; dead.

He sips at his own tea, Elian on his mind. He must take care of her, everyone expects him to; Sissy, Klim, Selina even. Usually he does not like to do what others expect him to, but this is so very different. *He* is so different, and it is all down to Elian Gould. He doesn't know what this young, nineteen-year-old girl done to him, former player, confirmed bachelor; but something happened to him out in Chernobyl. Before then, Kiev, even London maybe, definitely London, he nods an affirmation as he remembers how wretched he felt after he had slept with her and then left her in bed whilst he snooped through her private possessions.

And that's another thing to think about, how damn much he wants her. Because he doesn't want to just look after her, although that is a part of it, he craves her physically, he wants to be in that bedroom with her right now, not on the computer, but in the bed, in *her*.

He groans, because that is another issue. Elian still has to visit the clinic and have all the fucking tests to make sure that monster has not given her a life sentence, even after his death. He makes a mental note to ensure she goes through with an appointment and looks towards the closed bedroom door.

This can wait, Alex's feelings, he can control them. He mustn't crowd her. Mustn't scare her, for she has been scared enough already. No, the words that he wants to say to her, the outpouring of love and passion and the talk of forever, they can wait, for her sake.

Because she's not going anywhere.

Is she?

Epilogue
Russian Lev
Scheveningen 2015

Four windows, four girls all in varying states of undress. He stands tall, arching back ever so slightly to get the best view.

Rita is in the first window and she can see him down here in the street. She smiles coyly, hooks a thumb in the 'v' of her underwear, but he doesn't see what her next trick is, his gaze has already moved on from Rita.

It's not that he doesn't like Rita, rather the fact that he has been with her several times recently and a lot of people have seen him.

No, for what he needs to do tonight, it must be someone who is not known to him. There can be nothing to bring it back to his door.

*

Gabi Rossi hurries down the street, taking care that her spiked heels don't get stuck in between the cobblestones. There's a chill in the air, a cold front coming off the North Sea. She pulls her thin coat tighter around her and turns up the collar, thinking wistfully, and not for the first time, about Brazil, her home country.

The weather is the only thing that she misses about Bangu Rio. Here in Scheveningen, her home may be small and one that she shares with four other girls, but it is a palace compared to the favela where she was raised in a steel shanty shack.

And, it's safe here in The Hague. Just as she is musing on the fact that she's not known even a hint of trouble since she has been here, she hears a rough footstep on the road behind her and what sounds like the chink of a chain.

She stops walking and looks behind her down the deserted alleyway. A damp mist has rolled in from the coast and she squints into the gloom. There, a hundred yards away, there's definitely someone standing next to a dumpster. He is unmoving and seemingly looking towards her, silent and still. The whole scene seems strange, because this is a happy place. Even in her job, when some of the punters want something unusual or bordering on the perverted, it's never sinister. On the other hand, some of her punters might be timid, unable or unwilling to voice their desires. But this guy, he's neither exuberant nor shy. He's just standing, staring her down, observing.

Carefully, not making any sudden movements, she slips her feet out of her shoes. The cold cobbles draw a gasp from her and she backs up a couple of steps. He still hasn't moved, but now he takes his hand out of his pocket, drawing out a length of chain, presenting it to her, holding it as though it is a fine wine.

"*Filho da puta*," Gabi swears in a whisper and, after a beat, she turns and runs, leaving her shoes right where she slipped them off.

*

Lev leaves the slightly more upper class area of Geleenstraat and heads over towards Doublestraat. He stops under a bridge, pausing to light a cigarette when he hears the slap of bare soles on the street behind him.

The girl runs into him and when he reaches out a hand to steady her she smacks it away with a scream.

"Hey lady," he begins, and is taken aback when she does an about turn, leaps towards him, almost in to his arms.

She clings to him, sobbing into his coat.

"There was a man. I left my shoes . . ." is all she can manage to say.

Lev glances back the way she came and can see nobody in sight. "You really shouldn't be walking out here on your own," he says.

She seems to make a quick recovery, pushing him away from her and looking up at him with a sneer.

"You think I can't take care of myself?"

Well, no, he thinks. *Or you wouldn't be crying into my coat.* But he doesn't say it.

"As you were then," he says, holding out his hand in a gesture that says 'after you'.

With a final glare at him she walks away, treading gingerly over the cobbles.

He looks around once more, noting that this area between the two red light districts is deserted; a wasteland.

He puts his hand in his pocket, runs his thumb down the sharp edge of the blade that nestles there. With a smile, that is akin to a leer, lighting up his face, he sets off after the girl.

"Welcome to Schev, Lev," he chuckles under his breath. "I think I'm going to like it here."

Printed in Great Britain
by Amazon